From: Delphi@oracle.org
To: C_Evans@athena.edu
Re: The final showdown

Christine,

After Kwan-Sook's death and Lilith's new loyalty to Athena Academy, only one of Jackie Cavanaugh's offspring remains unaccounted for: Echo.

She and I have yet to meet face-to-face, but I've gathered a lot of intel on her over these last few months. Her unusual abilities—Lilith said Echo could stop bullets!—have warped her, I think. She's admitted to her sister that she wants to rule the world, that she believes she's unstoppable. But I have every confidence in my team of Athena agents. We will take Echo down.

We'll also retrieve the data she's stolen and prevent her from destroying millions of lives. I'm betting on our success, with my career… and my life.

D.

Dear Reader,

I just returned home from a ceremony honoring the students and instructors at my daughter's Tae Kwon Do studio. The instructors put on quite a show, demonstrating several martial arts traditions including Krav Maga, favored by many of our Athena Force heroes and heroines. It was exciting to see a young female Black Belt take on three attackers and make short work of them. She was a blur of ponytail and muscles, and her fierce, proud shouts echoed throughout the room. I was thrilled. I had imagined Allison Gracelyn fighting just like this, and here she was, lifted off the page for me just when it was time for me to say goodbye to her.

It has been such a privilege to write *Disclosure*. I can't believe how fortunate I have been to explore the world of Athena Force, and to delve into the character of Allison, surely the most enigmatic of all the heroines (at least, to me!). Allison is a fighter and a leader, but the biggest battle she faces is a war of the heart.

It takes a lot of courage to admit when one is afraid, or lonely, or lost. I know it has been difficult at times for me to admit to feelings like that. I was afraid when I started writing Allison's story. I wanted with all my heart to write a good book that would honor the fine work of the authors and editors who came before me in the world of Athena Force. Like the Tae Kwon Do artists at the ceremony tonight, I took deep breaths and made each move the best I could. It was a joy to tell Allison's story of courage, while at the same time losing my fear and finding my bliss.

Be bold!

Nancy Holder

Nancy Holder

DISCLOSURE

ATHENA FORCE
Published by Silhouette Books
America's Publisher of Contemporary Romance

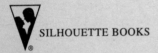

SILHOUETTE BOOKS

ISBN-13: 978-0-373-38983-4
ISBN-10:   0-373-38983-4

DISCLOSURE

Visit Athena Force at www.eHarlequin.com

Printed in U.S.A.

NANCY HOLDER

is a *USA TODAY* bestselling author who has published approximately eighty novels and two hundred short stories, essays and articles about writing. In addition to writing *Son of the Shadows* for Silhouette Nocturne, she is known for her tie-in work for TV shows such as *Buffy the Vampire Slayer, Smallville, Hellboy* and others. Please send letters to Nancy Holder, P.O. Box 26384, San Diego, CA 92196; or visit her Web site, www.nancyholder.com.

For Mr. Andy Thompson of Family Karate.
Thank you, sir.

Chapter 1

A dark, sharp wind threw autumn leaves against Allison Gracelyn's windshield as she put through her call to Morgan Rush, who was already at NSA for the emergency meeting. After the open and cloudless big sky of the Arizona desert, the frosty Maryland night grounded her in reality—her world was a lowering, stormy place; her safety zone as narrow as a grave; the situation as out-of-control as a nightmare.

No. I'm in control. I have a plan, she told herself. *I'm on my game. I can make this happen.*

She unrolled the window of her sleek black Infiniti and held out her NSA badge toward the security guard, who stepped from his kiosk to take it. The chill bit into Allison's ungloved hand. Beyond the kiosk, hidden by the night, the Men in Black patrolled the perimeter of the vast complex of the National Security Administration. The MIB were the crack security forces of "Crypto City"—suited up in black riot gear, armed with submachine guns and God knew what else. Not one of them would hesitate to open fire if given the order.

She knew at least one person who would gladly give the word. Her volatile new boss, Bill McDonough, was furious with her for having taken the day off with no explanation beyond the vague and unenlightening "personal business." NSA was sitting on top of a time bomb—literally—and the terrorist threat level had shot from orange to bright red around the same time that Allison's return flight to Washington took off from the airport in Phoenix.

Coincidence? She didn't know yet. She didn't know what her enemy was capable of. Lucy Karmon, a fellow Athena alum who'd been helping Allison with her "personal business," had described Echo's maniacal rage when Lucy had completed her mission to steal a spider necklace that contained a flash drive with the kind of information that could destroy the world as they knew it. "Wacko beyond bonkers. Way beyond. I've never seen anything like it."

That same black-and-gold necklace had dangled from Allison's neck on her return flight to the East Coast, hidden from view beneath a black turtleneck sweater. Allison had complemented the sweater with black wool pleated trousers and low-heeled boots, which was good, because she hadn't had any time to change her clothes after she landed, and they would work well in an NSA meeting about preventing hundreds of thousands if not millions of deaths.

Allison had flown to Phoenix yesterday specifically to retrieve the necklace from Echo's half sister, Lilith, to whom it had been bequeathed when Athena Academy's greatest enemy, Arachne, committed suicide. Arachne had left behind three genetically enhanced daughters and three flash drives that held the keys to the empire of evil she'd created before her death. Lilith wanted no part of the evil that came with her inheritance, while Echo had murdered men, women and children—and would have murdered Lilith—to steal Lilith's share as well as her own.

Still, a nuclear attack just didn't seem like Echo's style.

"Rush," Morgan said, the deep timbre of his voice caressing Allison's earlobe, the low, male rumble as pleasurable as running her cold hand along the warmed leather seat of her car.

"Yeah, hi, Morgan," Allison replied, adjusting her earpiece, keeping her voice neutral. Even during a national security crisis, Morgan threw her off. She had a feeling McDonough had assigned Morgan to her task force—Project Ozone—to keep an eye on her. Surely McDonough had no idea what working in close quarters with Morgan did to her insides. Or maybe he did.

"Meeting's set up in Conference Room A," Morgan said. "I ordered you a latte with soy milk and two sugars."

He remembered her beverage of choice. Any other time, she might have smiled.

"Thanks. I'm on site." Which he might already know, if he was keeping tabs on her. "I'll be up in five minutes."

"Hold on," he said. "I'm getting a red e-mail."

"Okay." Her adrenaline spiked. Red meant extremely urgent.

As she waited, she glanced at the time on her dash.

It was 7:35 p.m. McDonough had called the meeting for eight. She'd been on the go for nearly twenty-four hours, but she could make another twelve or so before she started getting sloppy.

"We got some more," Morgan continued. He was obviously referring to the team's successful cracking of chunks of the heavily encrypted chatter between the unstable Middle Eastern nation of Berzhaan and the despotic nation of Kestonia. "Big stuff. You called it right." His voice betrayed his anxiety.

Damn it, she thought. She didn't want to be right about a probable nuclear attack somewhere on the Eastern seaboard in less than a month.

"Brief me first, my office," she told him. She wanted to walk into that meeting fully informed.

"Will do. Something else is incoming," he announced.

"I'm holding," she said. She took her badge back from the guard, who waved her on to proceed. The white Jersey gate raised and Allison rolled onto the grounds of the most heavily guarded, mysterious facility in the alphabet soup of national and international intelligence agencies.

Allison heard the gentle ping signaling an incoming text message on her handheld.

SSJ: STAY OUT. U R COMPROMISED. CALL ASAP.

An icy chill washed up her spine. SSJ was Selena Shaw Jones, CIA, an Athena alum she'd sent to watch for intel at the headquarters of Oracle, the supersecret spy organization of which they were both members.

Selena's choice of words was telling. Employees stayed away. Spies stayed *out.*

"Okay, here it is," Morgan began.

"Morgan, save it. I'll be there soon." She disconnected. A microsecond later, her cell phone flared to white noise. She had reached the perimeter of the NSA's new and improved jamming field. She glanced at the handheld. Selena's message had disappeared. Nothing else electronic would work, not her laptop, nor her PDA, nothing.

"Damn it," she whispered, ticking her glance toward the central building, which rose into the night like a twinkling Rubik's Cube. Compromised how? By whom?

Echo, she thought. *She's made her next move.*

Allison pulled her car over to the turnout. Her face prickled as she kept her speed slow and easy, hanging a U back to the gate. No one else was leaving, and she knew her Infiniti was a conspicuous ebony dot on several dozen surveillance cameras as she unrolled her window and stuck out her badge for the same guard who'd waved her through. She remained silent; she was a top-level NSA agent, and there was no need to explain her comings and goings unless requested.

The guard's phone—a secured landline—rang as he took her badge. Her heart stuttered, her mind raced. Was it an order to detain her?

As he reached for the handset, she forced herself to look unconcerned. He swiped her badge and handed it back to her as he put the receiver to his ear. She left her window unrolled, on the chance that she might be able to eavesdrop. But he closed the door of the kiosk, sealing himself inside.

The Jersey gate had not yet raised.

Her gaze ticked toward the shadows, where the Men in Black patrolled. If she tried to bolt the gate, they just might shoot her.

Through the window, the guard's eyebrows raised; his forehead wrinkled as he looked at her through the window. She did not react, merely gazed placidly back at him, although her heart was trip-hammering against her ribs.

Then the barrier went up, signaling permission to leave. Her hands shook on the wheel as she drove through. She took slow deep breaths and kept her face slack and expressionless, picking up a little speed as she neared the NSA-only on-ramp onto the Baltimore-Washington Parkway, because anyone would speed up a little. It would look odd if she didn't. She fought the urge to floor it. She wasn't safe yet. She could still be summoned back. Shot at if she didn't comply.

She eased onto the on-ramp. Traffic was relatively heavy, and fat raindrops spattered on her windshield. She moved into "dry cleaning" mode—evasive maneuvers designed to reveal a tail, putting space around her car—in case she had to gun it and get the hell out of there.

With one eye on the traffic, she reached across to the passenger seat, where her leather briefcase lay facing her. She flipped it open and slid out her laptop. Using top-secret NSA data gleaned via the Oracle system, Allison had shielded her cell phone and wireless connections from eavesdropping with state-of-the-art sophistication; she should theoretically be immune to invasion, even this close to Crypto City. She popped the lid and punched in a macro, taking her eyes off the road long enough to scan the monitor windows showing a dozen views of Storage Unit #217 at Old Alexandria Self-Storage, just two short blocks from the new Oracle headquarters. The storage unit door was still bolted; her paint cans and tarps were undisturbed. Illuminated by a tiny light she had installed inside the otherwise empty paint can, the gleaming golden spider necklace still lay inside.

I'll kill you before I let you have it, she silently promised Echo. It was a promise she fully intended to keep—even if the Eastern seaboard blew up before the month was over.

Chapter 2

After Allison assured herself that the spider necklace was still secure, she kept her eye on the flow of traffic as she speed-dialed Selena Shaw Jones.

"Blackmail," Selena said by way of greeting. "I texted because I went straight to voice when I called."

Allison was mildly shocked. She hadn't even heard Selena's incoming phone call. Morgan's voice had captured her full attention.

"Go on," she told Selena.

"Oracle snagged an e-mail 'you' sent to an FBI agent named Phil Matsumoto. Looks like Special Agent Phil's in bed with Monya Kishinev."

"I don't know either name," Allison said.

"Kishinev's Russian mafia," Selena filled in. "The message was sent to Matsumoto's private home desktop, which is well-protected, but the sender cut through all the firewalls like a laser. If Matsumoto doesn't wire seventy-five thousand dollars into your offshore account in the Cayman Islands, you're turning him in."

"The Caymans? That's so last year," Allison quipped,

but she was shaken. Of course she hadn't sent the e-mail. It was a setup, and she wondered if this Matsumoto guy would buy it. If he was stupid enough to jump in bed with a criminal, he probably would. Or maybe he was smarter than that; maybe he was an undercover good guy working Kishinev, flipping him to the Jedi side of the Force. Maybe now Matsumoto would reconfigure his targeting system to probe the wrongdoings of a dirty NSA agent initials AG.

"How does it look?" she asked Selena, as a flash of lightning blazed across the sky.

"Anything but clumsy," Selena replied frankly. "It's a totally professional job. If I didn't know you, *I'd* believe you sent it."

Allison grimaced. "Except I'd never be this obvious."

"Agreed," Selena said. "But that wouldn't stop them from shipping you off to Leavenworth. Another one just popped in. Hmm, it's to a CIA manager. James Wrobleski. Hold on, I'm reading up on him. Gotta love Oracle. It snags more intel than I can get at CIA."

Allison didn't say anything in reply. She did love Oracle. She had designed it, built it, nurtured it. But she couldn't let Selena know that. Because right now, Selena didn't need to know that. No one did besides the head of Oracle—code name Delphi.

Aka, Allison Gracelyn.

She flipped on her windshield wipers and watched the traffic. Two lanes over to the left, a grubby white panel van passed a BMW on the right, and cut back in front of it. The Beemer honked his horn and flashed his brights.

"Here we go," Selena said. "Six months ago, three CIA agents and four Italian SISMI intelligence officials 'allegedly' kidnapped an Italian cleric in Rome. Our governments are denying it. Wrobleski is the CIA manager of the three agents and I'm willing to bet this is something very off the books that he has somehow managed to contain, workwise. I sure never heard about it. Your silence is worth eighty grand."

A produce truck rumbled up abreast Allison's passenger side, cutting off her view of the other right lanes. She dropped back and got behind it. In the next lane over, the white van was driving slowly about twenty feet ahead of her, and the trailing BMW was still angrily flashing his brights, insisting it yield so he could pick up speed.

"So do you know where this smear campaign is coming from?" Selena asked.

Allison remained silent. It had to be Echo, but Selena had no need to know that, not yet. The less Selena knew, the safer she would be. The safer she was, the easier to send her on a mission if need be; and Selena was one of the best field agents in Oracle. She had single-handedly defended the American embassy in Berzhaan from a terrorist takeover.

But would that be fair, to make someone fly blind straight into harm's way?

This is not a fair game to start with. No one in Oracle is blind, she reminded herself. *They agreed to work for the organization with their eyes wide-open. They knew some of it was going to be black bag ops. They knew they could die.*

"Okay, asked and answered," Selena said, signaling that she accepted Allison's silence. At some point in their tenure as Oracle agents, nearly every single one of Allison's operatives had asked Allison point-blank if she was Delphi. Allison had never confirmed it, nor had she denied it. She had merely remained silent, and no one had asked her more than once.

Her mind was racing. The Oracle mainframe would unpeel the layers of secrecy regarding any other threats and disinformation Echo was sending out in her name. Maybe if she personally watched the threads as they came in she would discover the pattern they wove. Trace them back, learn the location of the original signal and shut Echo down—if indeed she was behind this elaborate frame-up.

Allison's cell phone pinged as a message came in on her other line. She glanced at the number as well as the time. It was Morgan, and it was 7:51 p.m. She stayed on the line with Selena.

"I wonder who 'I'm' blackmailing at the NSA," she ventured. "I suppose I'm ensuring that at least one corrupt person in every intelligence agency will be gunning for me."

She heard Selena's staccato typing, popping like muffled gunshot through their connection. The Infiniti's windshield wipers *thwacked* back and forth, an edgy metronome. The white van lumbered along in the rain.

"I don't see anything, but it looks like you were right about Morgan Rush. His most recent message to McDonough is encrypted, but I'm running it through our codecrackers and your initials are part of the subject header." Selena grunted with disapproval. "All the good ones are married, gay, or spying on you."

Allison allowed herself a quick grim smile, appreciating the irony of such a statement from someone who was happily married and therefore, believed she had one of the good ones.

Another call came in. This one was Allison's boss, Bill McDonough, and she let it go to messages.

"Oracle just gave me one more," Selena declared. "No, wait, it's about the Marion Gracelyn scholarship fund. Someone just gave it a big donation. Two million dollars. Anonymous."

Allison grunted. "Wondering how much of that is my newly laundered blackmail money."

"Not seeing anything else on you directly right now," Selena told her.

"Then I'm listening to my new messages," Allison said, punching in her voice mail code.

"Allison?" Morgan queried. *"I'm in your office."* That was all. That was a hundred percent Morgan—a man of few words, someone who believed that actions mattered and talk was, well, talk. Which was ironic, given his choice of occupation. He was a damned good codebreaker, alert to the nuances in several foreign languages including Farsi, Mandarin, some Polynesian languages and dialects and Russian.

She went on to the one from McDonough. His voice came in loud and clear, and he had a little bit more to say. *"Rush said you were on your way up. Guard gate shows you left. Where the hell are you?"*

Allison exited her message system and checked back in with Selena. "Anything?"

"Still doing my search," Selena said.

"Then I'm putting you on hold again. Beep me if you need me."

Allison pressed redial to call McDonough back. He picked up immediately.

"Bill, I have an emergency," Allison began.

"*This* is an emergency," McDonough thundered. "This is the biggest goddamn emergency in the world. You are here in two minutes or you have no job and you never have a job again and I give you to CIA for debriefing until you die."

"Sir, with respect—"

"*Respect?* You have no respect! No respect for your teammates or your project or your country. Who the hell do you think you are?"

"Sir—"

"*One* minute, or I'm sending someone after you to haul your ass in here."

"Yes, sir," Allison said, disconnecting.

She pushed her foot down a little harder on the gas and went back to Selena. "My boss," she said flatly. "Wondering why I haven't shown up for our meeting. I guess that tells us I'm not blackmailing *him.*"

"No. So far Oracle has reported no evidence of Gracelyn-NSA corruption, you'll be gratified to know."

"Keep searching," Allison told her. "Not that I'm hoping you'll find any."

She saw what Echo was doing—setting fires, wreaking havoc. Allison moved her tense shoulders, rubbing her forehead as a headache threatened. She was tired down to the marrow. Her day had already been very long and incredibly tense.

She had landed at Washington's Dulles International Airport at one this afternoon, every cell of her body on extreme high-alert as she unclasped the spider necklace containing the precious flash drive and calmly placed it in one of the plastic bowls at the airport's security checkpoint. Of course the guard who took the bowl had no idea what was in that necklace—the last third of Arachne's vast web of off-the-books state secrets; corporate espionage capable of shutting down Wall Street; career-ending dirt on superstars; and life-ending intel on world leaders.

Echo already had the other two memory sticks; she needed this one to fully reweave her mother's web. Echo would stop at nothing to get it; Allison half expected the airport guard to reveal himself as a plant, pull out an AK-47 and gun her down as she walked through the metal detector.

Once on board the jet, she put herself beside a window exit and monitored the other passengers for the duration of the flight. She skipped the champagne and went for the steak, storing up protein in her body, staying loose and easy so she could go from zero to sixty if she had to.

In the airport parking structure, she swept her Infiniti a dozen times for both bugs and bombs before she drove straight to Old Alexandria Self-Storage, two blocks away from the new Oracle headquarters, still located in Old Alexandria.

There she ran an hour-long soft recon on the storage facility, studying the security cameras, staring into the shadows. Popping some button cams when and where she could, making sure the wireless uplink to her laptop was solid. Once assured of that, she forwarded the feed to the Oracle mainframe.

She left the you-store-it to buy some supplies so her

unit would pass cursory inspection—paint cans, a ladder, tarps. She did it alone; she told no one where she was and asked no one for help. She warred with herself about that decision as every step of the way she thought about the stupid little things that could happen: slipping on the newly washed floor in the paint store; getting hit by a car. But it was too late in the game to change her rules.

Returning with her purchases, she rented Unit #217 from the overly friendly, middle-aged man at the desk, surreptitiously adding more button cams under the ledge of the office counter as she filled out forms, paid cash and collected the keys.

She also installed a fully portable state-of-the-art laser security setup at #217, which she tied into the existing alarm system. It was identical to the system she had put in her town house in Old Alexandria, and at the new Oracle headquarters location.

Although Allison worked steadily, remaining focused, her nerves were screaming. She herself could task any number of satellites to track a target if she could lock onto it; she had to assume Echo had the same capability. Despite wiping down the necklace and the memory stick for homing devices, there was no way to be one hundred percent positive that even now, the flash drive wasn't signaling Echo as to its location.

That was why Allison hadn't hidden the spider necklace and its contents at the far more secure, brand-new Oracle headquarters. Keeping Oracle HQ off Echo's radar was every bit as vital as retaining possession of the necklace. If Echo took out Oracle's nerve center, she'd hamstring the organization. Allison knew Oracle was the only way to stop Echo; she had to keep the flash drive out of Echo's hands, and she had to keep Oracle intact.

Two top priorities—three, if she counted Project Ozone—one woman juggling all of them.

She'd told Selena to go to the new town house location and watch for intel that revealed Echo's next move. However, there were layers to Oracle's intricate data mining programming that Allison had reserved for her own eyes only, and now she debated about the wisdom of that as well.

I'm spread way too thin, Allison thought grimly. *And I'm playing a dangerous game with the lives of millions. Maybe it's time to change strategies and get more of my own players on the board.*

"Oh, no," Selena muttered. "Damn."

"Talk to me," Allison ordered her.

"Abductions. Three girls. They were all conceived via the Women's Fertility Clinic in Zuni," Selena bit off.

"No," Allison breathed, clenching her jaw. "No way."

"I don't recognize any of their names. Hang on, I'm pulling up Jeremy Loschetter's file." About half a minute went by. "Allison, he swore the full list was on that memory stick he hid in his shoe heel. But none of these names are on it."

"He lied to us. Imagine that," Allison said bitterly, feeling ill. She'd thought they were done with this, with the abductions of young women—with Loschetter, a loathsome human being.

"Oh, my God, Allison, I'm getting more pings. There have been *seven* domestic kidnappings that the FBI has gotten involved with in the last forty-eight hours. All girls. Their mothers were infertility patients at the clinic."

Ignoring her tumultuous inner state, Allison pro-
cessed the new information. Echo had still been in India
when the kidnappings began. Was that why she had
been so focused on stealing Lilith's necklace? Did it
hold more information about the technology Loschetter had used to genetically enhance eggs that had been
harvested at the Women's Fertility Clinic and place
them into gestational surrogates?

Allison had no idea what was on Lilith's memory
stick. She couldn't read it. She knew that Lilith had
downloaded some files onto a laptop back in India, and
she figured Lilith's mother, Arachne, had programmed
in a one-time-use code that she, Allison, had yet to
crack. Allison hadn't tried very hard. For all she knew,
activating the stick sent out a beacon. That might have
been how Echo had found Lilith in the first place.
Maybe when Arachne had created the three drives, one
for each of her daughters, she meant for them to find
each other and work together to restore her empire.

Acting as Delphi, Allison had sent the twins Elle
Petrenko and Samantha St. John to India to retrieve the
laptop, but so far they'd come up negative. That could
mean Echo had it—which might be how she'd known
which girls to abduct—or it could simply mean that the
sisters hadn't located it yet.

"Go on," Allison said tersely. She could feel her anger rising, and she forced it back down. She was the
AIC—Agent in Charge. She had to stay calm, strate-
gize, and proceed.

"I'm reading the FD-302 on one who was taken in
San Francisco. She's only five years old. Her name is
Cailey. She's just a baby." Selena was angry, too. Alli-

son knew Selena and Cole were trying to start a family of their own, probably through adoption.

FD-302 was FBI jargon for documents that could be used in a court of law as possible testimony, and therefore, were released over the Internet. The bureau was well-known for using the Internet as little as possible. Agents' workstation computers didn't even access the net; they had to use specially protected computers in another part of the building. That might explain why the files hadn't shown up in the Oracle system before; the feebs might have released them in a batch because another agency had requested them.

"I cut and pasted a list of the vics," Selena said. "I'll send your laptop a copy and CC Delphi. I'm calling Delphi now. I know she's told us to refrain whenever possible—"

"She probably already knows this is happening," Allison cut in. "I'd say if she doesn't call you within half an hour, call her then."

There was a pause. "Roger that…Allison," Selena said. "But we have to move fast. If she can get back to me asap…" It was clear that she was struggling not to confront Allison about Delphi's real identity. "I'll keep on it."

"Good. I'm going to make some calls. You stay at the town house. Make sure the mainframe is safe."

"Oh, I will," Selena said, grittily. "When I find who did this…"

"We will," Allison promised her. "And they will know Athena justice."

"They will," Selena said feelingly.

Athena Academy for the Advancement of Women was the most elite, state-of-the-art prep school for women in the United States. The school was founded by Allison's mother, Marion Gracelyn, to educate the cream of the female student crop not only in academic subjects but martial arts, spycraft and other Special Forces-style subjects. The ultimate goal was to groom women to penetrate the highest echelons of power and serve as a force for good in society. Marion's foresight was paying off, and there was a special quality among the students and alumni—an Athena Force—that was changing—and saving—the world.

"Have you found anything on that force field that went up around Echo when Lucy attacked her?"

"Negative. Still working." A beat. "There's a lot going on."

"I know," Allison said. "But we'll get it done, Selena. You can count on that."

"Roger that," Selena replied.

They hung up.

For a moment the bombshell fragmented Allison's thoughts. *More genetically enhanced babies. More mayhem. Faked extortion schemes. Echo's legacy from her mother—a vibration field that deflects guns, knives, bodies and bullets. Too many things to keep track of. Not enough time. Not enough of anything.*

Then piece by piece she pulled herself back together; in an almost Zen state, she rested her hands on the wheel. The windshield wipers droned. The rain spattered.

I'm the center of the storm, she reminded herself, using one of the oldest relaxation techniques she knew— which she had learned while a student at Athena Academy. *Never tell yourself how powerful the problem is. Tell the problem how powerful you are.*

Her heartbeat slowed. Then she rifled in her brief-case for one of the half-dozen prepaid handheld cell phones she routinely packed, along with the electronic device she used to distort her voice when "Delphi" made calls. This batch had been on sale at the local electronics store, probably because their cheetah skins were *so* last week.

She punched the number of the Oracle safe house where they were keeping Loschetter. Before the current crisis, Allison's recruits had their own lives first, and then ran missions for Oracle. But some of them had made special arrangements so that they were free to guard Loschetter around the clock. The smarmy scientist had sold Teal Arnett, an egg baby and a current Athena Academy student, to Kestonian leader Vlados Zelasco at a nightmarish auction in Venice. Zelasco had spirited her to Kestonia where Athena alum Sasha Bracciali had rescued her. Another Athena Academy alum, Lindsey Novak, grabbed Loschetter. Now Loschetter belonged to Oracle, and they were keeping him incommunicado in a heavily fortified safe house in Arizona, not far from the southern rim of the Grand Canyon.

Her cell phone connected, ringing once.

"Athena Construction," a woman answered. Allison recognized the voice of Katie Rush, and the image of Katie's older brother Morgan popped into her head. He was probably as furious and baffled by Allison's actions as Bill McDonough. She could see him now, pacing the way he did, running his long fingers through his prematurely salt-and-pepper hair—he was only thirty-two—blinking his heavily lashed eyes of intense indigo, setting his hard, square jaw.

She had seen him agitated before, seen him fight to keep his temper when they decoded a gleeful e-mail sent from Berzhaan to a terrorist cell in Kestonia, announcing that some poor thirteen-year-old had earned a place in paradise by blowing himself up in a crowded open marketplace. Morgan had nearly wept at the loss of life, at the depth of despair and/or hatred that would prompt someone to do something like that. Instead he'd balled his fist and slammed it against the wall of the pit, startling half a dozen military brass who were there for a briefing.

Then and there, she fell a little bit in love with him, moving beyond her omnipresent lust for his magnificent body to a deeper connection. *This is why we do the things we do, Morgan Rush and I. This is why our jobs are more important to us than our lives.*

This is why I am Delphi. And this is why he can never know.

Her secrets would keep her alone for the rest of her life.

"I'm interested in building a house," she said, knowing that her voice was being unrecognizably distorted by the device clamped over the mouthpiece.

"Delphi," Katie said, and Allison detected the awe in her voice.

"How's Loschetter?" Delphi asked. "Is there anything unusual about his demeanor?"

"Quiet, bored. He wants more DVDs," Katie said with disgust. "He says his brain is atrophying. We can hope."

"Katie, listen," Delphi said. "In the last forty-eight hours, seven girls have been kidnapped. Girls conceived at the Women's Fertility Clinic in Zuni." She let that sink in. "They were not on Loschetter's original list."

"Oh, my God," Katie murmured.

"Watch him. I'm going to send you some backup." There were three Oracle agents guarding him at all times. "If someone's stealing egg babies, it stands to reason they'll want him. He knows more about genetically altering chromosomes than anyone else on the planet."

"Roger that," Katie said fiercely. "I'll kill him before I let anyone take him."

Delphi thought for a moment about the teenage suicide bomber in Berzhaan. Then she thought about Morgan Rush, Katie's older brother. She could hardly imagine the grief and fury that would rage through him if anything happened to Katie.

"You…be careful," Delphi blurted, and it was so out of character, so *not* what Delphi would say, that she hung up before Katie could remind her that she would rather die than fail at a mission. Delphi knew Katie would say it, because Katie had said it before. And Delphi had told her that she was proud of her commitment.

She set the phone on top of her briefcase and swallowed hard. She was getting too personally involved with her people.

Another image of Morgan came unbidden into her mind—in a pair of loose track shorts that revealed his muscular calves and thighs, and a damp, sleeveless T-shirt clinging to his pecs. He'd mocked her fumble during a recent tennis game on the agency courts. A second later, she'd power-slammed a tennis ball at him inches from his foot, a volley he couldn't hope to return, and he had broken into full-bodied laughter, completely appreciative of how thoroughly she had just kicked his butt. She didn't suppose he was laughing right now.

She blew out her breath and gave her head a shake. Morgan was off-limits, now and forever. The thought penetrated, despite all the other thoughts her busy brain was entertaining.

Allison began putting everything back in her briefcase—PDA, personal cell, laptop, distorter—then the produce truck switched lanes, revealing the white van again. The BMW took advantage of the hole in the traffic flow and shot back around the slow-moving vehicle. The van was definitely pacing her.

On your mark, Allison thought grimly.

Without signaling, with no warning, Allison cranked her steering wheel to the left and shot across two lanes of traffic, heading for the off-ramp. Horns blared. Brakes squealed all around her—and behind her—as the van barreled after her in hot pursuit.

Go.

Chapter 3

McDonough proceeded with the top-level Project Ozone meeting in Conference Room A, but he dismissed Morgan from the urgent and critical sit-down, and ordered him to interrogate anyone who had ever met Allison, much less worked with her.

Morgan was extremely pissed about missing the meeting, but when he got past the red haze of anger, he had to admit that it made sense. Morgan had been "observing" Allison for McDonough ever since McDonough had signed onto Ozone, three months ago. It was a distasteful arrangement that Morgan would have ordinarily refused, except that it gave him more latitude to sniff around Allison, access her records and get his request for a wiretap turned down.

He fed McDonough enough tidbits to fulfill his job description, but he kept the good stuff for himself. Not that there was much. Spider files, incomplete. Someone named Arachne. Someone else named Delphi, or maybe it was a place. Those kidnappings of Athena students earlier this year. But never the full story. Allison kept the good stuff for herself as well, of that he was certain.

Allison Gracelyn was doing something she didn't want anyone to know about. Correction: didn't want *NSA* to know about. In Morgan's book, that was six kinds of wrong.

Morgan deliberately set up shop for his interviews many conference rooms away from the Ozone meeting. He kept his black suit jacket on and his dark gray tie crisply knotted. The visiting brass didn't need to know NSA had forgotten to microchip Agent Double-O Gracelyn or that she was on the lam.

His black double shot went untouched. He had snagged a sandwich from the conference room but hadn't stopped to take a bite. After a few interviews, the air smelled like mustard and roast beef, and Morgan chucked it in the trash can.

Nobody had anything to tell him, and so far, an hour into interviewing, he had no feeling that anyone was omitting information in order to protect her. She wasn't made of Teflon; she was just…boring. Again, wrong. Allison was not boring. She was a busy woman; yesterday's personal leave day was one of many (but not beyond agency guidelines, and he'd kept track.) Not showing up in the midst of a high-alert was bad, but hanging a U and then going incommunicado was inexcusable.

The clock was ticking, and he was getting more and more pissed off. Why the hell didn't she at least call in? Who the hell did she think she was?

He tapped his government-issue black pen on his legal pad and gazed up at his next interviewee, Kim Valenti, who came in and sat across the mahogany laminate conference table. Like him, she wore a simply, nicely tailored black suit—in her case, with a skirt. Like Allison and him, she was a cryptanalyst, and one of the best at the agency, which why she was with Ozone. She and Allison were good friends; on many occasions, when Morgan had been in Allison's office, IM's had come in through the internal NSA net from Windtalker2, which was Valenti's handle.

"She called you earlier today," Morgan said to Kim Valenti. He knew that because he had downloaded and examined both women's phone logs.

"Yes, she did," Valenti said after a beat, as if weighing how much to say to him. His bullshit-ometer ratcheted up two notches. What was she hiding?

"What did you two talk about?"

"It was personal business," she replied, crossing her legs at the knee and settling back, as if she had all the time in the world, and no cares at all. She was cool, she was steady.

Morgan knew her body language didn't mean a thing. His colleagues at the NSA might think he was simply an extremely proficient codebreaker, but he'd run a few covert ops for his government strictly off-the-books. More than a few. He had done terrible things on behalf of the free world, risked his own life countless times, sent willing men to their deaths. No one suspected, of course. He made damn sure they didn't. How did the saying go? The better the spy, the better the lie.

"You know she's missing."

"I know she's not here," Valenti countered.

"I can hook you up to a polygraph," he reminded

her. "I can hand you over for interrogation. Your head will spin."

Valenti gazed at him steadily. "She had some personal business, just like I said."

Morgan balled his fists, tamping down his irritation with her screw-you attitude, because that wouldn't get him anywhere. Allison's comings and goings had been worrying the agency for years. That concern had mushroomed in the last twelve months. He himself had moved from concerned, to highly suspicious, and finally to wondering what game she was running on her own. For all her unflappable demeanor, she was a loose cannon, and he knew more than most that a weapon with the safety off could be used against you in a heartbeat.

He had the scars to prove it.

Inside and out.

"Ms. Valenti, foreign nationals of unknown origin are plotting to blow up a significant target in your country in less than a month," he said. "If that occurs, thousands of people will die. Until we resolve that, there is no such thing as personal business. We're here to protect those people, and until they're safe, we don't belong to ourselves. So whatever, why ever, she's wrong."

Her eyelids flickered. He watched her struggle with a sharp retort, and he wondered if he'd gone too far.

"Standing down a little," he informed her. "I actually do know we're not living in Nazi Germany."

It worked. She moved her shoulders and tapped her fingers twice on the desk. "Okay. She's pregnant."

Or maybe she had just been making him sweat a

little, payback for trying to intimidate her. He did that. He intimidated and bullied. He threatened. He frightened. He used whatever weapon he had whenever he could. He was combative. He was driven. He did what he had to. And he had to find Allison.

"Oh, for God's sake!" Morgan thundered, slamming his fists down on the conference room table. Valenti didn't bat an eyelash. "You can't think I'd believe that."

But the truth was that the male part of him—the part that fantasized about Allison Gracelyn naked and in his bed, the part that drove him to cool down at the gym, take icy showers, pace sleeplessly in the middle of the night, that part—was shocked and angry. Almost as if Allison had betrayed him with another man—when he had no claim at all on her, of course.

"You are lying to me. She's a consummate professional," Morgan flung at Windtalker2. "That's not her style. That's soap opera crap."

Valenti raised her chin. Her dark eyes flashed at him. "She's pregnant, there's a problem with the baby and she thinks she might be miscarrying."

For one more instant, he believed her, because he remembered how gently Allison broached the subject of his missing mother when he'd been assigned to Project Ozone and she had to get him a higher-level clearance.

"You were twelve," she observed. "That's a rough time in life, even without something like that."

"No one can buy me by promising me information on my mother," he had replied bluntly, raising the barriers around his heart. Of course he'd been asked that before. And would be asked again. But it was the first time Allison and he had discussed anything about his personal life other than his sister—whom Allison knew, of course, since Katie had gone to Athena Academy.

Allison's lips had parted slightly, and he saw for the first time how big her brown eyes were, and how beautiful, flecked with gold and heavily lashed. He was startled, and flustered. The men he worked with had an office pool going that the Ice Princess was a thirty-seven-year-old virgin. She'd never dated anyone. There were secretaries who refused to work for her, saying she was too demanding. Which earned her the title of Queen Bitch in the eyes of many. Sexism was still rampant in the workplace. He was probably more sensitized to it because he'd heard stories from Katie.

Morgan read Allison differently. It wasn't so much that she was cold or unreasonable; it was just that she didn't give much back, and she needed her people to work as hard as she did.

But that one time, discussing his mother, remembering that her own mother had been murdered, he had felt as if he'd seen a part of her she was in a habit of concealing. As if a mask had slipped. Maybe she had a guy who knew how to take that mask off. Maybe they were having a kid together, and that kid was in trouble.

Allison as a mother. It had a certain…resonance.

"Rush," Bill McDonough said from the doorway. Sweaty and unpleasant, he had loosened his dark blue tie and he looked twenty years older than he had fifteen minutes ago. McDonough shot Kim Valenti a glare that might turn a lesser woman to stone and jerked his head toward the hallway.

Morgan gave Valenti another look—a chance to change her story—but it was obvious she was done. He followed McDonough out, masking his distaste for Allison's boss of three months—his boss's boss. McDonough was crude around his female staffers, and he stole credit from his people for their decryptions and analyses.

"How'd it go?" McDonough asked him.

"It's all bullshit," Morgan replied. "You?"

"Same here." He made a face. "Here's the sum total of what we know—someone's got a nuclear device and wants to kill the Great Satan. You know, I always wanted to be an astronaut." He slid a glance at Morgan. "Think it's too late?"

Before his mother had gone missing, Morgan had wanted to be a cowboy. He figured he still had time.

"Nothing new?"

"The terrorists are waiting for one of two messages. One is the code word to hit us. The other is to abort the mission. We don't know what either code word is. I suggested this." He said the most offensive version possible of "I'm having sex with your mother" in Farsi.

"You think it's coming out of Iran?" Morgan asked. "I was thinking of Berzhaan."

McDonough grunted. "I don't think so. The Berzhaanis are too unorganized."

The two men walked down the hall past the open pit of monitors, phones and codebreakers working on Project Ozone. McDonough had on too much aftershave, and he was a smoker. He smelled like the inside of a taxicab.

In the pit, there was a worried-looking general standing beside a harried-looking guy in a suit, both talking in low voices. Another trio, two men and a woman in a naval uniform, were paging through stacks of stapled printouts. The scene was noisy and appeared chaotic, but there was methodology in the madness, a through-line that the seasoned cryptanalysts of NSA knew how to find. A couple of crackerjack codebreakers gesticulated at a map of the Eastern seaboard with a dozen lights blinking—displaying potential targets for a nuclear attack.

Allison's office door was closed. McDonough pulled a swipe card from his pocket and ran it through the panel beside the door. The lock unclicked.

"Her little escapade stinks like a dead hooker," he said as he barreled in and flicked on the lights. "I was just in here, checking on things. This is what I saw."

He crossed to her desk and pointed at her computer screen. Morgan stared down at the screen—to see himself in profile, staring down at the screen. He turned and squinted, searching for the camera.

"It's a button cam on that picture frame—the one of her and her family when she got her black belt," McDonough said.

Morgan couldn't detect the camera on the black lacquer frame, which didn't surprise him. The photograph itself was very familiar to him, showing a teenage Allison dressed in an all-black martial arts uniform, belt included, beaming from the center of a loving family. Her mother had still been alive. Marion Gracelyn was murdered ten years ago, when Allison was twenty-seven. Morgan had studied the picture before, wishing he could see Allison smile that broadly in person, catch her in a carefree moment.

Catch her, period.

He wondered if McDonough's spycam had captured even one of the hungry, lustful gazes he, Morgan, had thrown Allison's way when he thought she wasn't looking. He should have guessed her own boss would be conducting illegal surveillance of her at the office. He wondered if McDonough actually was NSA. He had the codebreaking creds, but on the other hand, CIA employed lots of multilingual codebreakers, too.

"Watch what we've got. This was yesterday morning." McDonough pulled a miniaturized remote control device out of his black suit trousers and clicked it. An image filled Allison's screen—it was Allison at her desk, fingers racing across her keyboard as she frowned mildly at the monitor. She stopped typing and rested her hand on her chin. Clouds must have passed behind her window, dimming the light. Morgan could practically see the wheels of her brilliant mind analyzing strings of code as they blipped across her monitor.

Then her outside line rang and she picked it up.

"Yes," Allison-on-the-screen said. Her face changed and she sat up straighter in the chair. The room darkened perceptibly as her eyes widened and her lips parted. She looked…frightened.

"I'll get the cash," she said. "Give me time." Then she hung up, pushed back her chair, turned off the lights and left her office.

"Then she leaves," McDonough said, as the footage continued, the room cast in an eerie night-vision luminescence. "That was yesterday morning, before she took today off for personal reasons…and has been MIA ever since."

Morgan thought a moment. "Any corroborating calls

come in while she was gone?" He could comb back through the phone log himself to check.

"Nothing on my camera. I listened to all her messages, in-house and her secured outside line. I'd say that woman has no life except she clearly does, maybe working for the same guys who are trying to blow up the United States in time for Thanksgiving."

Listening to her messages involved some protected speech issues, but Morgan stayed focused. He was intrigued by what he'd seen, but he knew there could be a logical explanation. He simply had no idea what it might be.

McDonough glanced at him. "As far as I'm concerned, that bitch has made her move, and it's time for the bat signal, Batman."

Morgan kept his face impassive, and McDonough laughed mirthlessly.

"Yeah, I know about you. You've gone deep for the people of these United States. Risked everything. Almost gotten killed a couple of times. I know you want to do this. Go ahead and volunteer. I'll back you up."

Morgan doubted McDonough would backup his own mother, but he wasn't about to say no. He wanted to go after Allison so badly he could taste it.

"If you don't go get her, I'll send someone else who doesn't have a hard-on for her," McDonough continued.

Morgan nodded once, hopefully out of camera range.

McDonough nodded back. "You have everything you need?"

"I do."

"Then stop wasting time." McDonough lifted up his hand, snapped his fingers and pointed at the door.

Morgan bristled at the lapdog-style command, but kept his irritation to himself.

Without another word, Morgan left Allison's office.

McDonough stuck his head into the hall. "Call me. Check in. I don't want to have to send someone after you next."

Morgan kept walking.

As he strode past the conference room, Valenti rose from her chair and joined him in the hall.

"What are you going to do?" she asked, catching up.

He turned his head. The door to Allison's office was closed and McDonough was nowhere to be seen.

"What makes you think I'm going to do anything?" he asked.

She pursed her lips and raised her chin.

"Just tell her to come in," he said. "It's not too late. McDonough will back off."

Her expression never wavered. Morgan gave his head an angry shake.

"You're wasting my time," he said, and then he guessed that maybe that was the idea.

He took off.

Chapter 4

Allison flew down the off-ramp, gutterballing it as close to the shoulder as possible, and hit the turbo through a very yellow light. It was red before she was halfway across the intersection. More horns blared and she flicked her vision from the rearview mirror to the crimson taillights crowding her windshield. The grubby white van hadn't shown yet, but in this day of cell phones and satellites, that didn't mean a thing. For all she knew, her Infiniti had been painted by Echo herself, who was observing her nemesis via satellite as she flushed her out.

There was a nondescript strip mall up ahead. Allison scanned for entrances and exits where she might dump the car if she needed to.

A motorcyclist swerved around her and failed to maintain his speed. She braked hard, keeping her eyes on him in case he was trying to box her in. Her laptop and cell phones crashed to the floor on the passenger side. Sloppy. The motorcycle flipped her off and streaked away in the rain.

Making a command decision, she turned off her lights and shot into the alley behind the strip mall. There were no overhead lights, and the alley was narrow, bordered by two one-story brick buildings on her right and a quartet of oversize aluminum Quonset huts on her left.

She eased the car around an overflowing Dumpster, then glided around the far corner of the building. Leaning forward, she craned her neck and peered through the windshield.

The van was crossing the intersection.

She leaned down and grabbed up her personal phone, a more subdued black than the cheetah print prepaids. Punched in Selena's number.

"Yes, Allison," she said.

"I'm being pursued. White van." She gave her the license plate number.

"Checking. Is there anything I can do?"

"Negative."

"Staying with you." Selena's voice was taut with anxiety, but she kept on task.

The van pulled into the strip mall. It did not go into the alley, but advanced slowly down a straggly row of cars parked in the gravel lot, the majority of them clustered near Allison. A quick glance revealed that the building beside her was a bar.

Allison backed up slowly, reluctantly shifting her attention from the white van to check the alley behind her via her side mirror, which she cranked to a sharp angle.

Harsh white headlights blazed at the entrance of the alley. She froze. If she backed up any farther, the lights would brush her car. If the driver was working with the van, they'd have her.

"I'm exiting my vehicle," she informed Selena, then she grabbed up the spill of her phones and her laptop and crammed them into her briefcase, feeling for her hat and gloves in her pockets in case she didn't get to come back. She got out, leaving her umbrella; too much to carry. Her Glock was unloaded and locked in the trunk, a precaution required for entry onto NSA property. She sidled around the side of the vehicle, her destination the trunk.

She looked from the headlights to the other side of the alley. Above the buildings, a stand of evergreens rocked in the increasing downpour. Lots of places to hide, if you were on the run…or if you were a sniper.

Parallel with her, the back door to the bar opened. Allison jerked away from her car and melted farther back into the shadows.

A twenty-something man in jeans, a knitted cap and a sweater emerged. Cursing, his head down, he jogged a large wheeled black plastic trash can toward the Dumpster.

Allison slipped into the opened door and found herself in a small hallway, facing another opened door that appeared to lead into a small, dingy kitchen. The braided odors of wet wool, hamburger grease and beer wafted toward her.

On her left, the hallway extended into the bar proper, and she heard someone shout, "Hey, shut that damn door! It's frickin' cold out there!"

"Allison, what's your status?" Selena asked her.

Allison didn't answer. Dripping, she took a few steps into the hall, and then a few more, jerking when the man with the trash can reentered the door behind her. He was with a young woman carrying a flowered umbrella. She was dressed in a puffy down jacket and skintight jeans.

"I'll get my stuff," he told her. "I have to tell Andy they didn't empty the damn Dumpster again. I swear."

"Hurry," she pouted prettily, running a hand through her blond hair. "The movie starts in twenty minutes."

Had the woman driven that car into the alley? If so, that was excellent news, because she was harmless. Allison turned and walked up to her.

"Did I block you?" she asked her in a friendly, relaxed manner.

"Yeah, but it's no problem," the woman said. "We'll be backing out." She smiled questioningly at Allison's coat, then at Allison. "Get caught in the rain?"

"Yeah," Allison said, arranging the coat over her shoulders. "I probably look like a drowned rat."

"Kinda," the woman replied, wrinkling her nose.

"Hey, dude, what is your problem?" the same protesting voice yelled above the noise. "Shut the damn door!"

"What's going on?" Jeans asked Allison, craning her neck. "It's not the cops again, is it? Man, Bobby gave *one* girl with a fake ID a beer, and—"

It might be that. Or "Dude" might be looking for her.

Allison pushed around the woman and flew back out the door like a shot. The light from the door spilled over the alley, against a metal door ten feet away cut into the large Quonset hut. She hurtled herself at it, grabbed the knob and jerked. It opened. She darted inside and shut it after herself, feeling for a locking mechanism, finding none, moving on into the darkness.

She smelled oil, dust and dirt; her hand brushed against something serrated that felt like a large saw. The building was some kind of storage facility for machinery parts. She crept forward carefully, trying to keep herself moving in a straight line. Most buildings had two doors, an entrance and an exit. If she could find the way out...

"Allison, where are you?" Selena said in her ear.

Allison disconnected her and put the earpiece in her coat pocket. There was nothing Selena could do for her right now except distract her.

She snaked her arms through the coat sleeves as she tiptoed on the balls of her boots through the darkness. Her ears were primed for footfalls, voices, but she heard only the rain and the occasional clink when she ran into something. Dark shadows formed from darker shadows, retinal artifacts of her heightened anxiety and nothing more. Half a dozen times, she grabbed at objects as her knees or elbows or her briefcase collided with them, shutting her eyes tight, holding her breath.

With a pang of regret over her Glock, she tried to remember if she had taken everything else of value out of her car, if she had collected all the prepaids when her briefcase had fallen onto the floor.

It seemed an eternity before the toes of her boots pressed against the opposite wall of the building. She felt with her hands for a door, moving methodically to the right; then a sliver of light drew a line across the tips of her shoes.

Target acquired.

As she found the doorknob, an image of her mother flashed through her head. Allison had never meant to see the morgue photos, but she had by accident, and they'd been gruesome. Marion Hart Gracelyn had not died well. Fear rose inside her. She didn't want to die like that.

Then Morgan's face filled her mind, laughing exuberantly when she beat him at tennis. He rarely laughed. She doubted he would be laughing now.

She took a deep breath and turned the knob as soundlessly as she could. The door cracked open, the pressure making a soft *puh* that reminded her of a silencer. Rain sheeted down *ping-ping-ping* like spent cartridge casings.

Then she heard a noise behind her. Someone else had just entered the building. If they had a flashlight and a gun, she was in trouble.

She crossed the threshold. Stopped. Took stock, shivering beneath the downpour as she edged past the doorway, preparing to take out whoever walked through the door.

Then she realized she wasn't alone in the alley.

A stuttering streetlight strobed the scene, allowing Allison to piece together her surroundings.

Damn it.

Drenched by the rain, a tall, husky man loomed at the right end of the alley. He was wearing a bulky coat over a suit. He looked straight at her…and then past her, toward the other end of the alley.

She slid her glance to the left.

Equally tall, the man there was heavier, and bald, and dressed in an overcoat as well.

Bareheaded in the downpour, they began walking toward her. Adrenaline raced through her veins. She stayed light, got ready.

A flashlight flared from the exit of the Quonset hut. The man carrying it was at least six-four and dark-skinned, and his eyes were hooded as he saw her and held up a wallet. He must be showing her his ID, but she couldn't make it out in the dim light.

He said, "Allison Gracelyn, we'd like to speak to you."

"You are?" she asked steadily, not at all surprised that they knew her name. FBI? CIA? NSA? Echo's lackeys?

"CIA. We just have a few questions. Come with us, please."

Her heart jackhammered. No way.

She gazed left and right as the two other men continued striding toward her, blocking her escape routes. She wondered if their heavy coats concealed weapons.

"We can talk here," she said. Her skin sizzled with anxiety as her body prepared itself for flight or fight. "What would you like to know?"

"We just have a few questions," he answered smoothly. "It's nothing unusual."

The bald man reached her first. His heavy hand clasped her shoulder.

"Please, Ms. Gracelyn, let's go."

She kept her bicep loose as she said to the man facing her, "Unless you're FBI, and you have a warrant, you have no jurisdiction here." She glared at the bald man. "And I can have *you* arrested for battery."

"We only want to talk to you," the dark-skinned man repeated.

The hand on her shoulder dug in then. Her mind raced through possible moves to take all three of them out as quickly and efficiently as possible. If they were field agents, they had some martial arts training. Given the shape they were in, she probably had more. But her karate master had warned her to never, ever underestimate her opponent.

Then the bald man surprised her. He circled behind her, and the hard pressure of a weapon indented her back.

"This is a Magnum .357," he said. "You know what it can do."

"Christ, Wilcox." It was the third man, the husky one, who had been silent until now. "What the hell are you doing?"

"She has to come in. She's in some deep shit," the bald gunman—Wilcox—informed him.

"Hey, I don't know anything about that. Beck just said to pick her up," the husky man argued. She could hear the anger in his tone. "This isn't what we were told to do."

She noticed that the dark-skinned man wasn't talking. Was he in on it, then?

"It wasn't what *you* two were told to do," Wilcox declared. "I have orders to bring her in or shoot to kill."

"From Beck? No way," the dark-skinned man insisted, siding with the husky man. So he wasn't in on it. "You must be doing this for someone else."

She tried to remember whom she was supposed to be blackmailing at CIA. Wrobleski? She ran through the implications of dropping his name to see what happened.

The dark-skinned man reached inside his coat pocket.

"Raise your hands above your head," Wilcox growled, "or I'll bust your ass for obstructing justice."

Infuriated but impotent, the man did as Wilcox ordered.

"Wilcox is going to kill me," Allison said, as calmly as she could. "He used you to track me, and he can't let you survive."

"Shut up," Wilcox said, grabbing her and pressing the barrel against the back of her skull.

"I've drawn *my* weapon," the husky man announced.

"It's not loaded," Wilcox said derisively. "Check it."

The millisecond of distraction was the best she was going to get. If she died, she died two seconds sooner, that was all. She rammed sideways into Wilcox with an elbow strike hard to his chest, then immediately whirled around with her right hand around the gun. With a grunt she pushed back hard on his wrist. At the same time, she executed a very high jump-front kick, her toes leveraging beneath Wilcox's chin and snapping back his head.

Incredibly the weapon hadn't discharged. As Wilcox tumbled backward, his head smacked the cement in the alley with a loud crunch.

Not completely to her surprise, the dark-skinned man charged her from behind. She executed a backhand chop into his face with the gun as he began to wrap his arms around her torso. Then she whipped back around to face him, pushing forward with a knife hand strike between his ribs as she kneed him hard enough to drop him. With a grunt, she slammed her foot against his windpipe. Three times in the last two seconds, she could have killed him. But she didn't. He was only unconscious as his eyes rolled back in his head.

Aware that the husky man still presented a potential threat, she aimed the gun at him, left hand under the palm of her right as she distributed the weight of the weapon in a tripod formation. As he raised his hands over his head, she took a few steps away from both the supine men, in case they tried to sweep out an arm or a leg and take her down.

"Tell me who sent you," she said.

"I swear, I don't know what's going on," he insisted, staring down the barrel. "We were told to bring you in for questioning."

"By running me off the road?" she demanded.

He shook his head. "I don't know what you're talking about."

Her lips parted at his genuine confusion. She was in bigger trouble than she realized. "You aren't driving a white van?"

"No."

Damn it. "Who is Beck?"

"Our boss, CIA. I have to tell you, we're wired," he added.

"I'm betting your buddy had you disconnected," she observed. "So he could have a little more privacy when he killed you. Someone forced me here," she continued.

"Not us," he insisted.

"Then how did you know where to find me?"

"We were sent," he replied. "That's all I know."

Then something swooped off the roof and drove her to the ground, slamming her facedown in a puddle. She heard a snap as excruciating pain roared through her head to the backs of her eyes, and she tasted blood.

It was a fourth man, landing so hard on her back that she expected her spine to crack in two. A haze of gray dotted with red swam in front of her eyes. She forced herself to stay conscious.

"Who the hell are *you?*" Husky shouted.

The .357. Allison realized she had landed on top of it. Then she heard footfalls as the husky man charged the jumper.

Her attacker's weight shifted and she took immediate advantage, contracting her torso, quickly snaking her hand into the space and gripping the gun. She rocked, attempting to leverage herself onto her side so she could get a knee under herself and lift her body off the ground.

She heard a *snick snick snick:* Husky, still trying to make lemons out of lemonade with his unloaded gun. She wondered if he really was CIA. He didn't seem smart enough.

The weight on top of her shifted again. She scooted out and got to her feet, to discover Husky using standard martial arts techniques against the jumper, a skinny Caucasian in a catsuit, who was employing a variant of Krav Maga, favored by Israel's Special Forces.

Allison leaped to her feet, charging forward at the two grappling men, and brought the .357 down on top of the jumper's head. He went slack and collapsed against the cement. His face was gaunt. By his cheekbones and haircut, she judged him to be Eastern European—possibly Kestonian.

Husky stared at her. She stared at him. Blood and rain gunneled down his face.

She showed him the gun, aiming straight at him. He looked scared as he panted and kept his hands where she could see them.

"Start over," she said.

"Our manager is Jack Beck," he replied. "Swear to God, I didn't know it was a setup. I don't think Jack does, either." He stared at the gun through a curtain of rain. "But you're right," he said. "They should have heard this. They should be coming for us." He grimaced. "Wilcox played us."

"I think he's working for someone in CIA," she said. "I think you've got someone real dirty close to you." She was willing to bet Wrobleski outranked Beck, probably was his superior, and he was doing bad deeds on company time, with company equipment, funds and personnel.

"Come in and talk to us about it," he ventured.

She shook her head. "Another time, maybe. What does your vehicle look like?"

"Black Town Car," he replied.

Then she spied her briefcase, her gut clenching as she realized she hadn't closed it properly. The laptop was poking halfway out, and there was a cell phone lying in a puddle beside it.

He looked down at them, too.

"You tell them I'm clean. I'm being set up. When you wake up," she said to Husky, as she executed a side spinkick and clocked him hard against the temple.

As she whirled around, she watched her own blood spatter the corrugated aluminum siding in the weirdly strobing overhead light. It was from her nose.

She dropped down to her haunches; threw the phone and the laptop back into the briefcase; and soaked up blood with the arm of her coat as she sprinted around the building into the next alley.

Her car was where she'd left it, and she saw no one else in the alley. Most importantly, no black Town Car. She unlocked the door of her Infiniti, fingers crossed that no one had pressed a bomb or tracking device to the undercarriage, slid in and gunned it.

Grabbing tissues from a box in the glove compartment, she mopped up her face, grimacing when she touched her nose. She was pretty sure it was broken. She was panting and shaking as she crashed back down from the extreme high of her adrenaline rush.

The white van was gone. It would have blocked her getaway from her end of the alley if it was still here. Maybe the wheelman figured the leaper was gone too long and abandoned him. Maybe Husky had lied and CIA decided to wait until she left the parking lot before they attempted another interception.

The better scenario had the white van freaked and gone, and the CIA arriving to see what was going on and staying to do a mop-up, giving her time to put some distance between her and them. Maybe they'd ID the roof jumper, trace him back and discover…what? That a genetically enhanced woman named Echo was after a memory stick?

A memory stick the CIA would love to possess themselves? Did Oracle really want them to know that?

I can't trust anyone.

She grabbed the nearest phone out of her briefcase—cheetah print—and dialed Selena.

"Allison," she said, "God, are you all right?"

"The van," Allison replied. Her voice was ragged and muffled, as if she had a head cold. She pulled around the corner of the bar and straightened out, glancing in the rearview mirror to see if her luck was still holding.

"Nothing on the plates. Allison, you sound—"

Without warning, a red pickup truck backed out of a parking space in front of Jade's Bar. Allison hit the brakes but it was too late. Metal squealed on metal as she hit the rear wheel well. Her air bag did not deploy, but she was jerked, hard. Pain shot from the center of her nose and radiated like electric wires all over her face.

"Damn it, damn!" she yelled.

She backed up and swerved around it, flooring it out of there. She looked in her rearview mirror, to see a man run out of the bar. He was joined by another man, taller, wearing a ball cap, racing toward her in the rain, waving his arms over his head.

"Allison?" Selena shouted.

Allison gritted her teeth and kept driving straight, noting no fishtailing, no swerving. That meant she was still in alignment. Despite the impact, her car was in better shape than she was.

"Selena, you need to do something for me," she said. Then she hesitated. No one else in the world knew where that flash drive was. No one, except, perhaps Echo.

If I get picked up—or killed, God knows what will happen to that flash drive next.

"There's a storage facility." She grabbed more tissues and pressed them beneath her nose. It hurt like hell. "I've got it wired and you'll need the code to get in. It's on the mainframe, in a file labeled with the nickname of my favorite horse back at Athena Academy. You know that name. You'll need it to decrypt a disarming protocol. Don't try to go into the storage facility until you're absolutely sure of that protocol." *Because you will die.*

"Roger."

"There's a paint can in the library where you are now. It's a duplicate of one in the facility. Both are labeled with the color of my eyes. Take the one from the library to the storage facility and exchange it for the one you find there. When you get to the facility, disarm the alarm system. The protocol will also initiate a pre-recorded visual feed of the storage unit for the caretaker and anyone else who's watching. It will mask your entry, the swap and your exit."

"Understood." Everything Allison had described was SOP for covert ops, so no surprises yet for Selena.

"Once you retrieve the can, don't open it. Repeat, do not open. Box it up and ship it to Drop Point Alpha."

Allison was referring to their post office box in Athens. As bizarre as it sounded, the more out in the open they were about receiving their supplies, the less likely the bad guys would be able to locate and intercept them.

"Drop Point Alpha, Roger that. Is the can wired to explode?"

"Not by me," Allison said. "But I don't know if the contents are wired. Use extreme caution. Don't hold onto it, Selena. Get rid of it asap."

"Roger that," Selena said.

"Call my cell phone when you've done it."

"Will do," Selena replied. "Are you hurt? Do you want me to meet you somewhere?"

"No," Allison said firmly. "Do exactly what I just told you. Do it like the world will explode if you don't do it."

"Are you coming in?" Selena asked her.

"No. I'm going deep. I'm going to have to ask more of you to put Oracle first. Anyone who can make special arrangements to free up their time should do it. Spread the word."

Selena was quiet for a moment. "Understood."

"I'll be in touch." Delphi disconnected and raced through the dark, sharp wind.

Chapter 5

The rain was almost hail, ricocheting off Morgan's windshield as he left NSA headquarters in his black Lexus. His tie unloosened, his suit jacket laying over his briefcase, he merged onto the Baltimore-Washington Parkway, planning to drive straight to Allison's town house. There was something about that recording McDonough had showed him that bothered him, but he couldn't put his finger on what it was.

Shortly after he entered the flow of traffic, he intercepted a Maryland State Police dispatch call: hit-and-run and a possibly connected B&E concerning a parts store across an alley from a strip mall bar called Jade's. Dark sedan, possibly a Lexus or Camry, Virginia plates, numbers not caught. Suspect may be female with brown hair.

He narrowed his eyes as he glided through the traffic like a shark. Could that have been Allison?

The only thing Morgan had to go on was the proximity of the incident to Fort Meade. That and the sixth sense he sometimes had about these things. Still, he wavered as he pulled up the GPS coordinates for Jade's

Bar on his handheld. What if it had nothing to do with her? What if she was at her town house right now, throwing a few fake passports in a bag and shredding incriminating evidence?

Sometimes he used a team when he was on a mission, and he thought now about making a few calls. He could go to the Jade location and someone else could go to Allison's home. Another someone else could ask some questions at Athena Academy in Arizona. And a fourth teammate could scare the crap out of Valenti until she gave up her friend.

His people were good at coordinating their efforts, but he was moving awfully fast. He'd have to bring them up to speed and he wasn't sure he could spare the time. For the moment he had the element of surprise on his side. If Allison was looking over her shoulder, she would never dream of seeing him in her rearview mirror. As far as she knew, he was a codebreaker and nothing more. If one of his guys inadvertently tipped Allison off—if, say, she spotted a tail—and he lost her as a result, she would be a whole lot more difficult to find.

But he *would* find her. It just might take more time.

Better to travel light for the moment. It was just Morgan versus Allison, and he knew who was going to win.

Or am I simply giving her a chance to come out of this intact? A chance to tell me what's going on before I drag her in by her hair? he wondered. He wasn't sure he had the luxury of extending kindness or mercy. He had no doubt McDonough had a list of trackers he could and would call if Morgan didn't bring her back.

He took the off-ramp, racing to beat the cops to

Jade's. Since no one had been hurt, the Troopers might take a little time getting there. Good news for Morgan. That would keep the crime scene fresh.

There it was, the bar, seedy and run-down, and an older man in a ball cap stood hunched out in front, waving at him from beneath an umbrella.

Morgan pulled up. The man jogged into the lot as Morgan rolled down his window.

"Did you call in a hit-and-run?"

The man nodded. "I'm Andy Nelson. I own the bar. Are you a detective?"

"Yeah. Can you tell me what happened?"

"This woman in a black car ran into Hunter's truck." He pointed to the truck, which featured a good-size dent dead-center above the wheel. The tire looked to be losing air. "Happened about fifteen minutes ago."

"What did she look like?" Morgan asked him, because if she was a blond or a redhead, he was history.

"Well, before I go into that, I gotta tell you something else," Nelson said conspiratorially, glancing over his shoulder, in the direction of the bar entrance. "I was, you know, walking the perimeter while I was waiting for you, and I found some blood in the alley behind the parts store."

"I see," Morgan replied, cool and collected, even though his heartbeat picked up and he was sure his eyes had widened. "And do you believe that is connected with the hit-and-run?

"Maybe," the man replied. "Listen, I ain't told anyone in the bar about the blood. I gave Hunter—it's his truck—a shot of tequila on the house. He's mad enough to kill somebody. It's all he got in the divorce settlement. Bitch took his house. Let me show you the blood first. It's back there." He surreptitiously jerked his head. It was clear that he was thrilled to be of service; he was splashing around in drama and he liked it that way.

"All right," Morgan suggested, rolling the window back up and easing away. There was no way he was going to invite Andy Nelson to hop in out of the rain. One glance at the lack of police computer and comm system, and Morgan's jig would be up.

Morgan drove past the bar and slowed at the alley. A row of large upside-down U-shaped buildings made of corrugated aluminum faced the back entrance of the bar. He slowed, glancing in the rearview window at Nelson, who gave his head a shake and gestured for Morgan to keep going.

The rain pummeled his windshield as he complied, rolling slowly to the other side of the aluminum buildings and stopped the car. They were faced by low brick buildings and beyond them, towering evergreen trees whipping in the storm.

Morgan stashed a few manila envelopes containing some routine NSA business under the spotless passenger seat and glanced around for other evidence of his true identity. Then, as Nelson caught up with him, he grabbed his broad-beam flashlight from his glove compartment, and his umbrella, and got out of his car.

"Can you walk me through the evening?" Morgan asked, pressing the umbrella open.

"Well, this guy came through the bar like he was looking for someone. He left the front door open and it was pissing off my regulars. Bobby's girlfriend was in the back talking to some lady, and she went out of the bar in a hurry. The lady, I mean. Lee remembers a black car in the alley because the lady asked her if she was blocking her."

Morgan's sixth sense tingled again. "Lady?"

"Yeah, I guess she was pretty. I didn't see her. Bobby and Lee took off for the movies. If you want to interview them later, you can call the bar. I have a business card." He had been holding it the entire time he'd been talking, waiting to hand it over to the law, prove that he was helpful.

"Thanks," Morgan said, placing it in his coat pocket.

"I was going out to look at the Dumpster. Bobby came to tell me the trash guys didn't empty it again. I swear, I'm going to sue the management company, they raise the rent and then what, they stop collecting my trash?" He shook his head importantly, a businessman weighed down by the ineptitude of others.

"I hear you," Morgan said, clicking his teeth sympathetically.

"And I saw the door to Fred's Parts Supply was open. So I went in to check. There's mud tracked in and the back door was open. Fred's coming by to see if anything was taken." He shrugged. "I didn't realize you guys would come this fast, or I would have waited to call until Fred got here."

"That's okay, Mr. Nelson. You did the right thing. Do you have Bobby and Lee's home phone number?"

Nelson shook his head. "They're in the middle of moving in together. He hasn't updated his W-2 paperwork. I gotta get on him about that. Lee has a cell but I don't know it."

"Okay." He looked at the open door halfway down

the alley. "Did you go through the parts supply store when you walked the perimeter?" *Thereby contaminating a possible crime scene?*

"Yep. That's Fred's store. Let me show you the blood. I almost didn't see it."

Pulling a flashlight from his pocket, Nelson led the way down the alley, past the open door. There, beside the jamb, dark spatters rode the accordion folds of aluminum. Morgan was curious why the man thought they were blood; as Nelson shone his common flashlight over them, they washed to dark gray in the yellow light.

Morgan got closer and aimed his stronger light at the spatters. Sure enough, he saw a red tint. In the strange ways of the universe, an overhang had protected the evidence from the rain. Which meant that there may have been a trail the rain had erased. He ran his flashlight over the aluminum folds, then down onto the blacktop, washed clean by the pounding rain.

"Okay, thanks. This is very useful. It would be better if I worked alone here," Morgan said. "I'll come down and talk to the hit-and-run victim in a few minutes."

Nelson nodded knowingly. "Collect the evidence, secure the scene. Sure thing. It was just Hunter's *truck*. *He* wasn't hit. He'll sit tight for a few more minutes." He winked at Morgan. Actually winked. "Especially if I give him a few more shots of tequila."

"Good plan," Morgan assured him.

"Glad to help," Nelson said. Then he jogged up to the open door, and hesitated. "If I go in there, I'll contaminate the crime scene," he ventured. Then he winced. "I probably already did, huh."

"It's no problem," Morgan lied. "But it might be better to go around the way we came."

"Gotcha." The man smiled. "I watch *CSI*."

Morgan smiled back. "So do I."

"I'll keep Hunter from getting too drunk to talk."

"Good."

Nelson jogged back into the alley. Once Morgan was sure Nelson was gone, he returned to his car. He grabbed a pair of latex gloves out of a kit in the trunk, put them on and walked back toward the blood. The guttering streetlight was more annoying than helpful, but he'd take what he could get. He hugged the row of metal buildings on his left, sweeping with his flashlight as he went.

He looked at the spatter pattern, trying to imagine where it'd come from. Facial injury? Person had to be about half a foot shorter than he was. Maybe Allison's height. She came up to his shoulder. Perfect for kissing.

He didn't like thinking that way right now.

She's here…why? She gets attacked. She hits a guy's car making her escape…

Or she was never here in the first place.

He took one of his tissues, wiped it across the blood spatter on the wall and dropped it into a paper evidence envelope in his pocket.

He made his way back to the open door and aimed his beam into it, noting several sets of dirty shoeprints, one set significantly smaller than the others, exiting this way. He was guessing heeled boots. Allison had boots.

Could still be someone in there, hiding in the shadows, armed with an Uzi or a rocket launcher. He put it on his list of things to keep track of and started to head back to the car.

The rain was hitting the blacktop unevenly, indicating an object on the ground. He arced his beam downward again, and saw a portable phone. Some kind of animal print—leopard, maybe. He squatted down, grabbed it and stuffed it in his pocket.

In the distance, the thin wail of a siren prodded him to hurry. Swearing softly, he glanced up. Maybe he should go up on the roof…

The siren was getting louder. Morgan was a little surprised, and wondered if Andy had told another member of the Maryland State Police that he'd found some blood. Why else rush on a rainy night to a vehicular hit-and-run with no injuries?

Betting against the likelihood that the State Troopers would be searching for advanced bugging equipment, he reached in his pocket and pulled out a small plastic container of microphones no larger than fleas, which were adhesed on strips that looked like tiny bandages. He picked up the tiny pipette included in the package, squeezed out the air and tapped one of the microphones with the tip, creating suction. Then he placed it on the interior section of the doorjamb, two inches lower than his own mouth, and tapped it onto the surface. Morgan was six foot two.

He dashed back to his car and fished a small black metal box out of his trunk. Nonstandard issue for cryptanalysts, highly standard issue for black ops. Morgan wished he had some sexier stuff on hand. He hadn't restocked his car after his last assignment—Fairfax—because he'd intercepted comint—communications from intelligence—that NSA was going to recommence random searches of employee vehicles. One of Project

Ozone's tasks included beta-testing encryption protocols for mini-mics, so he could explain why he had them.

He flicked the box open, felt around for his earphones and looped one around his ear. It was set to the frequency of the tiny microphone on the jamb.

He hurried back to the button mic.

"Test, test," he said. He heard himself in his earphone. He also heard the siren—in stereo—distinct from his voice and the rain. He had good reception, and he was about to have company unless he got the hell out of there.

Back to the car, then, he put his flashlight in the glove compartment and calmly drove away. He went through the intersection and looped back around to get back onto the parkway. Sure enough, a Maryland State Troopers vehicle was just taking his original off-ramp.

Still wearing his gloves, he pulled the animal-print cell phone he had collected out of his pocket and hit the code to redial the last number that had been called.

"Athena Construction," came a voice. His *sister's* voice.

He drove on autopilot for a few seconds, dumbfounded. *Athena.* As in Athena Academy?

Katie said nothing more; she was obviously waiting for a reply. That raised the likelihood that there was some kind of coded response—which Morgan didn't know.

He listened to the white air. They were still connected.

She was his sister, for God's sake. If he ID'ed himself—

Everything in him told him to shut down the call. He shouldn't tip his hand. Frown lines creased his forehead as he clicked the phone closed, put it back in his pocket and drove straight to Allison's town house.

* * *

Allison kept to surface streets as she tried to staunch the flow of blood from her nose. She was certain that it was broken. Her head was pounding and her vision was blurring. She was worried about a concussion.

As soon as she had verified that there was no one following her, she pulled over to a weed-choked shoulder, staggered out and threw up.

Her mind bounded ahead, clearing a path to her goal. She would have to dump her car. She would have to get to Arizona. She would have to stay alive.

Slinging herself into the passenger seat, she dug in her briefcase for some ibuprofen and a bottle of water. She rinsed out her mouth, then swallowed a double dose of painkillers. Her body was trembling. She had to find the calm center. She had to take control, not be controlled. But she was on the verge of freaking out. Her body was still in battle mode; she had both fought and fled, and her central nervous system knew very well that the dangers were not over.

She breathed deeply, aware that seconds mattered right now. Nanoseconds. But she had to take the time.

Once she was more composed, she grabbed one of the prepaids, slapped on her distorter and called the Loschetter safe house again.

"Athena Construction," Katie Rush said.

"I'm interested in buying a house," Delphi answered, using her voice distorter. "Status."

"Delphi. Did you call before without speaking?" Katie asked.

Allison blinked. Alarms went off like hand grenades. "No. When?"

"I logged it. About ten minutes ago. Nine minutes and forty-eight seconds, actually."

"Hang on," Delphi told Katie.

Despite the fact that several Oracle agents had the safe house phone number, Allison had a feeling that things had just escalated from worse to worst. With her free hand, she opened up her briefcase. She had put six prepaids in there. There were four. The one she was on made five.

She shut her eyes at her terrible blunder. She must have left the one she had used in the alley. Who had found it? Her mind ranged over the possibilities, from CIA to assassins unknown to Echo. A good spy would be able to trace the call with satellite equipment. She'd done it herself in the past.

"Pack up. Be ready to leave on my signal," Delphi ordered her subordinate. "Your location may be compromised."

There was a beat. "Roger wilco, Delphi."

"Switch to the alternate phone number. I'll send a memo. I'm going to check in with you every hour on the hour starting now," Delphi continued, checking her dashboard clock. "It's 6:57 p.m. where you are, correct?"

"Yes, ma'am."

"You'll be called hourly. Always by an Oracle agent. Do *not* identify yourself as Athena Construction. The agent calling you will identify herself first with a new code word." She thought a moment. "The code word will be *'Gordita.'* Respond only to *'Gordita.'* Do you understand?" That was the nickname of her horse back at Athena Academy. The same code word she had told Selena to use.

"Yes. *'Gordita.'*"

"Next call will be eight your time, and then nine. Around the clock. On the other phone."

"Understood."

"Concentrate on Loschetter. Maybe he's figured out a way to contact his masters."

"No way. Not on my watch," Katie insisted.

"We might have underestimated him," Delphi cautioned her. "We don't get extra points because we're the good guys. Never assume we have an edge. Things are moving fast. Stay on him."

"I will." She liked Katie. The twenty-six-year-old was mature, frosty and aggressive—like her older brother.

"I'll get those reinforcements to you," Delphi continued. "If you have to abandon the safe house before they get there, I'll contact them with the new location on my end." They had another safe house set up, but she didn't want to transport Loschetter if she didn't have to. Let the fox out of the foxhole, he might figure a way to run—or someone might swoop down in a Black Hawk helicopter and spirit him away.

"You just say the word," Katie assured her.

"Stay alert but don't do anything you don't have to do," Delphi cautioned her, even though Katie was one of the most level-headed young women Allison had ever met.

"You can trust me, Delphi," the young woman promised her.

"I know."

A wave of vertigo swept through Allison. The hand holding the cell phone shook. She needed to get medical attention, or she would never make it to her destination. It would be so much simpler if she could hop another plane at Dulles. She wished she could keep her car. Her

Infiniti was a powerful weapon in itself: a movable wifi, fully loaded with a GPS and a built-in computer that would give her the locations of the closest food, gas, lodging and feeder airports.

"Delphi, are you still there?" Katie asked her.

She was spacing. "Yes. If you get another silent call, or any call that doesn't follow the new protocol, call AG or SSJ immediately. If you can't reach them, call me. But only in extreme emergency."

"Roger that," Katie said.

She took a breath. "Katie, your brother may personally contact you. I tasked Allison for something very urgent and she's going off the grid. Her employer is distressed." That would be NSA, and Katie would know it.

Katie hesitated. "Is something going on between him and her?"

Allison's face tingled. "Could you be more specific?"

"I mean, on a personal level. You know it bothers him that I'm doing things with her that I don't talk about. But I think it's more than that. He hasn't been dating much lately." She laughed humorlessly. "If you can call what Morgan does 'dating.' And he's mentioned her a few times. Little questions, like is she seeing anyone?"

"They work together," Allison said tersely. She knew about Morgan and his "dating." And despite her having fallen in love a little with a passionate man with bone-deep convictions about protecting innocents and bagging the bad guys, she doubted Morgan Rush had fallen in love with her at all. "What else has he been asking?"

"Well, he's pushed, actually, asked me if I knew

very much about her. I said of course I did. We both
went to Athena Academy. He asks me about the Spider
files, Arachne, those things. I haven't given him anything. But maybe if he knew that she was working undercover, he'd—"

"Agent Rush, he is not to know. You swore an oath
that you would serve Oracle first and foremost. Are
you still committed to that oath?"

"Yes," she said firmly. "I am, Delphi."

Allison softened a little. "I know he's your brother,
Katie."

"Everyone in Oracle is my family, too," Katie responded. "We're sisters."

Another wave of protective emotion rushed through
Allison, and it alarmed her as much as the first one. She
couldn't go soft. That was altogether inappropriate
behavior for Delphi.

"So we understand each other," she said, forcing her
tone to sound as hard as nails.

"We do," Katie concurred. "I'll wait for the next call.
Meanwhile, we'll pack."

"Good. One hour."

Chapter 6

As she glided through the pouring rain, Allison debated the wisdom of continuing to use the same prepaid phone. The public might not realize that calls from such cell phones could be traced, but she worked for NSA and she knew better. She gazed up through the rain and the trees to the twinkling night sky, where the satellites sniffed out signals like bloodhounds and alerted their masters when they were on the scent. She got out her personal phone, went online and ordered six dozen prepaids from a wholesale source. She had them shipped to the drop point in Arizona.

It was eleven at night Eastern standard time, and she wanted to drop.

She sent text messages to three more Oracle agents to get to the safe house asap—Jessica Whittaker, Chesca Thorne and Sasha Bracciali, who had recently joined the ranks of Oracle.

Then she got out another phone, clamped on the distorter and dialed Sam St. John in India.

"Yes," Sam said.

"Delphi. Have you found the laptop?"

"Negative," Sam replied. "No one has seen it. But they've been very busy here." There was an edge to her voice. "They're burying their dead. It was a massacre, Delphi. Echo mowed down simple villagers. Buddhist monks and Catholic nuns. And *children*." Sam's voice was so brittle Allison thought it might shatter. "Thank God Elle packed some vodka."

Allison's own fury silenced her for a moment as she gripped the wheel with white knuckles. "More egg babies have been taken," she continued. "One's only five years old. We know of at least seven, but those are only the ones that have been reported. There may be more. We didn't know about any of them. If there's a list on that laptop, we can warn them while we move in to guard them."

"Damn it," Sam muttered. "Is it Echo?"

"We assume so."

"What's she up to?"

"Unknown as yet," Delphi told her. "Maybe she's looking for one child in particular. Or maybe she's going to sell all of them to the highest bidder."

"Not going to happen," Sam insisted.

"Did you contact Lilith?" The beautiful daughter of Arachne had already taken a flight back to India with Tarak, her fiancé.

"Yes, she checked in. She described where the laptop should be. It wasn't there."

"Find it," Delphi urged. "When you do, notify me asap. If you can't get me, go to Allison or Selena."

"Roger that," Sam assured her.

They hung up.

With a groan, Allison rested her aching head on the steering wheel. Then she drove on, gliding deeper into the woods, where the streets were potholed and dark; the small houses and occasional businesses—liquor stores, pawn shops—ramshackle and stressed.

After half an hour of searching, she saw some half-rusted old cars inside a chain link fence. A hand-painted canvas sign that said Carlas Cash Or Tradein We Support Our Troops drooped across the fence, beneath a limp string of faded American-flag motif outdoor lights.

A small brick building sat beside the lot. The blue haze of a TV was on, and the red tip of a cigarette betrayed the viewer.

Allison took a deep breath and pulled down the illuminated makeup mirror on the sun visor. She had successfully cleaned off her face, but her nose was terribly swollen. Maybe she could work that to her advantage.

She took a nail file out of her purse and set to work prying off her parking sticker and her dashboard VIN—Vehicle Identification Number. Then she collected her car registration, her insurance card—everything she could think of—and put them in her briefcase. She methodically went through the car's computer, wiping it clean of her inputs—routes home, her address, the addresses of her father and brother, everything she could think of. She had a small toolbox in the trunk, and she got it out and removed her license plates, which she also put in her briefcase. There were VIN numbers elsewhere on the car, not easily erased; she'd have to leave them.

As a final precaution, she counted and recounted the prepaids, and checked the charge on the laptop. Then she pulled on her coat, her hat and her gloves, and retrieved her umbrella.

Next she popped the trunk. Shielding her briefcase as best she could from the downpour, she swayed as she walked to the back of the car. Her Glock was there, and a small box of ammo. Also, her karate bag and gear. She put the Glock and the ammo inside her karate bag, zipped it back up and slung it over her shoulder.

She walked past the window with the blue haze and the cigarette glow. Saw the glow shift and point in her direction.

She walked up the weed-choked pathway to the peeling front door. A motion detector light went on, revealing a sign that said Office Closed.

She made her knock sound tentative; after a few seconds, the door opened a crack, held in place by a chain. Allison smelled not cigarette smoke, but marijuana.

"Are you a process server?" The woman had a whiskey voice.

"No. I—a friend of mine told me about you."

She saw a rheumy eyeball, which widened as it took in her face.

"What the hell happened to you?"

"My…husband," Allison choked out, trying to sound desperate and frightened. "I just need some…I want to sell you my car. I need to get out of town."

The eye disappeared. "Not interested," the woman said. The door began to click shut.

"My Infiniti," Allison added.

The door opened again.

Morgan had never been invited to Allison's home. He hadn't been invited now. It didn't take much to disable the commercial alarm system and break in, which surprised him, and made him edgy. He wondered if he was on a more customized surveillance system right now, and if she was watching him herself.

"Come in, Allison," he said aloud. "McDonough can be dealt with. Let's hit reset."

There was no answer.

Still dressed in his business suit, he moved stealthily through her house, examining it as he went. He had snuck through embassies and palaces, armories and laboratories, and he had developed an eye for telling detail. Allison's town house was graceful and understated. The antiques, hardwood floors and creamy drapes and upholstering said East Coast, but there was a spacious, airy feel to the rooms that reminded him of the Southwest. He knew she was from Arizona. Her father had recently retired from the Arizona Supreme Court. And there was a lot of warmth here, too, from the plethora of family photos hung on all the walls, including a shot of a horse in a magnetized Athena Academy frame on her refrigerator. He plucked the picture off the fridge and admired it, turning it over.

"Gordita," he read. He smiled faintly. That meant "Little Chubby One" in Spanish. Odd name for such a beautiful horse.

He placed a mic on the frame.

About fifteen minutes later, he was in her bedroom, his leather satchel of spygear and flash drives at his feet, pawing through her underwear, searching for the elusive clue that would tell him where she kept the good stuff. He'd downloaded everything off her desktop system. For what it was worth, there were no phone numbers for high-risk obstetricians on her computer or in her hard copy address book—which was one of the items on top of the tidy little stack he was going to take with him.

He whistled low in his throat. He had had no idea that beneath her classy executive suits, Allison Gracelyn wore silky push-up bras and thongs. And he was enough of an animal that thoughts of her in these sexy under-things—she wore thigh-high stockings, oh man, who knew?—were making him hard.

"Ice Queen, my ass," he muttered. A band of black satin gleamed in the moonlight from her bedroom window. "She must have a gold card at Victoria's Secret."

Exhaling, he yanked the drawer out and felt along the runners. Above. Below.

While he searched, he listened to the chatter of the State Troopers at the Jade's alleyway crime scene through his earpiece. They were more interested in the vehicular hit-and-run. That made sense. Troopers were practical people, and blood spatters were more esoteric than dented trucks.

There had been no one inside the parts store; nothing had been taken; and from their conversation, they had already walked over the assorted muddy footprints and didn't seem interested in lifting them anyway. Nothing was missing. Time for the gang to head back to the doughnut shop.

Morgan had already done a cursory and illegal search on the unlisted number the prepaid had called—the one for Athena Construction. It, too, was a prepaid cell phone. No sales or activation records for either phone were immediately available, but he had the means to do a more in-depth search. He figured that for a dead end, with phony IDs and useless landline numbers in the blanks on the registration papers. But the area code for Athena Construction was the same as that of Athens, Arizona, the closest town to the Athena Academy.

So either Allison had been in that alley; someone had lifted a prepaid phone off her and then lost it in that alley; or someone really had dealings with "Athena Construction"—no business by that name being listed in the Athens phone directory—and someone who sounded very much like his sister worked there. It was possible he had been mistaken about her voice. He hadn't talked to Katie much lately.

However, he had never been a fan of coincidences. Which slammed shut doors number two and three.

His cell phone rang. He looked at the number. It was Juliet, who worked in a crime lab twenty minutes away. Morgan had contacted Bobby Guardino, an Alexandria-based P.I. who occasionally worked for him, and had him courier over a section of the shredded bloody tissue Morgan had collected at the scene. Juliet agreed to check it out for him stat—and off the books. Juliet was part of his network. She and he used to date.

Okay, used to have sex. Good sex.

"Hi, Juliet," he said.

"It's AB neg," she replied. "Rarest type there is."

He knew Allison was AB neg. He'd already checked. One percent of the U.S. population had AB negative blood.

"Can you get a pregnancy reading off it, too?"

"Oh God, Morgan," she said in disgust.

"It's business," he said.

She knew that he had an extracurricular life in service to the nation because she did, too, now, thanks to him.

He hadn't meant to use sex to recruit her for covert activity and in retrospect, he wouldn't have slept with her if he'd known they were going to be working together. It was difficult to regret something that had felt so good, but their relationship had degraded about as fast as your average corpse left out in the noonday sun. Definitely his fault—it always was—but he was genuinely sorry about it.

"All right," she muttered. "But I'm violating someone's civil rights all to hell and I could get fired, so it had better be vital to national security, or I'm kicking your ass."

He almost smiled.

"Thank you," he said sincerely. "I do appreciate it."

"Whatever, Morgan. By the way, I'm dating a doctor now. We really date. He's a good guy."

And I'm not, Morgan translated. *I don't have time to be a good guy.*

"I'm glad," he said, and he meant it. "Invite me to the wedding."

She snorted. "As if."

"Call me when you get results, okay?" He repeated his cell phone number.

"Oh, for God's sake, I still have your number, Morgan," she said. "I'll call you. And *I* really will."

He knew what she was saying: He hadn't called, after a while. Maybe he'd gotten distracted with assassinating a drug trafficker. Or maybe he'd gotten scared because they were starting to actually date.

"Thank you, Juliet," he said.

"Later," she said, and disconnected.

He started gathering up Allison's unmentionables, replacing them in the drawer, trying to quell the images of her that rose in his mind. His conversation with Juliet reminded him that he was a dog and that while Allison was his professional target, her very silky—sheesh, transparent—intimate apparel demanded his respect.

He thought again about the recording that slime bucket McDonough had shown him. Why would Allison Gracelyn need time to get some money? Why would she be getting scary phone calls at the office? It just didn't work or make sense to him.

He was mulling it over, seeing it in his mind, remembering the timbre of her voice. And something occurred to him; it was the answer to what had bothered him about the video feed, which had finally hit the little bell in the pinball game that was his mind.

At the exact same time, he opened the next drawer down, which was filled with athletic socks rolled into neat little balls. He pushed them aside like bubbles in a fish tank, and a fillip of excitement jittered through him as he picked up a matte-gray container and flicked it with his thumbnail. It opened like a hydraulic clamshell, revealing the sweet pearls inside: button cams just like the one on her picture frame in her office. Nice. Useful.

He grunted aloud at his good fortune, shut the clamshell and set it on top of the dresser beside an elegant enameled vase filled with white roses that were starting to wilt.

"Let's see what else you've got," he muttered aloud.

Beneath a pair of bike shorts, he found a printout of an article. *Force Fields and Electromagnetic Shields in Nature.*

"Huh?" he said aloud, skimming it. *Anecdotes in Science Fiction... Particle Accelerators... Quantum*

Physics... Insects That Can Concentrate Electrons to Create Actual Force Fields...

"Is she on some special woowoo task force to create the ultimate defensive weapon?" he muttered, flipping over the page. "Or has she finally cracked under pressure?"

He was engrossed, intrigued and highly skeptical as he kept reading.

And that was probably the reason he didn't hear the crepe-soled shoes creeping up behind him and didn't feel the butt of the Skorpion as it crashed down on his skull.

An unnamed island in Micronesia

"We're approaching the target," the accented South African voice said into Echo's earpiece, which was fashioned to look like a six-carat canary diamond post. The man who had created it for Echo was dead now. She was neither glad nor sorry about his death. Emotions were a distraction and she was a very focused individual.

Except, of course, for her pesky temper.

Stilettos clacking on the metal catwalk, Echo glided to the state-of-the-art overhead plasma screen and pressed it on. It hung within easy reach; she was six feet tall. Below her in the black maw of the half-built lab, a welder's torch arced like a distress flare. A saw whined like a torture victim.

The angular, light-brown face of Max Zabuto filled the screen. Max was the leader of the LeClaire extraction team. Knees, shoulders and Uzi barrels crowded the picture, and she knew he was packed inside the panel truck with his team.

"There will be no witnesses to deal with, correct?" Echo queried. There had been a witness during the San Francisco extraction. Briefly. There wasn't one now.

He raised his chin as if he were affronted that she would dare ask. Then and there she decided that after the mission, he would be eliminated. As attractive as he might be, a man who thought for himself was not a useful man.

And as for Max's other premier talent…there were other attractive men who pleased her just as much in bed. One was there now, in fact, waiting for her.

"I have confirmed it," he said. "No witnesses. Her parents are in Bisbee running some errands and the neighbor's on a trip."

"Good," she stroked him. "Go silent until you've completed the extraction. No more communication."

"Roger that," he replied. "Going silent."

The screen went blank.

Poison, she thought. Slow and painful, because of the combative way he had raised his chin. He would know he was dying and he might even realize why.

Then she pressed another button on the screen, and the holding cell for Max's target gleamed into view. It was made of a Kevlar-titanium-Mylar alloy, a state-of-the-art building material that was heat-resistant and unbreakable. Its inventor had not realized that Echo's mother, Arachne, had stolen his proprietary secret the moment he e-mailed the specs to the U.S. Patent Office, in the pathetic and useless attempt to protect his amazing discovery.

With a few simple keystrokes, Mummy had framed him for the murder of a young college student. A job well done, and Echo knew there were many more examples of her mother's brilliance she was not yet privy to. All would be revealed once she had the third packet of Arachne's vast network of information— Lilith's share. That poor, misguided idiot had placed her trust in the wrong people—Allison Gracelyn and her little supersquad of spygirls. Echo was ninety-nine percent certain that Allison was this "Delphi" who was proving to be a constant source of irritation. So Echo had devised a two-pronged plan: part one, ruin Allison's life as thoroughly as possible and part two, kill her.

The plan was going very well.

And so was the Big Plan, which was also two-pronged—find and acquire all the missing egg babies Jeremy Loschetter had not told Team Allison about and finish reweaving her mother's web, so Team Echo could get back to the lovely work of ruling the world.

She cocked her head. "Not exactly ruling it," she said to the lovely but empty cell. "Controlling it."

A far better term. She really didn't care who ruled it. There wasn't a lot she actually *cared* about. Like the cell, her heart was very lovely, but quite empty. Things like caring—loving, hoping, emotions—were like weather, fleeting and unpredictable. A sign of weakness. One had to stay focused.

Echo was focused. She needed, wanted, the egg babies. But she had to have that necklace.

She balled her fists so tightly she nearly drew blood. Not in hatred, for hatred was an emotion, and so was rage. For a moment, all she saw was the color red. It swam before her like a sea of blood. Then it faded to gray, and then it disappeared altogether.

"Champagne," she said, unfurling her fists. "To cel-ebrate."

She blew a kiss at the image of the empty cell and turned off the monitor. Her heels clacked busily on the catwalk as she left the lab. She did a little tango step, listening to their rhythm.

Clack, clack-clack-clack, clack-clack.

Kill Allison Gracelyn. Kill Allison Gracelyn.

Then she went into the Spider Room, where she kept her two beautiful necklaces, and sat with her mother for a while.

Echo was in bed with her exhausted lover when her earring vibrated again. She got up and glided naked into her bathroom, slipping on a black silk bathrobe.

"Yes."

"Target acquired." It was Max.

"Ah!" she cried happily, as she pressed the view screen beside her makeup mirror. The interior of the panel truck filled the screen. Still wearing his black flame-retardant catsuit, Max reached down and lifted up the head of a pale, dark-haired girl. She was unconscious. And very pretty.

Sleeping beauty.

"Report," she ordered him. "Problems? Casualties?"

Max hesitated. "One casualty. Johnson."

"How?"

"He moved in before she was fully sedated," Max answered, glancing warily down at the girl. "She fried him."

"You observed her in action," Echo said, pleased. "She really is a firestarter."

"Yes." Max swallowed hard. "It was…unbelievable."

"This is very good. The casualty, of course, is unfortunate. Johnson was a good man." She had no idea who he was. Johnson was such a common name. Anybody with any style would have changed it. "Contact me again when you leave the country."

"Yes, madam," Max said.

His image disappeared, to be replaced by a field of black. Echo glided back into her cavernous Louis XIV-style bedroom and picked up the bottle of champagne in the silver bucket. They'd killed it. She rang for another.

"Ian," she sang out, jostling her bedmate. "Wake up."

Her exquisite English eye candy opened one bleary eye. Tousled blond curls, golden pecs. Enormous penis. Not a brain in his head.

He groaned. "Again, luv?"

Groaned!

"Yes." She threw off her black robe. "Again. And again."

He did his best to accommodate her, which was delightful. She loved riding her men, loved being on top, loved to see them give into the pleasure and in that vulnerable moment, put themselves completely in her power.

As she slid up and down, gazing at his face with his closed eyes, listening to his labored breathing, she decided that Ian would die by strangulation. With piano wire.

Echo was one for the classics. No one groaned when Echo told them what to do.

And no one *ever* called her luv.

Chapter 7

"Okay, *mi amor,* you're all set," Hector Gonsalvo informed Allison, as he stepped back from Carla's kitchen table to admire his handiwork. *Casino Royale* was on Carla's TV and it seemed fitting somehow, since Carla had just helped a superspy out of a jam.

Hector wore a grinning skull do-rag and a T-shirt that read Heaven Don't Want Me And Hell Didn't Even Answer The Phone. After a liberal dose of whiskey—a glass for Allison, a glass for Carla and a glass for himself—he had straightened out Allison's broken nose and laid a bandage over the bridge. He was more concerned about the big bump on her forehead, and the fact that she was dizzy.

Carla had called him to come over to help, and it sounded like she had interrupted a robbery or something equally illegal. Half an hour later, he had blasted right over on a pimped-out Harley-Davidson, very flashy, roaring and blaring just in case no one noticed his midnight arrival.

Once Allison's nose was shoved back into place, the three ambled out to examine the car she wanted to ditch. They stood under umbrellas, which did little to protect them.

Carla examined Allison's car the way some men stare at naked women. She whistled under her breath and lit a cigarette. Then she took a step back, cocking her head at the dented front end and chewing the inside of her cheek.

"No deaths, right?" Carla fished a piece of tobacco out of her mouth and rolled it away into nothingness between her thumb and forefinger. "Your old man, he make that dent when you ran him over, something like that?"

"No, but you should make sure you get rid of every single identifying number on it, or else you should just help me set it on fire," Allison told her. Which didn't sound like a bad idea.

"No way I'm torching a beauty like her," Carla insisted, shaking her head. "You're sure you didn't kill anybody with it? Because I'm not about to become an accessory to murder."

"Obstruction of justice," Hector corrected her.

"Whatever."

"I swear to you," Allison said seriously. "But people will be looking for it. You'll have to be thorough."

"Don't you worry," Hector said, sliding his arm around Carla. Their umbrellas knocked together. "I'll help Carla if she'll let me ride in it. Carla lets me ride, don't you, baby?" He nuzzled her cheek with his stubbly chin.

Carla snorted, slammed into him with her hip and pulled a fresh cigarette out of a box pack in the front flap of her jean jacket.

"Hector is a sex addict," she said to Allison. "He has admitted his powerlessness over his need to get laid."

The two burst into raucous laughter. Allison's head

hurt. She felt as if she were about to melt into a puddle, she was so tired.

"What's the payback?" Carla asked her. "I can give you all the paperwork, legit if you want, on one of my cars." She jerked her head at the rusting hulks behind the chain link fence.

"Which one will last the longest?" Allison asked.

"Me, baby," Hector said, snorting. Carla rammed him again.

"I got a blue Corolla back there. She looks like hell but she'll run good on the open road."

Allison craned her neck. Then she nodded and held her hand out. The two women shook.

"Hector will drive your Infiniti into my garage. You can sack out on the couch."

Allison took a deep breath and slid the key off her key ring. "I can't stay. I have to hit the road."

"And get a DUI," Carla said. "Girl, you've had some booze and you're a mess. Get some sleep. I'll make you some breakfast in a few hours."

"She cooks like an angel," Hector said, putting his arms around her. He grinned at Allison with his very few teeth. "Serious, though, *amiga,* you need to lie down for a little while. You're in no shape to drive. Take it from a pro."

He and Carla laughed as if at some private joke.

"Listen, honey, we know all about injustice, Hector and me. Hiding out from the man. You're safe here," Carla promised her.

Allison didn't know about that. She didn't know if Hector and Carla would decide to call the police in the hope that there was a reward for her capture. Or maybe they would murder her for her laptop and her credit cards.

Or maybe, Carla would take Hector to bed with her in her bedroom, and tiptoe out in the middle of the night to drape an extra blanket on Allison. Allison had been dozing between sending rafts of e-mail.

FROM: Delphi@oracle.org
TO: AGracelyn@virginia.rr.com
BCC: Samantha St. John
Kim Valenti
Selena Shaw Jones
Diana Lockworth
Lynnette White
Katie Rush
Lindsey Novak
Chesca Thorne
Jessica Whittaker
Dawn O'Shaughnessy
Sasha Bracciali
ALERT: Echo is stealing egg babies. See attached.
Other attempts likely. Report readiness asap.

FROM: AGracelyn@virginia.rr.com
TO: C_Evans@Athena.edu
cc: KaylaRyan@YoungtownPD.org
Christine & Kayla,
Intel reports indicate that attempts to kidnap Athena Academy students identified as superegg babies will resume. Please discuss security procedures and get back to me asap. Thank you.
AG

Allison didn't work from her Oracle account and she didn't sign her message as Delphi. It made perfect sense that Allison, an NSA agent who had taken her dead mother's position on the Athena Academy board, would have her finger on the pulse of the heartbeat of Athena.

Next she checked to make sure her agents knew the new safe house phone number and ID code word. Selena had called Katie to verify the new procedure. All was well.

Allison knew she couldn't constantly monitor her people. She needed to trust them or she wouldn't last another forty-eight hours. Someone in her position couldn't micromanage. But every part of her wanted to. She wanted to remind them all to stay off the radar as best they could. She wanted to remind them to survive. That was when she knew she had to get some rest. She was losing it.

So she tried to let it go, tried to believe that even when she was off-duty, her people continued the mission. These women had dedicated their lives to the greater good that Oracle represented. She was not in this alone.

So why did she feel so alone?

Maybe I have a force field, too, she thought, noting that Oracle had added a half-dozen more articles about quantum physics to her folder about Echo's ability to deflect weapons. *Mine keeps me "safe" from other people.* Drifting, not quite asleep but too exhausted to stay conscious, she twisted and turned in the night, groaning; she dreamed of running from monsters and giant spiders and Marion Gracelyn, her face torn away, holding out her arms.

"It's so nice to be dead," she whispered to Allison. "The dead can rest."

In the morning, Allison woke up as bone-weary as if she hadn't slept at all. Hector checked her nose and promised her he'd done a good job.

"It might have a little twist to it is all, *ese,*" he added. "Give you an edge."

"Where, in a boxing ring?" Carla snorted.

Carla clucked at Allison and told her she was a bad sleeper, but maybe Allison had cause, if she needed to get rid of a dented car. Listening to the news on a small TV in the kitchen, Carla made hashed browns, scrambled eggs and bacon. There was no mention of a runaway NSA agent or a hit-and-run on any of the several channels she watched. Nor of the fact that NSA was working day and night to decrypt SIGINT—signal intelligence—about an imminent nuclear attack. Allison watched Carla in the kitchen, whistling to herself and smoking a cigarette, smiling when Hector nuzzled the back of her neck. Ignorance was bliss indeed.

Allison ate as much as she could hold down. Carla loaded up her plate again and asked her if she'd thought about checking into a battered women's shelter.

"Or you could stay here," she suggested, so offhandedly that Allison realized she had thought about it long and hard before she made the offer.

"Thanks, but I have to go," Allison said. "I'm grateful to you."

Carla flicked her cigarette ashes in a metal tray shaped like a marijuana leaf. "I'm kind of worried about you being out there alone," she ventured. "You seem awfully fragile."

"I'm not," Allison promised. Maybe it would make her feel better if she knew that Allison had sustained far worse injuries than a broken nose.

Or maybe not.

She took a brief nap at Carla's urging. She was going to wait for the morning commute rush hour traffic to subside, and then she was going to get out of the area. The prospect was not inviting, but it was what had to be done.

Morgan saw stars and heard fuzz as his assailant crashed his weapon over Morgan's head. Then his finely honed reflexes took over and saved his life.

He wrapped his hands around the edge of Allison's bureau as he crumpled forward, fought for consciousness and kicked his feet up and back, connecting with the attacker's face. As the man was thrust off balance, Morgan pushed away from the bureau and crashed on top of the man, his back to the man's chest, flattening the son of a bitch against the floor.

Should have grabbed that big-ass vase, Morgan thought.

The attacker fought back, savagely. Morgan was woozy and wobbly, but he batted and kicked for all he was worth, aware that he was smacking the floor more than fifty percent of the time, but now and then he pounded flesh. He worried about the guy grabbing his tie.

His attacker's gun went off. It was equipped with a silencer that didn't do much good; it wasn't like the movies. A sizzle of heat zipped along Morgan's right arm. Penetration? If yes, then it should have caused worse damage. He was only grazed, then. Good. The arm should still work.

Thoughts flashed through Morgan's brain faster than a speeding bullet: from years of missions and of learning by others' fatal mistakes. He straightened the arm and rocked himself to the right; luck was his and he pushed down hard on the guy's wrist, forcing it to the floor. He doubled up his left fist for power and jutted back his elbow. He heard bones crack. He did it again. Again. Again.

The attacker's gun hand went limp. Morgan wrenched the gun away from him and whirled around on his knees, straddling the assailant's chest. Moonlight shone through the window; the man's face was a pulpy mess. His dark blond soul patch was matted with blood.

"Who? Why?" Morgan demanded.

"Sent…" The man coughed and gurgled. He had a French accent, and Morgan thought he might be drowning in his own blood.

"Who? Why?" Morgan said again, lifting the guy's head up. Blood trickled out of his mouth and ran down his chest. The man coughed and gagged harder. Morgan pressed the shiny blue steel Skorpion against the man's temple as he rolled him onto his side.

"Ouch! I don't know why. It's just a job," he rasped.

"You weren't after me," Morgan guessed.

The man shook his head. "Target was Allison Gracelyn. This is her house," he added, perhaps in the unlikely event that Morgan didn't know that. "Was she yours as well?"

"Yes," Morgan replied.

"*Merde.* Competition!" He sounded almost jolly as he blinked blood out of his hazel eyes. "Did you get her?"

"Not yet. How did they hire you?"

"The usual. A call. An offer." He almost laughed, but it came out as more of a sob, his face contracted as if he were in terrible pain. "I *thought* it was too easy to get in here."

Morgan could read the worry lines on his face. The man was pondering the possibility that Morgan had been sent to kill him, too.

"How much were you getting?" the man asked.

"Twenty-five. Euros," Morgan said. He knew that was the going rate for highly placed government workers.

"For one or…two?"

"One," Morgan replied. Then, just as the man visibly relaxed, he added, "There was an extra ten for taking you out, but only if you had already made an attempt and failed."

The man groaned. "*Ten?* For *me?* Only ten? *Putain de merde,* they've lost faith in me." He swore some more in French; then he coughed hard, spitting a tooth onto the floor. "I make you the deal, *mon vieux.* Let me go, I let you have her. And I pay you full price, including the bump for me."

Morgan didn't let him up. "What guarantee do I have that you won't come after her again?"

"Monsieur, I'm injured. I'm going to need a lot of surgery at this rate," the man said, still full of good humor. "It was just a job to me. I sign off, I walk away. You can have her. If you kill me, you'll have the mess to worry about," he added hopefully.

"You can't just walk away. You have a reputation to maintain."

The man groaned softly under his breath, moving restlessly. "Pfft, I've been thinking of a career change anyway. Maybe I'll go back to university. My parents always wanted me to become a physician. You appreciate the irony, *non?* The code of medicine is 'First do no harm.'" He laughed, which set him off to coughing again.

"If you quit, your bosses will need another house painter on the payroll." Morgan deliberately used the Mafia term for "hit man" to see if he could shake anything loose.

"Are you looking for an introduction?" the man asked.

Morgan remained silent.

"*Eh bien,* I have no boss," the man scoffed. "I am a, how do you say, independent contractor. But first, please, *mon ami,* release me so I can sit up. I feel… rather terrible." Incredibly he chuckled. "This is all so absurd. I didn't want this job. Since the 9/11, I hate flying to the States."

"I want your name," Morgan said, forcing the guy to stay prone.

"I'm called Rousseau, like the philosopher. You know, the Frenchman who thought we would be better people if we were allowed to remain uncivilized."

Right now I'd take a lot of satisfaction in being uncivilized, Morgan thought. This man—Rousseau—had broken into Allison's house to kill her. Morgan wrestled with his desire to do the same to him with all the ferocity of a man fighting off a tiger. But this was Allison's home, and trace evidence might link her to the killing. It looked as if she had enough to deal with.

And Morgan was not a killer. An assassin, maybe, if he had to be.

"Who hired you? Don't be stupid. Just tell me," he ordered Rousseau.

"Then I *would* be stupid." He grunted when Morgan put the gun against his temple. "Ah, *bon,* he is Greek. I call him Achilles. Please, be discreet." He coughed up more blood. Maybe he'd die on his own. "After you leave—"

"We're both leaving together," Morgan said, sitting back on his haunches and dragging the man up to a sitting position.

Morgan's cell phone went off. He wondered if Rousseau was thinking what he was thinking: that accomplished hit men didn't do moronic things like leave their ringers on. Maybe Rousseau had just silently taken back his promise to first do no harm because he assumed he was dealing with an amateur.

Maybe Morgan was going to have to kill Rousseau after all.

He took off his tie, finally, and stuffed it in his pocket. "Let's go," he said, roughly dragging the bleeding man to his feet. There was a lot of blood all over everything; it probably wouldn't add much to the cleanup if he popped the guy right now. But that was just his anger talking. It made more sense to keep Rousseau alive and trace back the contract on Allison as far as it would go.

He slung Rousseau's arm over his shoulders and half-carried him out of Allison's bedroom. They were trailing blood. He decided it was time to call in some help, get one of his guys in here to clean up, get another one to spirit him and Rousseau away. By the way the guy was gurgling and wheezing, Morgan considered requesting a body bag.

"Stay," he told Rousseau, laying him down on the floor of her living room, near her desktop, and placing a foot on his neck. Rousseau managed a chuckle at Morgan's sarcasm.

Morgan checked his phone. The caller had been McDonough. He made a mental note to punch his lights out, but he didn't call McDonough back. Instead, he tied Rousseau's hands behind his back with the coaxial cable from Allison's cable box and located the monitoring handheld for the button cams in the same drawer he had found the matte metal case. He pressed a button cam on the frame of her desktop monitor. Then he placed one on the Athena Academy magnet frame on her refrigerator. He added two more in her bedroom and the bathroom.

He had three left. He slid the case in the back of his black suit trousers as he demon-dialed Liam Gruebel, the head of his mop-up crew, and gave him Allison's address. Then he called Zorba Vares, his wheelman, and did the same.

Then, because his sixth sense was tingling again, he returned to the man he had cuffed and left to bleed on Allison's high-end hardwood floor, sliding the monitor into his raincoat as he slipped it back on.

Rousseau's eyes were wide-open, but the light had left them. Morgan knew men could die like that, quietly, while you were busy doing something else. One guy could be shot six times and walk away. Another, you hit him wrong once, and he died, while you were talking on the phone.

Adieu, Rousseau. You'll never have to fly to the States again.

With a heavy sigh, he moved away from the body and packed his lock picks and his burglar alarm code descrambler into his leather satchel.

He was about to add a handful of unused mini-mics when Allison's desktop pinged, signaling incoming e-mail. He looked at the screen and saw no indication of an arrival in her in-box. It was something secure then, delivered behind firewalls she had erected specifically to receive sensitive material.

He almost laughed at the timing—he had had all the time in the world for something juicy to show up before he'd been attacked, but now he was knee-deep in a crime scene complete with a corpse. Didn't matter. Allison's town house and especially her computer were ground zero until he found Allison herself. Since he was first and foremost NSA, the most likely receptacle for the clues that would help him track her down were her e-mails.

Morgan reached into the leather satchel and pulled out fresh latex gloves. Rather than plant his blood-soaked trousers in her nicely upholstered desk chair, he leaned over the keyboard, grimacing at the droplets of blood and sweat that spattered on the polished cherrywood.

His gloved fingertips clicked on the keys as he ground through her security, attempting to trace the message, finding himself blocked at every attempt. He attacked layers of protection, moved to different routers, used alias ISPs. Nothing worked.

"Huh," he said aloud, slipping a fresh flash drive out of his pocket and sweeping everything new onto it—cookies, caches, anything.

His cell phone rang again. It was McDonough again. This time Morgan took it. They needed to have a little chat.

"So, is she pregnant?" McDonough said without preamble.

Morgan wasn't surprised that McDonough had bugged the conference room and listened in on his interrogation of Valenti. Or that he'd digitally assembled his surveillance "recording" of Allison from bits and pieces of other surveillance events. He was that kind of spook.

The tip-off was the change in contrast. It had altered at least twice during her five-second conversation, too quickly and too intensely for it to be natural. Although it was a pretty good job, Morgan was used to the best; he had simply been too preoccupied to notice it when he'd watched it in her office.

Because it was Allison. Because I've let her get under my skin.

Morgan had no idea why McDonough was setting up Allison. He wondered if McDonough was the one working for the guys who wanted to blow up the East Coast.

"Pregnant? Don't know yet," Morgan replied, evenly, calmly, as if he didn't suspect a thing. "My money's on negative."

"Damn it," McDonough groused. "You know, don't you. The video was such a damn mess. I didn't have enough time."

"I'm glad to hear that," Morgan said. "I just figured you thought I was an idiot who'd buy anything."

"I had to make sure you'd listen to me. In case you believed Valenti's bullshit."

Morgan felt a disconcerting chill on Valenti's behalf. Despite the fact that she had probably lied to his face, he hoped she was all right. Allison's associates were like cats; they usually landed on their feet. Just like the queen tigress.

So far.

"Did Valenti change her story after you confronted her?" Morgan asked.

"Don't be stupid. Why would I confront her? If she wants to hang herself, I'll let her take all the rope she needs. Maybe you should give her a call, check in with her, get some more perjurious statements for my miles-thick dossier on her."

"Have you sent out backup on me?" Morgan asked. *Such as a hit man code named Rousseau?* "I should know, so I don't pop him."

"You just do your job," McDonough said, "and I'll do mine. You see anybody you think you should know, just say 'Marco.' They'll say 'Polo.' Speaking of your job, have you got anything on her whereabouts? Whereabouts are *you?*"

Then Morgan's sixth sense did not just tingle. It gave him a jolt. The burglar alarm system of hers had just been too easy to disarm. And it seemed awfully early for McDonough to be checking in with him. Maybe McDonough wanted Morgan as gone as Allison was.

This is wrong. I'm in trouble.

Getoutgetoutgetout.

He dropped the phone and the flash drive into his satchel.

Don't use the front door. Getoutgetoutgetout.

He grabbed the satchel and raced for her bedroom.

"Rush?" McDonough's voice chattered from inside the satchel. "What's happening?"

Redalertabandonabandon.

In the bedroom, he grabbed the big enamel vase and hefted it at Allison's bedroom window as hard as he could. The gods loved him; it cracked diagonally, giving him a weak spot to target. Ducking his head, he flung himself at it. Pieces gave way as he crashed through.

He was plummeting gravity-ward through the beating rain when the town house blew. Bricks and wood, metal and glass shot sky-high. Fireballs singed his feet and legs, melting the soles of his shoes. A volcanic roar split the air around him, pummeling him as he collapsed onto icy brown grass in a fetal position around his satchel. Heaving, he kept his head pressed against his knees. He waited one, two, three; and more explosions rattled his eardrums and his teeth.

He couldn't hear a thing, but he knew there would be screams and sirens any second now. And cameras. And helicopters.

Semifunctional, he felt in the satchel. His cell phone was still there. Maybe McDonough was still bellowing. He couldn't tell. He disconnected anyway. He felt through the rest of his stuff for the Skorpion and the memory stick.

They were not there.

Shit. They must have fallen out.

Flames lit up the sky and he grabbed at a shape. It was a rock. Another. It was a pebble. A third. The third one was the drive. He'd settle for that.

He threw it in the satchel and scrabbled to his feet. Then he wrapped his arms around the satchel like a running back with the pigskin, tucked in his head and ran like hell.

Chapter 8

Tired and hurting, Allison stopped at a walk-in health clinic in eastern Kentucky. The eager young intern there gave her a shot that numbed her entire head before he stuffed some fresh wadding up her nose. Next he considered wrapping her ribs below her breasts, which probably meant she'd whacked some cartilage, but she talked him out of it. He wrote her a scrip for some heavy-duty painkillers and told her to go home and rest. And then he asked her for her phone number.

She deep-sixed the prescription and bought some more maximum-strength painkillers at a local strip mall, as well as six more prepaid phones. She had them all activated via one of her many dummy registration IDs created expressly for that purpose. She checked in with the safe house and verified that no one had phoned Athena Construction without first saying *"Gordita."*

Athens Police Lieutenant Kayla Ryan had put local law enforcement on notice, and Christine Evans was grateful for the beefed-up security provided by Athena alums Lucy Karmon and Diana Lockworth. Athena Academy was in lockdown mode and the young Athena students were badgering Christine to let them patrol the perimeter.

Selena had sent the paint can.

Sam and Elle had not located the missing laptop in India.

Allison checked into a flea-bitten motel and studied the information Selena had sent her about the ongoing kidnappings. There had been three more. The FBI had also noticed that all of them had been conceived at the fertility clinic in Zuni. The feebs were asking good questions and connecting useful dots. Of course they had no idea that their firewalls had been blasted through by the power of Oracle, or they might not have been so forthcoming with the details of their investigation. Generally, the FBI was very good at keeping information off the grid, preferring phone conversations on secured lines and face-to-face discussions. Allison assumed such was the case now as well, and that she didn't have the big picture. However, she was pretty good at dot-connecting herself.

She forced everything from her mind and willed herself to sleep, but it wasn't good sleep. It was erratic and chaotic—she dreamed of taloned spiders crawling all over her face, slicing it apart; then her mother's face, then Morgan's face. When she woke up, she was crying.

I can't lose it, she thought. *This is only the beginning. Things are going to get much worse, but we'll win in the end. We always have before.*

We have to now.

Regretting her decision to throw out the heavy-duty pain prescription, she took some more ibuprofen and turned on the TV, waiting for it to take effect before she got back on the road. Channel surfing past the local news, she stopped clicking the gummy remote when a familiar face popped up on the screen.

It was the TV reporter, Shannon Connor. Allison smiled faintly at this small gift from the gods—a reminder that she, too, had sisters. She and Shannon had recently patched things up after years of enmity. Shannon had been unjustly expelled from Athena Academy and had incorrectly believed Allison to be responsible. For years, Shannon had dug up every speck of dirt she could find on Athena Academy—until she took on Echo's deformed half sister, one of Arachne's three children, Kwan-Sook, and proved herself to be resourceful, courageous and persistent—an Athenian through and through.

Shannon's forehead was wrinkled, her eyes shiny with tears. Either Shannon was "presenting" a tragic news story or she was genuinely upset. Intrigued, Allison turned up the sound.

"This is Shannon Connor for the ABS network," the blond, brown-eyed newscaster said. "We are…we are live at the scene of a horrific fire in Old Alexandria, Virginia." She could barely speak.

The camera panned past her, and Allison's mouth dropped open.

Oh my God. That's my town house.

The twin Dutch maples that shaded the walkway were charred skeletons. The path itself was covered with ash, and the brick structure was a gutted ruin. Firefighters were still spraying water on the smoking hulk from enormous hoses. The camera panned upward to show a helicopter dumping liquid on remnants of the slate, gabled roof.

"ABS has verified that this was the home of Allison Gracelyn, a highly placed government employee, and the sister of U.S. Attorney General David Gracelyn." Shannon's heavily glossed lips pulled down in a moue of sincere distress. In the old days, Shannon would not have missed the opportunity to mention Allison's mother's murder. Now that she and Allison had buried the hatchet, she never spoke of it on the air, despite being pressured by her producer to do it because it was "sexy."

Allison's personal cell went off, and she muted the TV. It was her brother.

"*Oh* my God, Allison, are you all right?" He was nearly shouting with fear. She could feel it through the phone.

"I'm fine," she said. "I'm okay. I'm not even in Virginia. Hold on." She turned the sound up again.

"Fire Chief Bruce Radcliffe will be issuing a statement in just a moment," Shannon continued. She pressed her finger against her ear. Her face went white, and she swallowed hard. The camera pushed in, just a little, intruding on what was clearly a difficult personal moment. Shannon lifted her chin, fighting for control.

"I have just received confirmation that a body has been retrieved."

"Oh my God," Allison said. She went numb as she leaned forward toward the set, as if she could physically pull more information out of Shannon. *Who was in my town house? Don't let it be one of the Athenas. Don't let it be an Oracle agent.*

"Allison?" David said. "What's going on?"

Shannon bobbed her head slightly, listening to her earpiece, then shut her eyes tightly and looked back into the camera.

"Sources investigating the blaze tell us that the body is definitely that of a man, and his identity is being withheld pending notification of his family. No other bodies have been located at this time."

A man. Someone who got past my state-of-the-art laser alarm system, a duplicate of the one I used in the self-storage unit and the one I installed at Oracle HQ. Was it someone Echo sent? Was it Echo herself? Oracle has multiple backups, but—

"Damn it, Alli, talk to me," David demanded.

Her other line went off. It was her father.

"David, Dad's on the other line." She put her brother on hold. "Dad, I'm fine," she said, connecting with her father. "I'm nowhere near my house."

She watched the screen. There was a cutaway to the interior of her kitchen. Her kitchen towels and drapes were gone. Flames had chewed through the wall. Then there was a close up of her refrigerator where, remarkably, the photo of Gordita wasn't even smudged. A chill shot down Allison's spine as the camera moved in on the picture of the horse, and held, almost as if the camera operator were trying to make some kind of point.

Was Echo sending a message via someone on the scene, taunting Allison that she had cracked her code as well as her security system? Had Echo already broken into the self-storage facility and taken the necklace, leaving a fake for the unsuspecting Selena to retrieve?

If she had what she wanted then she'd leave us alone, right? Allison thought. *She would have all three flash drives, and we would have nothing. So there would be no reason to go after us. Maybe she's trying to throw us off, make us assume she has it…make us scramble to check on it. So she can see where we go.*

Maybe she watched Selena move it.

Or maybe Allison was pushed to the brink and saw signs and portents in everything. If she opened the motel-provided bag of Lipton's to read the tea leaves, would she see a spider?

"Sweetheart," her father said hoarsely. "The first thing I thought of was your mother." His usually robust voice was whispery.

"I'm here, Daddy," she replied. *And it's because of Mom that I'm doing this. I'm carrying on her legacy.*

"Where?" he asked.

"I'm on company business," she told him. It was only half a lie. "Something big."

"I wish you were here." He sounded old, fragile. It hurt her heart.

Her other line beeped. David had disconnected and redialed.

Allison's head pounded. She wearily closed her eyes and reminded herself that her men were concerned about her because they loved her. But right now, she needed a moment to collect her thoughts.

"I'll come as soon as I can," she promised her father. "I'll be careful. This was just a freak accident." She would say anything she could to ease her father's terror. "Dad," she said gently, "David is on the other line."

"Allison," her father began. His tone of voice told her

that he wasn't buying her "freak accident" scenario. He exhaled. "Talk to your brother."

"Okay. I'll let you know what they find." She reconnected with her brother.

"What the hell is happening?" he thundered. "I'm watching Shannon Connor on ABS. The fire chief is saying possible arson."

Damn you, Echo. Allison wearily closed her eyes. Her nemesis was pushing all the right buttons, flushing Allison out, making her vulnerable. If indeed it was Echo. Maybe she was simply pulling the strings so someone else—Wrobleski, Matsumoto—would do it for her.

"I'm launching an investigation," he declared. "I'll get some people to look into it—"

"David, no. Back off."

He was silent for a moment. "Tell me why."

"Just don't. You're the U.S. Attorney General. It'll look like nepotism. Like you're using taxpayer money for personal reasons." *And I don't want anyone investigating Delphi.*

"Don't be coy," he said angrily. "I know you work off the books. I don't know who you work for, or what you do. But I know you're like Mom. I know you fling yourself wherever there's a problem. You have this superhero complex. She was *murdered,* Allison. And someone set your house on fire. Who was it?"

He was fishing. He didn't know anything. She knew if their situations were reversed, she would be just as pushy and insistent. But that didn't matter. Right now, family didn't matter. No one mattered. The mission was the priority.

"I can't discuss this with you right now." She

forced the emotion out of her voice. "I need to find out who was in my town house. It may have been a friend. I need to call my insurance company. I have neighbors I care about. I want to make sure they're all right. I—"

Her own words hit her full force.

It may have been a friend.

Her stomach contracted as if she'd been gut-punched. She sucked in her breath and blinked rapidly, afraid to let herself think. Because if she did, a name would form in her mind.

The good ones are either married, gay, or spying on you.

"Ally-cat?" her brother said, using his very oldest nickname for her. He hadn't called her that in a long, long time.

She went blank. She swallowed hard, staring at the TV screen while her heartbeat roared in her ears. "I'll call you later."

She watched them wheel a body bag out on a gurney. A black lump on a steel bed, grim-faced EMTs, and Shannon Connor, trying to do her job.

"Do not hang up on me! Let me in, goddamn it! Talk to me!" David pleaded.

She hung up. There was a text crawl along the bottom of the screen: *Man's Body Discovered In Town House Fire Details At Eleven.*

She punched in Shannon's private number, shaking hard. It went straight to voice. She moved on to Selena. Acid churned in her stomach. Fresh pain bloomed behind her eyes.

"Allison," Selena said. "I've been trying to call

you. Your phone's been busy. Do you know about your town house?"

"There's a body. Is it…can it be Morgan?" Allison blurted without preamble. She wasn't Delphi the superhero at that moment. She wasn't even calm, cool, collected Allison Gracelyn, Oracle field agent, checking in with the home office.

I didn't know I felt this way about him. She couldn't take her eyes off the screen. Off the body bag as it was wheeled into a waiting ambulance. Beyond the yellow caution tape and the lines of police officers, the faces of curious onlookers strained to see what was going on. She saw no one familiar.

She suddenly felt horribly alone.

"Are you saying that you think Morgan might have come looking for you himself?" Selena asked slowly.

"Yes." She took a deep breath. "It's a possibility."

"Well, we know he's been monitoring you for McDonough. When you went MIA, he might have come after you. But Katie said—"

"*Selena,*" she gritted. White noise followed. She knew Selena was putting the pieces together. She felt exposed and raw. And terrified.

"Allison, I'll check. Right now."

"Thank you." Allison massaged her aching temple. "Don't let him know anything. Throw him off. Have Katie call, pretending to be worried about me." Allison had the presence of mind to think at least one jump ahead. But she needed to see the whole game board. She couldn't let her judgment be clouded like this.

But she couldn't see past that body bag. Or the crawl at the bottom of her TV screen.

"We'll do it right," Selena promised.

"Do it fast," Allison said.

"Allison, you and Morgan…" Selena left the rest unsaid.

"No," Allison said. *He doesn't work that way. I don't think he's even wired that way. I know what the loss of your mother can do to you.*

"Hang on. We'll let you know asap."

Wiry and freckled, Zorba drove Morgan to his place in his black panel van, brimming with weaponry and spy craft goodies. Liam called it the Opsmobile. Zorba owned a historic carriage house made of brick and trailing with ivy. It was loaded with white plaster statues of naked Greek goddesses and a poster from the movie *Zorba the Greek*.

Stationing Morgan on a pile of towels atop an oak bar stool at his well-stocked wet bar, Zorba dressed the graze on Morgan's arm and helped him figure out if he had a concussion or any other brand of internal injuries. Morgan watched the proceedings in the mirrored wall behind the wet bar, glistening with elegant bottles of high-test alcohol. He looked like an extra in a zombie movie.

As soon as he could hear again, he called Liam and canceled the cleanup assignment at Allison's former place of residence.

"So, we're on a new mission," Zorba ventured, squinting into Morgan's left eye. "Your pupil's normal," he informed him.

"Yeah," Morgan said. "New. I'm still getting the big picture."

Zorba snorted as he checked Morgan's right pupil. "Did the big picture include a free ride to Mount Olympus?"

"That tiny detail got omitted," Morgan answered dryly. "Someone's ass is mine for that one."

Zorba nodded slightly and straightened. "You got anything for me yet?"

"Not yet."

Zorba nodded placidly.

That Morgan was withholding information was not unusual in their line of work. Data usually got doled out piecemeal as the team was assembled and their assignment was defined. Morgan's public professional life was intelligence—how much of it was useful, and what would just confuse and distract. In his private professional life running black bag ops, he always told Zorba—and everyone else—what they needed to know when they needed to know it. His lead, his call; they didn't like it that way, they didn't have to sign on. So far, no one had ever walked off a Rush-run op.

Morgan's cell phone rang. He was amazed that it still worked.

He expected McDonough, and he wasn't sure which way he was going to play that card. Should he go silent? McDonough would eventually learn that he hadn't died in the explosion, but should Morgan be the one to tell him?

He didn't have to decide just yet. Caller ID revealed his little sister, Katie's number.

Zorba gave him a *Should I stay?* look. Morgan gave his head a quick shake—his brain seemed to slosh inside his skull—indicating that it was nothing for the

Greek to be concerned about. Nodding, Zorba drifted away down the hall, ostensibly to give Morgan some privacy.

Morgan raised the left side of his mouth in a half smile as he connected. He was going to enjoy this.

"Athena Construction," he said calmly.

There was dead silence. "What?"

The silence lengthened. He was the soul of patience, having learned long ago that if you waited long enough, people who might otherwise keep their secrets told them to you, just to end the tension. Unfortunately Katie was a lot like him, in that respect. But she could rarely withstand his taunting at any level. He hoped she hadn't changed. He'd been too busy to notice if she had.

"Are you still there?" Katie said irritably.

Bingo.

"I am. What is Athena Construction? I heard your voice. When I called Athena Construction a few hours ago."

"Not a clue, Morgan. I have no idea what you're talking about." She sounded as if she didn't care if he believed her or not. Scrappy, that kid.

He tried another tack. "Tell Allison to come in. Now," he said. "Convince her, Katie."

"Oh my God, have you talked to her?" Katie cried. "That's why I called. She's not at work and she's not answering her phone. You do know her town house burned down, right?"

"Yes," he said. "I know her house…burned down. But I don't know where she is. I called her cell and left a message but she didn't call me back. She was supposed to come to a meeting at work but she didn't show up."

"Oh?" Katie said. "And then her house burns—"

He decided to go for it. "So after she didn't show, I went looking for her, and I found a cell phone in an alley. It looked like there had been a fight. I called the number, and I heard your voice."

"A fight? Allison was in a fight?" she echoed.

"*Your* voice. Katie, I'm your brother. Don't BS me."

"What alley? What kind of fight?"

He took a breath. "If you hear from her, tell her to get in touch with me. She's in danger."

"What kind of danger?" Her voice shook. She was *good*. "Morgan, what's going on?"

"I need to speak to her," he persisted, "asap."

"Morgan…" She sounded as if she wanted to tell him something. He waited. She remained silent. Morgan wondered at her discipline, her sense of loyalty to Allison. He admired both Katie and Allison more than he could say, and he wished he could make either one of them listen to him.

"Tell her not to trust her boss," he said, unsure of the wisdom of going there. He thought about warning Kim Valenti through his sister, but the problem was, he was still after Allison. If he warned off all her friends and associates, he would have no leads. Valenti was a big girl, and he was a bloodhound, not a rescue dog.

He gingerly shifted his weight on the wooden bar stool, wincing at the discomfort it caused him.

"Tell her I have to talk to her," he told his sister.

Zorba reappeared with a plate of feta cheese and pita bread and a bowl of olives. He set the Greek food down within Morgan's reach, then crossed around to the wet bar and snagged two dark blue glasses and a bottle of ouzo. He set the glasses and the ouzo down, not leaving, which irritated the hell out of Morgan. It wasn't like Zorba to loiter when he was on the phone.

"I'll tell her," Katie said, "if I can find her."

"I'll do the same," Morgan said, flaring with frustration as Katie hung up.

He picked up a piece of feta. Zorba still had his back to him. He was pouring the ouzo…and studying Morgan's reflection in the mirror with narrowed eyes. Zorba's expression was cold and appraising.

A frisson rocketed up Morgan's backbone. It was not the kind of expression he would have expected from someone on his team.

When Zorba realized Morgan was looking at him, he relaxed his face and set down the bottle of ouzo.

A Greek code-named Achilles hired Rousseau to kill Allison Gracelyn. Zorba is Greek, and we're both fully connected in the bad-guy network. I would never even bother with such a flimsy link, if I hadn't seen what I just saw in the mirror.

"What is it this time? Do we have to go back to Managua? I hope not, because my eyebrows still haven't grown back." As Zorba turned around, he pointed to his face with the glass in his right fist, where, sure enough, sections of his thick black eyebrows were still missing. It gave him a mangy look.

Morgan had known Zorba for five years…and three months ago, Zorba had driven a Jeep through a flaming brick wall to save Morgan from having his eyes blown out by a very pissed-off narco-baron. Zorba could easily have not shown up. He had definitely and deliberately put himself in harm's way to save Morgan.

But Morgan found it telling that Zorba was bringing it up just now—as if to remind Morgan that he was a loyal friend. Why would Morgan need reminding?

In the black bag world, three months could be a lifetime. A man could be bought overnight—with a big enough bribe or a great enough threat. That was why guys like Zorba and Morgan didn't have wives and babies—or even serious girlfriends—for their enemies to dangle by their ankles over balconies seventy stories up. You might do anything to keep them from letting go…including flip your loyalties and kill the man you once risked your life to save.

What about gals like Allison? What would it take for her to go rogue?

This is a rotten business, Morgan thought, tipping his head back and allowing the liquor to burn a trail down the back of his throat. *It makes you stop trusting everybody. Including your wheelman. And your own sister.*

"I don't know what it is yet," Morgan told him. "Or where it is. Just that it is."

"I hope it's not Managua," Zorba said again. He handed Morgan another glass and kept one for himself. "Drink up, my friend. It's not every day you dodge a bullet."

"Yeah," Morgan said. "You're right."

They toasted, threw back their ouzo and slammed their glasses onto the oaken counter of the wet bar.

Morgan thought about the Skorpion that was missing from his satchel. And his equally sexy Medusa revolver, which was not.

* * *

"Morgan's okay," Selena told Allison.

Allison closed her eyes. "Thanks."

"He told his sister that you're in danger, and that your boss is dirty."

"Oh God, have 'I' blackmailed McDonough?" Allison groaned.

"He didn't say. I think he's withholding so you'll call him. He wants to talk to you. Directly."

"No," she said, ignoring the dusting of tingles over her collarbone and shoulders at the thought.

"Katie got the impression that he's actively searching for you. Did you find any evidence of that?" Selena asked.

"Well, I don't have a town house anymore." She couldn't imagine that he had anything to do with it, but she needed to consider all the possibilities.

"He told Katie to tell you that he wants to help you."

She put that aside for the moment. "Did you contact Diana?" Diana Lockworth was at the safe house, which was near the Army base where she was stationed.

"Yes. She's fueled up a Bombardier Learjet 40 and she wants to know what destination to put on her flight plan."

That was a figure of speech, Allison knew. There was no way Diana would announce to the world where Allison was hunkered down. The choice of a civilian aircraft was a good one. It would keep their mission further off the radar.

"Hold on," she said. She glanced at the motel's address on the receipt for the room. "I'll give you half on the phone and e-mail you the other half as soon as we disconnect." It was an old trick, one some people used to give out their social security numbers, passwords and other sensitive information. It was a very broad stroke that wouldn't fool anyone who was paying attention, but something was better than nothing.

"She's on her way," Selena told her. "Try to get some rest."

As soon as they hung up, her phone rang again. The caller ID was restricted. She let it go to voice, and then she listened.

"Allison? Morgan. McDonough's dirty. He showed me a fake recording that compromises you and he's probably sent other trackers after you. I know you're in trouble. Call me."

Her heart stuttered at the sound of his voice. Not very many minutes ago, she had been afraid that he was dead.

Compromised. Other trackers. Do you want to help me or to trap me?

Why was she surprised that there might be more to Morgan than met the eye? Maybe the two of them had more in common than she had realized. Maybe that explained the way she was drawn to him. She had assumed it was the job they did, the values they held.

But maybe it went much deeper than that. Maybe he was…like her. Working deep, and dark, for the greater good, yes, but deep inside, accepting that she was a protector, a warrior. She was set apart, and would be, for her entire life.

Could Morgan be a warrior, too?

She thought it through. She had always noticed his sinewy physicality and figured him for a fitness buff. But maybe he needed to stay in shape to dog his quarry, fight off assailants. She'd been impressed by the way he seemed to absorb double meanings and nuances that other cryptanalysts let slide. He thought like an operative. Like a spy.

He was circumspect about his downtime. Whenever he came back from a vacation, he rarely said two words about where he'd been or what he'd seen. She'd always figured it was because he'd taken some woman along; Morgan might have flaws when it came to relationships with the opposite sex—as in, he didn't have relationships, he had sex—but he was not the kind to kiss and tell.

Besides, despite the fact that she was five years older than he was, she liked to flatter herself that maybe she was on his list of potential conquests. She had caught him sizing her up the way men do when they're on the prowl. He would have enough sense—and class—not to brag about his adventures with one woman when he was working out his strategy to land another.

Is McDonough sending him after me, or is it someone else? Is it someone who has lied to him, the way my husky friend got lied to? An adversary who has shown him proof that I'm a remorseless blackmailer who needs to be stopped? Or someone even worse?

Or did he volunteer for the mission, because he and I both know I've held back? A guy like Morgan doesn't like being on the outside looking in. He would make no apologies for digging through someone's trash or picking their lock. Hell, we do the electronic equivalent of that where- and whenever we can.

What can I tell you, Morgan Rush? What should I tell you?

She carried the phone to the bed and curled it under her chin. She played his message again. She listened to his voice, deep and rumbling, full of insistence and maybe some concern. Or was that just something she wanted to hear?

"Allison? Morgan."

He had her attention. She played the message again. And again.

But she didn't call him.

Chapter 9

"Allison, you'd better wake up now," Diana said.

Allison jerked awake and looked into the face of the hazel-eyed strawberry-blonde, who was no longer strapped into the pilot's seat in the cockpit. Allison didn't think they were airborne anymore.

"I wasn't asleep," Allison insisted, yawning and blinking her eyes. Her ribs hurt.

"You needed it. You need about a year of sleep."

"It's overrated. So I hear," Allison shot back.

"Trust me, it's not." Diana smiled. "I would almost rather get a good night's sleep than have sex. *Almost.*"

"Well, sex is not overrated, as I dimly recall," Allison said, her thoughts straying to Morgan.

Stretching, she turned her head and glanced out the window of the little Learjet. They were sitting on a private airstrip just outside of Athena Academy—a little something that had been put in as a courtesy to visiting dignitaries who wanted to avoid commercial flight or the commute from the Air Force base.

They deplaned. Allison felt like a sack of cement. Her mouth tasted like one, too.

An unmarked sedan idled at the edge of the tarmac. Another Athena alum, Kayla Ryan, was at the wheel, and as Allison and Diana approached, she exited the vehicle and opened her arms as if to hug Allison. Allison held up her hands.

"Sore ribs," she said.

"What happened?" Kayla asked.

"I'll catch you up when we meet with Christine." It would be a heavily edited version. Every version Allison told was edited, even to other Oracle agents.

Neither Allison nor Diana had any gear to stow in the trunk. Diana rode shotgun up front and Allison took the back. Allison had impressed on both of them that they needed to move rapidly and without calling any attention to themselves. As they sped away, she spared a fleeting thought for the post office drop. The necklace wouldn't be there yet. Maybe tomorrow, maybe the next day. It was killing her to have the necklace out of her control, wending its way through the U.S. Postal Service. She couldn't second-guess the wisdom of sending it through the mail. It was done.

Dusk had sent the desert sun behind the Tank Mountains, causing them to shimmer like mirages. Cracking the window, Allison closed her eyes briefly, savoring the mingled scents of cooling dust, white sage and creosote, through her cotton-stuffed nose. Smelling the bouquet of home was the best medicine on earth.

A hawk wheeled across the sky-wide washes of purple. An owl hooted. Her thoughts strayed as they often did to the nuclear crisis Project Ozone was struggling to defuse. How she wished she could call in and see how it was going. She'd check in with Kim as soon as she could.

Allison dozed off again in the backseat. She woke to see Principal Christine Evans waiting for their car beneath the flagpole at the entrance to the campus of Athena Academy. Allison's mother, Marion Gracelyn, had handpicked Christine to be the principal of the school, and she had been an excellent choice.

The years had been kind to the gray-haired former Army officer, and Allison's throat tightened at the sight of the woman who had known her own mother so well. Christine still moved with the disciplined grace of a military woman. An accident had rendered her blind in one eye—the military's loss and Athena Academy's gain.

"Allison, my God," Christine said, giving her a once-over.

"Little scuffle, a couple of injuries," Allison replied. "When we debrief, I'll elaborate."

"You'll go to the infirmary first," Christine overruled her. "Come with me."

Christine walked her there as if Allison were a new student again, awed by all she saw, and a little lost.

Dr. Singh had joined the Athena staff a few months earlier. She examined the job the doctor in Kentucky had done and pronounced it good.

Allison, Christine, Diana and Kayla walked out of the main building toward Christine's bungalow where, Christine explained, they would eat dinner in private. The Academy students, including Kayla's daughter Jazz, were in the mess hall for spaghetti dinner. Day was done, gone the sun; Allison felt a stillness, a peacefulness.

A calm before the storm?

"Hey, Allison," Lucy Karmon said, joining them in Christine's comfortable residence. The scrappy redhead brought high energy with her as she picked up a dish of spaghetti and dug in. "All secured," she told Christine.

"Lucy," Allison greeted her. Lucy was the one who had brought Echo's half sister Lilith from India to Athena Academy to give Allison the spider necklace. "Long time no see."

Lucy didn't smile, didn't meet Allison's eyes. Allison knew she was furious with herself for not taking Echo down. No one blamed her. She and Lilith had gotten the prize—the necklace—and that was huge. But she knew Lucy didn't see it that way.

Allison forced herself to eat a generous meal, knowing she was burning calories at a prodigious rate. As they ate, she brought Christine and Kayla up to speed, omitting significant portions of information such as the fact that she was Delphi; there was an impending possibility of a nuclear attack; and that Jeremy Loschetter was locked up in a safe house in the Arizona desert. Mostly she discussed the FBI results of investigation about the kidnappings of children conceived *in vitro* at the Women's Fertility Clinic in Zuni.

"One of them was especially troubling," Allison said. "A girl named Natalia LeClaire was abducted not far from here. Her parents were in Tucson and she was alone when she was taken. The feebs suspect the parents had a hand in the kidnapping. They were very reluctant to cooperate and the Special Agent in Charge found a fireproof cell in their basement. It had a bed, a toilet and a sink."

She looked at each woman in turn. "There were burn

marks on the cinderblock walls, and the sheets on the bed were clean, but looked like they'd been singed."

"Oh, my God," Kayla breathed. "An egg baby who can set things on fire? That's just too…science fiction."

"As opposed to someone whose skin is toxic?" Lucy asked her dryly, referring to Lilith. "Or a psychic?"

"Point taken," Kayla replied, blowing her bangs off her forehead. "So…what do you think? Was the mother a willing surrogate? Or do you think that couple got tricked into raising a little girl who could set them on fire? So when someone offered to take her off their hands, they agreed to disappear for a while to make it easier?"

It was clear to Allison that Kayla was having trouble wrapping her head around either scenario. The police officer came from a close-knit Navajo family, where children were loved and wanted. Kayla had given up a lot when she had discovered she was pregnant in her senior year at Athena Academy. But she had also gained a tremendous amount—a fantastic daughter to love and cherish.

"Does this involve the same parties as before?" Christine asked. She took a sip of the red wine she had served with the spaghetti.

"And does it have something to do with Lilith's necklace?" Lucy cut in.

Wishing her meeting with Lilith had been done less publicly, Allison nodded. "I can't say more than that," she told Christine apologetically.

Christine considered. "Athena Academy has remained free of influence peddlers," she said. "I argued with your mother about making this a high school. I thought we should open a college. But she was right.

There would have been more governmental oversight, interference and a lot of jostling to compromise our independence," she elaborated. "So many things have happened—your mother murdered, the egg superbabies among us… I come from a military background, and it's ingrained in me that might helps right."

She frowned at Allison. "It's hard for me not to ask for a thousand troops with heavy artillery to surround this place and protect my girls."

"Me, too," Diana said. "I'm Army. But I'm Athena first. And we have to do it ourselves."

"So maybe we should seed the outlying desert areas with land mines," Lucy put in. Allison could see that she was only half joking. Lucy was a demolitions expert, and hotheaded to boot.

"We can't go to your boyfriend. Or your grandfather, either," Allison reminded Diana. Diana was dating Gabe Monihan, the president of the United States. And her grandfather, Joseph Lockworth, was once the director of CIA. Now retired, he was still called in occasionally to consult. Allison wondered who at CIA had seen the faked e-mails of her blackmail attempts. And if anything else had filtered up via Echelon, the international global surveillance system created by NSA—but not as powerful as Allison's own Oracle.

"I concur," Diana said.

"Agreed." Christine raised her wineglass. "To Athena."

The women clinked their glasses, the tinkle of glass a bright moment in a dark night.

About half an hour later, the meeting concluded. Allison said good-night to Christine and to Diana, who was staying in guest quarters. Kayla said she was going to check in on Jazz, who lived on campus.

Allison had a bungalow of her own, down near the stables. Gordita was no longer there, but Allison smiled faintly at the commingled odors of hay and horse dung. She wished she could go for a soothing ride. But her nose and ribs were too sore, and she had urgent business.

Oracle business.

Lucy came in and sat down. She raked her fingers through her red hair and stood back up, pacing.

"We almost had her, Allison. We almost had Echo. We let her go."

"Lilith got the necklace," Allison reminded her. "That was your objective."

Lucy huffed and shook her head. "We blew it."

"There's no way you could have fought against the force field she threw around herself," Allison persisted. "I don't know how we're going to penetrate it." She felt the eyes of the woman on her. "I don't know *yet,*" she added. "But we will."

"Yeah," Lucy said glumly. "And when we do…" She clenched her teeth. "Lilith told me what Echo did to those people in India. There is nothing inside her to stop her from doing horrible things. No conscience, no moral compass. If she wants it, she'll take it."

And she wants me dead, Allison thought. *She wants the necklace.*

As soon as she closed and locked the door behind Lucy, she powered on her desktop. Far more powerful than her laptop, it was loaded with custom applications that would allow her to tie directly into Oracle. She got to work, taking the reins so Selena could leave the Oracle town house and show up for work at Langley. If Selena stayed out much longer, there would be questions.

Once she was in, Allison sent Selena a dismissal e-mail through the system. Selena received it, replied and went home to her husband. Maybe they'd get lucky tonight and make a baby.

And I will keep that baby safe, Allison vowed.

Oracle kicked out the coverage about Allison's town house. It also revealed the ME's report on the as-yet unidentified man whose body had been found inside her house. He had not died in the fire. He had been beaten to death.

So there had been two people inside Allison's town house. *Why? How?* She reran the scenario in the alley. One guy put into play with a seemingly legitimate order to pick her up for questioning, the other a double agent intent on murdering them both?

Morgan and an accomplice? Maybe even McDonough? Had Morgan killed an attacker? Was Morgan even there?

Too many questions, and not enough time. So she'd skip ahead to the answers…if she could.

At Zorba's place, Morgan showered and asked to borrow Zorba's blow-dryer. That rated a raised eyebrow but Morgan made no explanation. While Zorba was opening up a second bottle of ouzo, Morgan blow-dried the flash drive he'd used at Allison's just before the town house went up. Since his own clothes were filthy, he accepted one of Zorba's long-sleeved dark gray sweaters, a pair of jeans that were a little baggy on him, and a pea coat for later. Zorba's feet were smaller than his, so he was stuck with his caked, bloody shoes.

Then Morgan had helped Zorba kill that second bottle of ouzo and didn't squawk when they moved on to retsina. He didn't drink all the alcohol Zorba poured for him, but he kept things realistic.

He bided his time until Zorba staggered into his bedroom and started snoring. Then Morgan powered up the desktop in Zorba's small office, inserted the flash drive with Allison's last two e-mails and popped open the contents. Micronesia…and nothing else.

He dove into NSA and passworded himself through layer after layer of security.

Still, all he got was Micronesia. And he never got anywhere near the other e-mail. Allison's firewalls had firewalls.

He ejected the memory stick and slid it into the front pocket of his borrowed jeans. Next, via Echelon, he traced the cell phone number for Athena Construction to a section of the Arizona desert. He pulled up navsat—the images from the navigation satellites traveling in space—and wrote down the latitude and longitude coordinates. It was deep in the desert—hotter than hell even on winter days—and hard to get to.

He hacked into the NSA phone logs for his section and noted that McDonough had made a call from his office well after midnight. Long hours for Mr. Taxicab. Morgan captured the number and started running it. Then he captured Kim Valenti's personal cell phone number off her personnel file records.

McDonough had called someone named Wrobleski. CIA. Morgan started wading as deeply as he could into

Wrobleski's business without triggering an alert. Huh.
A lot of deletions, a lot of No Access Permitted. That
was unsurprising, given that Wrobleski was a spook.

Then he gave Valenti a jingle.

"Hmm, yeah," she murmured, then snapped awake.
"Hello?"

"It's Morgan Rush," he said. "I want to tell you a few
things. Are you awake?"

"Yes." She was instantly alert. "Go ahead."

"You know I'm looking for Allison. I was in her
town house. A guy showed up with a contract on her.
He's the body. I don't know if he was connected with
the explosion but I don't think so."

"Explosion? We thought it was a fire."

"The explosion caused the fire. Whatever she's
involved in, she needs help."

"And do you want to help her?" she asked suspiciously.

"Yes. I do."

He heard her moving around and wondered if she'd
started taping him. Or if she was trying to trace him. If
she could manage it, she was in for a surprise.

He had taken Zorba's van, and he was idling inside
Valenti's parking garage. The security attendant had
dozed off…after Morgan had shot him in the neck with
a little tranquilizer dart.

"Help her how?" Valenti asked.

He blinked. Finding her had somehow mutated into
leading her out of the snake pit she was in. Things were
catching up with Allison Gracelyn. Bad things and bad
people. Maybe it was deserved.

You don't think that.

He did. He was worried about her, but he still didn't trust her.

"You do a lot of things for McDonough. Like monitor Allison's activities at work," Valenti said. "But you're a mathematician. Not a bounty hunter. So why did he send you after her?"

"Don't trust him," Morgan said. "Ever. He doctored up some surveillance footage to make her look bad. Maybe he figured I needed a nudge to go after her."

"But you didn't, did you? Need a nudge?" Her tone was sharp. "You were just itching for an excuse."

"She's got a lot of secrets."

"I think you have some too, Morgan. Care to share? Like, did McDonough set the explosion?"

"I don't know," he said honestly. "I didn't ask him. Speaking of the office, what's the status of our project? I wasn't at the meeting," he reminded her unnecessarily.

"We got chatter about a radius," she told him. She meant the range of a potential nuclear detonation. How many people would be incinerated, how many would die horrible, lingering deaths from radiation sickness if they weren't treated. "Not looking good."

He gritted his teeth. It was killing him not to be there.

"McDonough is watching you, too. He heard you telling me about Allison's 'pregnancy.' Not your finest hour," he observed. "You need to attend a lying workshop."

"Have you been spying on me, too?"

"No. McDonough did that all by himself. I just spy on Allison."

"A one-woman snitch. What a relief."

"So you'd better be damn careful at work," he continued.

"I always am, Morgan."

He waited, hoping she would elaborate. The silence lengthened between them.

"She needs friends," he tried, but that was stupid. Allison had lots of friends, and both he and Valenti knew he wasn't one of them. "Strike that. Tell her I called you and I want her to talk to me."

"I will," she said.

He disconnected.

Then he got out of the van and dropped down at the rear of Valenti's nice white Lexus, jerking and creaking like an old man because he was so bashed up. He pressed one of Allison's button cams on the undercarriage of the Lexus, then added one of his mini-mics. He had heard that some guys kept condoms in their back pockets. It must be nice to live like that. Not that he was whining.

It was 5:07 in the morning. He was pushing it. People would be getting up for work soon and he didn't want any of them to run into him in their haste to get to the nearest Starbucks.

He took the elevator straight to Valenti's floor, the sixth. The elevator opened out on a mirror beneath a large vase of silk flowers. He looked tired and beat-up, with dark black circles underneath his dark blue eyes and a few scattered cuts in the hairline of his salt-and-pepper hair. He moved silently along the floral carpet, placing cameras and mics in inconspicuous spots along the way, like bread crumbs, violating civil rights the way some people eat popcorn. It bothered him, but it didn't stop him.

Looping his earpiece in place, he got back into Zorba's van and drove quietly to the security gate, which rolled open for him. The guard was starting to come to. He was going to have a headache.

Wind rustled the bushes as Morgan drove onto the street. He glanced at the clock in the dash. Five forty-five. From Zorba's stash of goodies in the hidden compartment beneath the van's floor, he got out a parabolic microphone and an LL—a wand-shaped laser. The microphone would probably pick up Valenti's voice but the laser was a snoop's dream come true, albeit with limitations—it had to hit a window and she had to be standing near it. She lived on the sixth floor, and her kitchen was the tenth window across. She had mentioned in casual conversation at work that she was a big believer in breakfast, which she cooked every morning.

A minute later, he heard the ringing of a phone line, outbound; Kim was making a call. Excellent. He loved this woman.

The connection was made.

"Gordita," Valenti said.

"Check." Even better, he could hear the other speaker. Damned if it wasn't Katie again! That stubborn little brat! "You're early. Everything is nominal. Loschetter is still PMSing or whatever."

"This isn't your check-in, although I'm glad everything's quiet. Your brother called me on my cell about twenty minutes ago. He said the body in the town house was a hit man sent after *her.* Also, that McDonough made some fake tape to convince Morgan to go after her."

Katie grunted. "My *brother?*"

"Katie, please tell me. Does Morgan have some kind of private life like we do? He's been spying on Allison at work, but it's weird that he would be sent out into the field like an operative."

"Spying? On Allison? That jerk," Katie said. "Who for?"

"Allison's boss. And I got the feeling he thought her boss might have engineered the town house explosion. It was a bomb, Katie, not just a fire."

"I thought so," Katie said. "I've been replaying the footage from Shannon's station and the debris field is indicative of that. About Morgan? I've wondered. After all, *I've* got a lot going on that I don't tell *him* about."

And what would that be? Morgan wondered, holding his breath. *Spill, Katie. Tell me.*

"I think I need to tell you we've been seeing e-mails that falsely incriminate her in a number of extortion schemes," Valenti said. "We think that's why people are coming after her."

"Who's sending them? Echo?" Katie asked.

Echo again. Who the hell is Echo? Does this have anything to do with those Spider files?

"Probably," Valenti confirmed. "But *I* can't even trace them back. They're spoofed but good, and they're stirring up trouble. So if your brother is hoping to catch her, he might have to take a number and stand in line."

"Morgan doesn't want to 'catch' her," Katie insisted. A beat. "Does he?"

"Yes. He's tacked on the incentive of offering to help her, but I'm not sure how he can."

He was mildly affronted, but Valenti had a point.

Allison didn't appear to need a knight in shining armor, not that his armor was all that shiny. Maybe an extra pair of fists in a street fight, or a rocket launcher…

Zorba has a rocket launcher in here, he thought. Also, grenades, a few Uzis and body armor. If Homeland Security stopped Morgan, he would have some tap-dancing to do.

"Morgan's actually a good guy," Katie said. "Even if he's all screwed up about women because of our mom."

Whoa!

"Well, we both know that the worst of the bad guys think they're the good guys," Valenti said back. "You're saying you trust him?"

"Yes. I do," Katie said.

Morgan smiled grimly. *Thank you, sis.*

"She's heading out your way," Valenti said. "Meanwhile, you'll get a check-in call at the usual time."

"Roger that," Katie replied.

The women disconnected.

Morgan drove, parsing what he'd heard. Check-in calls and extortion schemes. Was it possible Allison and Kim Valenti were playing his sister? Were they running some kind of op together and duping her into helping them?

Your sister's FBI, he reminded himself. *It would be pretty hard for anyone to fake her out.*

But not impossible.

Valenti had said that Allison was on her way. Maybe he could catch up with her.

He set the GPS for the middle of the stinkin' desert and opened the window so the cold air would keep him awake. Once he was out of town, he'd load up on coffee and fuel.

He had a long drive ahead of him.

* * *

Allison woke up in her bed at Athena Academy at nearly 10:00 a.m., groaning when she saw that she'd missed a call. She cursed herself for sleeping through it, and gave her message a listen.

It was Kim, telling her about Morgan's call, and also telling her she had called Delphi. Allison called the Delphi-dedicated line in Oracle HQ and listened to that message, too, which was a rehash of what Kim had told Allison.

Allison wasn't too surprised about the hit man. But she was very worried about the disarming of her town house's state-of-the-art alarm system—the first line of defense. As far as she could piece together, the only system that had been active when Morgan had broken in was the commercial one, and that should not have been the case.

She tried to call Kim back, but she went straight to voice mail on Kim's cell. She left a request for Kim to call her back.

A student brought her breakfast. Allison had a complete wardrobe in her quarters; she greeted the girl dressed in baggy olive pants and a black spaghetti-strap T-shirt—definitely not her usual tailored, professional look when she came to visit Athena Academy. But she had left the war room. She was in the field, preparing for battle. She could almost feel Echo doing the same. Allison wondered how it would come down—would they be two generals deploying their forces, or two lone warriors battling in hand-to-hand combat?

Scrolling through Oracle's busy night via her desktop, Allison had just tucked into her Denver omelet when Diana arrived. Allison took another bite, wiped her lips with her napkin and pushed back from the desk.

"Can you get me a vehicle so I can drive to the safe house?" Allison requested.

Diana hesitated. "Waiting until dark would be better."

"That's a whole day away," Allison argued.

"You could use a day," Diana countered. "We should get the necklace first, then go to the safe house. Less travel that way. Fewer chances to spot you."

Allison huffed. Diana was using Allison's own argument about laying low against her. The other piece of logic was that her desktop was Oracle West, and she could probably do more good monitoring it than she could checking up on Loschetter in person. Either she trusted her agents to guard him or she didn't. She admitted—privately—that it wasn't a matter of trust. It was a matter of…being a control freak.

Diana reached into her pocket and held up a post office box key. The agents of Oracle had sets of keys for over a hundred drop points located all over the world.

"I'll run into town and check for it after the post office boxes are stuffed," Diana promised.

"It's too soon for it to arrive," Allison said, running her hands through her hair, then dropping them to her lap. "Some of my alleged blackmail victims are trying to check in with me. Wrobleski's taken some personal time and Oracle kicked out his round-trip reservation to the Cayman Islands on a commercial flight. I'm embarrassed that 'I'm' dealing with someone so obvious."

"The stupider, the more likely he is to get caught," Diana said. "And if that happens, he might try to give you up in return for immunity."

"I thought about that, too," Allison said. "I'm wondering if that's 'my' plan. Kim said Morgan Rush wants to help me. Do you think he's referring to any of this? How can he help me? He's got to be working for someone."

"NSA?" Diana asked.

"No. Someone more…active," Allison argued. "NSA collects communications intelligence. We don't blow up town houses."

"McDonough's off the books. There could be other people off the books at NSA," Diana ventured.

"Okay, I'll give you that point. Meanwhile, someone is trying to blow up the East Coast and I'm not getting much. That tells me that the FBI and the NSA are dealing with it face-to-face." She slid a glance at Diana. "Army Intel has joined the party."

"And we're *good*," Diana said. "I'll feed you anything that comes my way if it doesn't kick out on Oracle first." She cocked her head. "We can still hope Echo's blowing smoke with some fake terrorist scheme, just to keep us looking in the wrong place."

"Been there, thought that," Allison said. "That's a dangerous assumption."

"I know. It's only an assumption." She pointed to Allison's bed. "Rest while you can. When it hits, it's going to hit big."

"Don't I know it," Allison whispered, clenching her jaw. A muscle jumped in her cheek.

Diana narrowed her eyes. "I've never seen you this stressed out. You don't have to carry the load all by yourself. We're a team, Allison. Use us."

"I am. I will," Allison told her. "We're headed for the showdown, Diana. I can feel it."

"Bring it on," Diana said. "Echo has a lot to answer for."

"Damn straight," Allison replied. "But it's not about payback. We have to stop her once and for all. And we will."

"Damn straight," Diana replied. "We're Athena."

Then she turned around and shut the door behind herself. Allison scooted back to her computer.

"Get some *rest*," Diana said through the door. "And, if you talk to Delphi, tell her we're ready to rock and roll."

Echo's new laboratory
An unnamed island in Micronesia

"Mom?" the young firestarter murmured as she awakened. They'd kept her sedated on the flight out of Arizona to Los Angeles; then on to Japan, then on to the atoll in Micronesia.

Her dark hair tumbling over her shoulders, Natalia LeClaire sat up very slowly on the concrete floor, one hand pressed against her forehead. Her hand dropped to her side as she gazed up and around at her patented prison.

Clad in an exquisite black Stella McCartney evening gown, with Harry Winston jeweled cuffs on either wrist, Echo stood well out of sight—and out of range—on her observation catwalk, angled forty-five degrees above the enclosed bunker. A plasma screen magnified every pore of Natalia LeClaire's skin. Microphones picked up each syllable and unsteady breath as the girl walked to the clear front panel and tapped it.

"Hello? Hello, someone?" she called. "Is anyone here?"

Watching, Echo smiled and remained silent. Shivers of anticipation skittered up and down her spine. She was hoping for a demonstration from her little torch.

"I'm sorry," Natalia whispered. She began to cry. "I didn't mean to hurt the man. I'm so sorry!"

Echo cocked her head and watched as Natalia's muzziness morphed into anxiety, then hit the turbo into full-on panic as she screamed, "I didn't mean to do it!"

Natalia slammed her right fist against the clear barrier, then her left, then both. Sweat beaded her forehead. Her face turned red; then a flush blossomed across her collarbone and zoomed up her neck. And then, incredibly, she began to smoke.

Lovely.

Flames erupted all around the girl, shooting to the roof and walls. With the first gout of flame, all her clothes burned off. But her dark hair, thick lashes and lovely skin remained untouched as the fire rose higher, shot farther, burned hotter.

Exquisite.

"Where's my mom!" Natalia LeClaire screamed. "Help!"

"O, brave new world," Echo cooed, as she gazed into the monitor at the girl. Imagine. A human torch. Truly Mummy had consorted with geniuses—men of vision, men who could make dreams come true.

Men Echo needed.

She touched the two upper quadrants of the screen. Images clicked on in the cells of two other recent arrivals, who were still unconscious. Little Cailey, who was five and had uncannily good eyesight, and Willa the eighteen-year-old superhacker, had also been sedated during their extractions. Then the sleeping beauties had been flown in separate private jets to a nearby atoll, and from there, ferried to her private dock by minisub, then driven in separate armored cars through the security checkpoints to the tunnel. And now they lay sleeping like sweet cherubs, in her brilliant new lab. She had the full set now—thirteen lovely egg babies Jeremy Loschetter had kept out of his records. Arachne had listed six of them on Kwan-Sook's memory stick, and seven of them on Echo's.

She was willing to bet there were some more names on Lilith's flash drive. And that Eric Pace, the disgraced former Army Chief of Staff and collector of information on very special children, had even more. He also had a great wealth of knowledge and expertise on the subject, and from reading the Department of Defense's classified files on him, and putting it together with what she had, she knew he had withheld a lot. She wanted everything he had. That was why she was going to break him out of jail.

Both Cailey and Willa had actual beds. Each of them was being guarded by one of Echo's favorite sort of expendable security—big, beefy men who weren't smart enough to be devious. They followed orders to the letter because they were afraid of pain—and of her. Simple equation, simple men.

Easy come, easy go.

There were no guards in Natalia's cell, of course. But there were two out in the passageway that led to her bunker. Echo clicked on the remote camera, and studied them in the lower right quadrant of her monitor. Both were tall and bulked up from steroids. One was bald;

one wore a very outdated ponytail. They wore Kevlar vests and held Uzis across their chests, and they looked frightened. Obviously they had heard about the operative Natalia had burned to death soon after her capture.

The immolation had obviously traumatized Natalia. This could only be good. She would need someone who understood what she was going through.

Echo was very good at understanding—or pretending to. She didn't give a damn personally about Natalia, or any of the other egg girls. She did give a damn about what they could do…for her.

After all, she was her mother's daughter.

She blew a kiss at Natalia, who was blazing away in a fetal position, crackling and weeping.

Then she went in and checked on "Silk" and "Shadow," also known as Mary and Elizabeth, the two little Goths she had located some months before in London. They were twins, and they loved her very much. Their parents were afraid of them—just like Natalia's were of her—and they had thrown them onto the street. But Echo's people had successfully located them, and Echo, of course, had welcomed them with open arms.

They lived in their own part of the laboratory, decorated with their manga and their anime and posters of vampires. They had asked her if any of the egg babies were vampires. They'd been very disappointed to hear that she hadn't found any.

"Hello, darlings," she said, as she breezed into their room. "Penny for my thoughts."

The pasty-faced teens with black-and-blue hair smiled at her and took each other's hands. Their fingernails were painted black, and they were wearing long-sleeved red and black blouses. They could only read minds when they were touching each other. Echo thought that was charming. She held that thought on purpose, of course, because she wanted them to read her highly complimentary opinions and then do whatever she asked them to. Echo limited her visits precisely because she didn't want to slip and think something that might disturb her little girls.

"You're dressed up for a party," Mary said.

"It doesn't take a psychic to figure that out," Echo said, amused, as she twirled in a circle.

"You've found more kids like us," Elizabeth offered. "They didn't want to come."

"They've been so traumatized by their terrible parents," Echo said sadly. She leaned forward and kissed each of them on the forehead. "We'll have to be very patient with them."

She turned away.

She was going upstairs for a little housewarming party, to thank all the local politicians who had paved the way for the construction of her beautiful new home, high atop a dormant volcano. They didn't know about the underground laboratory inside the dormant volcano, of course. Or the fact that she'd just sent a team to break Eric Pace out of jail.

Natalia would be good for jailbreaks.

And speaking of jailbreaks...

"We're going to America," Mary said, her eyes widening with excitement. "We're going to free one of your scientists."

"His name is Jeremy," Elizabeth put in. "We're going

to ride in a special airplane that's difficult to see. It's a spy airplane!"

"Very good." Echo clapped her hands together. "It will be such fun." She blew kisses at them and left their room. She walked into the dampening field, sagging from the effort of controlling her thinking while in the presence of the twins.

Clack clack clack, stilettos on the catwalk.

"Jeremy," she sang, "get ready. We're coming to get you."

Clack clack clack. Stilettos straight through Ian's balls.

At the last moment, she had decided against the piano wire. She liked being unpredictable that way.

Chapter 10

Day Two since Allison had driven away from NSA.

Now Allison drove "alone" into Athens in the pickup truck Kayla had lent her. Her backup team was strategically positioned up and down Olympus, the main drag. Although Diana Lockworth's older sister, Josie, wasn't specifically Oracle, she was an Athenian, and she had arrived in town to help. Now she and Diana were parked across the street. To add a sense of normalcy, Kayla Ryan was on patrol in a marked police car.

Allison wore a black wig and sunglasses, a long black skirt, a concho belt, a white blouse, black cowboy boots and a wide-brimmed black cowboy hat. She parked in front of the satellite post office and picked up her department store shopping bag. She took a moment to signal her backup—adjusting her sunglasses—then walked straight into the building and headed for the grid of burnished post office boxes, some the width of three magazines, others large enough to contain suitcases. There were about a hundred of them, and Oracle's was

one of the largest. As calmly as she could, she inserted
the key and opened the door.

Yes.

Selena had sent the can in a plain box and addressed
it to Christine Evans. Allison calmly put it into her in-
nocuous shopping bag.

She went back outside, adjusted her sunglasses again
and got back in her car. She hadn't dared to open the
package inside the post office, and she had decided to
take it out of town before she did.

She had also followed Diana's advice to make use of
the team. First, she sent Kayla on a grocery store run to
buy some wine and steaks. Then, she activated Lynnette
White and her boyfriend "Patrick Torrell," formerly FBI
Special Agent Nick Barnes whose cover had been
blown. Nick was in the Witness Protection Program, and
the two were living in Arizona. So she asked them to join
the team that was, for the moment, based at Athena
Academy. Lynn's supposed father, Jonas White, had
used her to steal valuable art objects, and Nick had been
the AIC on the case against Jonas, going undercover as
his bodyguard. Among Lynne's special enhancements
was superhacking, so Allison put her in charge of monitoring Oracle West while she, Allison, went to the
mountains.

Remembering the night before when Allison had
forced herself to calmly drive away from NSA HQ, she
glided out of town, down the suburban streets headed
for the 10, to her family's getaway, an aerie retreat up
in the mountains an hour north of Athena Academy. She
would get there first, and open the can alone. If anything
went wrong, it would happen well before her father and

brother arrived. Then, if she was still alive, they were going to have dinner together.

She had presented the get-together to her family as her way of assuring them that she was all right. That was partially true, but the primary reason for that dinner was that she wanted to see them before things got crazy—to tie up loose ends and to say goodbye.

Just in case.

Her throat tightened. She couldn't let them know that. They loved her; of course they'd try to stop her from putting herself in harm's way. But she had never gotten to say goodbye to her mother. She wasn't about to make any Gracelyn endure that again.

Soon she was out on the open road, beyond the metro area and headed up into the rugged and beautiful White Tank Mountains. The hard granite range, rising from the desert floor to over four thousand feet, was crosshatched with ridges and canyons, caused by infrequent heavy rains. Flash floods carved out deep depressions— tanks—that filled with water. Scatters of creosote bushes and agaves dotted the landscape, and saguaro cacti raised their arms toward the winter sun.

The bag was on the passenger seat. She was itching to open it and confirm that the necklace was inside. It was, or it wasn't. She had to stay patient. In control. Move ahead according to plan.

Her thoughts shifted to Morgan. Kim said he hadn't surfaced at NSA, and McDonough was treating Kim like his new best friend. There was progress regarding Project Ozone. Kim's team had translated messages indicating that the terrorist cell planning the attack was called the Circle of Justice, and they were waiting for the signal to move into place. There was also a code phrase that would abort the mission, and McDonough had put several team members including Kim on that task. But without Allison and Morgan, the team was shorthanded, and everyone was working around the clock. Tempers were growing short and people were asking pointed questions about the whereabouts of Gracelyn and Rush.

If we could access Arachne's web, we might be able to find the code words to abort, Allison thought, as she pulled up to the beautiful old stone cabin hanging over the side of a mesa. Nestled among pines and winter wildflowers, the old aerie was a reminder of happier days, when Marion Gracelyn was alive and her busy family would meet here for a few days to unwind and enjoy each other.

She stopped the truck, turned off the engine and closed her eyes. Her ribs hurt. She didn't want to die.

I am the center of the storm.

Then she picked up the sack and climbed down, shutting the door.

Kicking up dust, she moved past a large cluster of prickly pears and squatted down. She took the box out of the bag and pulled the box cutter she had brought out of her pocket. She sliced right through and opened it quickly. There was the paint can that looked exactly like her paint can. Her eye color: chocolate-brown. There was even the silly little cartoon horse head she had lightly drawn on the rim—an unexpected touch of whimsy from serious Allison Gracelyn. Of course, any attentive operative could have forged that, too.

She took a breath and used the other end of the box cutter to pry up the can lid.

The slanting rays of the afternoon sun burnished the gold spider as she lifted it by the chain. She gazed at it for a moment, then turned it over and flicked open the section in the thorax that cradled the flash drive.

It was there.

She pulled it out and closed her fist around it tightly. She thought she would heave a sigh of relief, and that the tension in her shoulders and neck would ease. But nothing remotely like that happened. She was as keyed-up as ever. Registering mild disappointment, she replaced the drive inside the necklace, and fastened the chain around her neck.

Then she got to her feet, retrieved the groceries from the truck, and let herself in through the back door, passing through the airy washed-wood-and-leather living room and into the kitchen with its matte metal appliances and marble countertops. She picked up the landline and called Diana.

"We're in business," she said. Then she called Selena and told her the same thing.

She brought in her overnight bag, leaving her duffel bag with her body armor, satellite phone and weapons in the truck. No need to bring the war to her family.

She opened the bottle of simple red table wine Kayla had purchased for her, rinsed the dust out of a wine goblet and poured herself a glass. She sipped it as she began dinner preparations, her chief tasks being to mix a marinade for the steak and make a salad.

After the steaks were soaking, she called Lynnette on a secure cell.

"I'm here," she said. "Anything?"

"Not yet," Lynnette replied.

The two hung up. Allison carried her wine to the back window and stared out at the breathtaking view. After a few minutes, she realized she was bracing for something, anything, that required her immediate attention. Silence crept over her like a lightweight bedspread, and she realized with a start that Delphi had some downtime.

The steaks were soaking; so could she. She undressed as she walked toward the bathroom, boots first, then skirt, blouse and bra. She wasn't wearing any underwear.

In no time, the whirlpool bath in the large bathroom was churning scented bubbles. She set her cell phone on the small stone table beside the tub, her one concession to her duty. After taking off her wig and pinning up her dark hair, Allison eased herself into the hot, frothy water. She had brought her wineglass with her. It occurred to her that she might have brought a magazine in with her, or even a book. The idea of having enough time to read a novel for pleasure boggled her mind. Maybe someday, after the world was finally, completely safe.

She smiled wryly to herself and sank up to her chin in bubbles, sipped wine, and luxuriated.

Morgan finished eating his greasy cheeseburger— pure heaven—and took a deliberately noisy slurp of diet soda. In their younger days, Katie had insisted that Morgan invented the "pig" in "pig out." He put the drink cup on the nightstand of his motel room, next to his most excellent Medusa, a K-frame revolver that, due to its unique spring system, could hold and shoot different calibers in the same chambers. Morgan had fired .380 auto rounds, .38 Colts, .38 Specials, 9 mms, and .357 Magnums all from this one gun. It came in very handy when ammo stores of one caliber dwindled. The handle had been etched for him by his Pentjak Silat *guru*. Pentjak Silat was Morgan's martial art, a savage tradition involving knives and backup moves for backup moves, designed for fatality and not for style. In Morgan's world, there was no such thing as cheating in a fight. There was surviving, and dying.

He scratched his chest and took a deep breath. His room smelled like bubble-gum—cheap deodorizer—but he had smelled much worse scents. Yawning, he stretched his hand behind his head. Then he picked up his cell phone and dialed Allison.

"Yes," she said tensely.

His brow went up. "I didn't expect you to answer. I had a prepared message all ready."

There was a pause. "What was it?"

"'Allison, this is Morgan. How are you?'"

"I'm fine." Another pause. "How are you?"

"Great. I just had a cheeseburger and now I'm going to work on the fries. Suicide by saturated fat." *Was that a chuckle?*

"We're having steak."

We. He didn't think he should ask who that was. It might remind her that they were actually having a pleasant conversation.

"I heard you haven't been showing up at work," she continued.

"How's Kim doing?"

"Have you heard about the Circle of Justice?"

"Of course. I'm not in the office, but I'm on the job."

He was also listening to Kim Valenti's phone conversations and monitoring her car, but he decided not to mention that.

Another pause. "What job would that be?"

"I want to help you, Allison."

She hung up. He sighed, frustrated. Then he got up, brushed his teeth and stripped down for bed.

His phone rang. He grabbed it eagerly.

"Yes?"

"She's not pregnant," Juliet informed him. "But I am."

He smiled. "That's great. Congratulations."

"So we're getting married."

"That's really great."

"So maybe I will invite you."

"I'll bring a date," he said.

"Don't get her pregnant."

"Wouldn't dream of it."

They disconnected.

He dozed off.

And he did dream of it. In his dreams, he wrapped his legs around Allison and took her, hard; then they shot bad guys; and then she died.

He bolted awake covered in sweat.

"You look tired," Allison's father said, after their delightful meal. She was drying the dishes and he was putting them away. David was artfully arranging some cheese and fruit on a platter, his contribution to their dinner. He'd also brought a very nice bottle of Port.

"It's the bruising caused by *her broken nose,*" David said meaningfully. "Which she broke *slipping* on the icy walkway to her town house. Before it *burned down.*" He violently plucked red grapes off their stems.

This wasn't going quite the way Allison had hoped. She picked up her glass of Port and carried it into the living room, sitting down on one of the leather couches. She had another headache. She felt foolish for the way she'd talked to Morgan. What had gotten into her?

"I'm sorry. I don't mean to push," David said softly, holding out his fruit and cheese plate. It was beautiful. She took a grape as a peace offering. He set the plate down on the coffee table in front of her and plopped down beside her on the couch. "It's just…I've lost our mother. I don't want to lose you, too." He sighed. "I have to check in with my office. The work of the Attorney General is never done."

He walked off in the direction of his room. Allison watched him go, then returned to the kitchen, where her father was pretending to dry the same dish he'd been drying when she left the kitchen.

"Everything okay?" he asked.

She wondered if he'd heard the whole thing. "Yeah."

"Then why isn't my broken-nosed little girl smiling?"

She took a moment. This subject was hard for her to discuss. There was no part of her that wanted to cause her father distress. But in case this was the last time she saw him, she had to put this on the table.

"I want to talk about Mom," she began.

He raised a brow and paused. Then he put down the plate and leaned against the counter, cocking his head and gazing at her.

"Something got your nose out of joint?"

She actually smiled. One of the many things she loved about her father was his quirky sense of humor. It had seen him through dark days. Add that to his idealism, and he would be okay if she died in the line of duty—if he knew why. She would have to try to make it possible for him to know. Ask one of her Oracle agents to serve as a witness to the truth, if it came to that.

Her smile faded and she took a breath.

"It's about Eldon Waterton." He was the senator who had been tried and convicted of Marion Gracelyn's murder. "Dad, I don't think he acted alone. I think there was at least one other person involved."

He was quiet for a moment. She chewed the inside of her lip and ran a finger along a trio of waters droplets on the marble countertop. "Do you have proof?"

"Nothing conclusive. But I've been doing some digging. Winter found out a lot of things, but I think there's more."

He was silent for a time, his expression impossible to read.

Then his features softened, and he cocked his head as he looked at her, almost as if he were apologizing to her.

"Sweetheart, the jury was satisfied. We got a verdict."

His response surprised her. She had assumed he had lain awake many nights, trying to parse together the chain of events that had led to his beloved wife's death. Allison didn't think a plan to murder her mother sprang full-blown into Waterton's head. Sure he had motive and opportunity, and Marion wasn't the only person he had murdered. Maybe that was evidence of Allison's arrogance—that her mother's status as a victim should be different, more special, as elevated as her family's grief.

"If you can't find something solid, you have to let it go, promise me?" His gaze was very kind. "Let *her* go."

"Dad…"

"Let her go," he repeated. Then he pulled Allison into his arms. "The hardest thing I've ever done. Letting you go, letting you grow up, was the second hardest."

"But you did. Thank you." She nodded, and he smiled.

"It comes with the job, if it's done right." He folded up the dish towel and looped it around the rack on the pantry door. "Hey, let's get your brother out here and break out the cards. I'm feeling lucky."

Allison's father *was* lucky. An hour after they had begun to play, he'd cleaned out both his children. The men both got a little drunk, but Allison stayed alert. She kissed them both good-night, and rehashed the evening as she crawled into bed. She'd done well. She'd come clean and said goodbye.

If this was the last time they saw each other, it would be a good end.

After his second vivid dream of having sex with Allison, Morgan jerked awake to hip-hop on the motel alarm clock and groaned. He showered, brushed his teeth and went on down the road to the all night mini-mart, since his motel didn't crack open the doughnuts and coffee until 6:00 a.m., and it was only midnight. He could sleep after he died.

Zorba's van had not been vandalized, which was a

blessing to all gangbangers everywhere, because bad things could happen if it was tampered with. After disarming the security system, he jumped in and zoomed back onto the highway.

The GPS said he had five more hours until he reached Athena Construction. Too damn long, but there was nothing he could do about that. So he hovered at the speed limit, because for all he knew, Zorba had reported his van stolen. It didn't seem likely, given the contents of the vehicle and the questions a police inspection would raise, and besides, Morgan still wasn't sure if Zorba was involved with the Allison situation.

He plugged his cell phone into Zorba's car charger—his entire team carried the same brand, just for situations like these—and tapped his fingers on the dash, debating about calling Allison again, or maybe Athena Construction and saying the magic word. *Gordita.* But he figured he'd spooked everybody enough for now. And lest he forget, he didn't know who Allison had steak with last night. It could have been Katie, the Kestonian dictator, or the leader of the Circle of Justice. Or a guy she picked up in a bar.

Scratch that.

One hour, two. He was still alert and driving straight. He figured he had a future as a trucker if NSA didn't work out. Three. Four. He looked down at the GPS and out at the stretch of desert. He was supposed to turn here, and barrel through the sand. Slowing, he inched along, searching for some indication of an actual road. He saw none.

What the hell, he thought, making a right and rolling from blacktop to desert sand.

The van proved to be the equal of the environment as it shushed along. After about half an hour, Morgan turned off the headlights, allowing the moon to guide him. According to the GPS, he should have ten miles to go.

Like a large black shadow, a mesa rose ahead of him, jutting perpendicular to the desert floor, rising up toward the moon. Athena Construction should be perched on top. But as he drove a little closer, he saw that the sky was tinged with red light.

He cracked open his window.

There was smoke, thick and oily. And he heard the echoic *blam-pop!* of mortar fire. Fireworks lit up his windshield.

Crap. They're being attacked!

His sister's face filled his mind; then Allison's superimposed it and Morgan floored it, every cell in his body drenching with testosterone as he switched over to fight mode. He could feel his mind running possible scenarios as his body focused on the immediate mission of delivering himself to the battle. Figuring one more party guest wasn't going to matter, he flicked on his high beams, searching for a way up the mesa. He thought he had one, and started to race up the steep incline. But it was too steep for the heavily laden vehicle, and the van slid backward.

He caught traction and surged forward, locating another flat wash dotted with pebbles. The van clung on and started to climb. The plosive backblow of an explosion rocked him like the yaw of a slingshot turn in an aircraft. He alternated between staring at the horizon and watching out for his tires. The smoke was growing thicker. He cracked the window again and listened to the *crackcrackcrackbam* of submachine gun fire.

Damn, what the hell?

Rocketing upward, Morgan bore down on a boulder at least ten feet high and ten feet across. He guided the van around it….

…And then he slammed on the brakes so hard he nearly went through the windshield.

About two hundred yards ahead of him, on top of the mesa, the roof of a one-story bunker was on fire, and the wall facing him had been shattered into rubble. The place was entirely surrounded by armed troops shooting the hell out of an electrified fence. Four female shapes were silhouetted on the roof, wielding machine guns at a Black Hawk helicopter chopper as it shot straight up into the night clouds and disappeared.

Oh God, if she's in that mess…

As he threw himself out of the truck, he grabbed his cell phone.

And his rocket launcher.

Chapter 11

Here we go.

As soon as Allison got Katie's call, she shot out of the house in her nightgown like a madwoman, leaped into the truck and drove away. Her duffel bag was where she left it, stuffed in the catchall in the cab. She reluctantly placed the pendant under the driver's seat.

She drove with one hand as she called Katie back. She could hear explosions in the background of the safe house.

"They got him out," Katie shouted into the phone. "Loschetter is gone."

"Damn it!" Allison shouted back. "How?"

"They hit the tunnel. They knew where it was. I don't know how."

My God. Do we have a mole? Maybe Echo hacked into Oracle and found the plans. She couldn't imagine either possibility. They were both too terrible.

The safe house itself was actually underground, through a tunnel and down several flights of stairs. The attackers had hit the tunnel.

"Status," she said to Katie.

"We're okay so far," Katie informed her. "The super-structure's mostly gone but we have the bunker for coverage. We're returning fire. There's a chopper and they're trying to pick up some ground forces that must have been the first wave. I don't know if they have orders to eliminate us or just get their people out."

"Hang on. I'll bring reinforcements," Allison said. "I'll be there in fifteen minutes." If she pushed the truck to a hundred miles an hour, she'd make it.

"Roger that. Appreciated."

Allison dialed Diana and told her what had happened. Diana and Josie would be in the air in ten minutes. Allison didn't know if they had ten minutes.

Then her phone rang again.

"Allison." It was Morgan. "Your people are under attack."

A tremendous explosion blared in the background, and Morgan's cell phone went dead.

Oh God. She stayed on the line. "Morgan, Morgan, do you copy?"

Her call waiting pinged. She took it.

"Switched to radio phone," Morgan said. "I'm going in. Do you have anyone else coming?"

"Are you attacking us?" she demanded.

"Negative. There's a Black Hawk above me. There's troops on the ground—"

The radio phone went out.

Oh God, oh God.

Allison hurtled along the winding road to the highway, mentally cursing herself for spending the night off-site when she knew the risks were sky-high. Better she had left her personal business unfinished than be this far away from her people. She floored the truck, lips set in a grim line, blurring down the tarmac.

I am the center of the storm.

Oh God, Morgan. My agents....

I am the center of the storm.

And she was, as she reached the eastern road that would take her to the top of the mesa. A cold calm washed over her, shielding her warrior's mind from distraction as her body was galvanized into attack mode. She pushed the truck as hard as it would go, until it was rattling with stress. She kept pushing. If it gave out she'd run the rest of the way.

Cacti guarded the road—little more than a path—as she began to climb. The sky glowed white with explosions and red with fire. As she reached the top of the rise, she saw that the safe house exterior was ablaze. Four silhouettes danced on the roof, shooting skyward. Katie, Lindsey, Nikki, and Chesca. No one looked hurt.

She was watching them so intently that she almost didn't see the shape in the middle of the road. She swerved, registering only afterwards that it was Morgan, his back to her, armed with a rocket launcher— aimed at the safe house. At her people.

She slammed to a halt and flung herself out of the truck in her nightgown and her slippers. She was about as vulnerable to injury as if she were naked; more importantly, she was unarmed. It didn't stop her as she cut the distance in half between her and Morgan, cut it again; if that bastard got off a round at the safe house—

When she was two feet behind him, she bent her knees and pushed off as hard as she could, sailing against his back. He lost his grip on the launcher, which was all she cared about at the moment.

Then Morgan stopped himself from falling by making a tripod with one giant step on his left, straightening and aiming for his assailant's temple with a outward crescent kick. Allison saw it coming and blocked it with her forearm, then pushed forward again, folded her right leg and bringing it through his wide stance and up, to his private parts. He bellowed but lost no concentration as he tucked into a forward roll, sprang to his feet and hauled ass right at her. He tackled her, grabbing her around the waist and driving her backward onto the dirt. She gripped his biceps and jammed her forehead against his as hard as she could.

He fell on top of her and would have knocked the wind out of her, if Allison hadn't exhaled sharply first. The force against her ribs was excruciating. She ignored it as completely as if it belonged to someone else.

He scrabbled to pin her but she kept one hand free, curling her fingers to deliver an eardrum-bursting punch…if it came to that.

Then the whine of a bullet and a shower of dirt clouds smacked her face. Someone was shooting, hopefully at Morgan.

"Freeze!" she heard a voice. It was his sister, Katie.

Morgan pushed himself upright, so that he was straddling Allison. His eyes flared for a second, and then he was on his feet and yanking her up with him. Allison could have used any number of breakaways to get free, but unless he planned to hold her hostage against his own sister, the fight was over.

Allison ticked her glance past him to the safe house.

The battle on the roof was over as well. She counted five silhouettes—all five of Katie's fellow guards.

Katie had a radiophone, which squawked. She thumbed a button and pressed it against her ear.

"We're airborne, going after target." That was Diana.

"In an unarmed Learjet 40? Tell them to abort," Allison told Katie.

"Roger that. Abort, Diana, abort mission. Do you copy?"

Allison became aware of Morgan's gaze on her nightgown again. It was coated with sand and striped with blood—Morgan's, she hoped, and not more from her nose. The right strap had ripped away, revealing all but the nipple of her right breast. Now she did execute a breakaway, snapping herself out of his grip—he didn't fight it—and covered herself.

To his credit, he didn't smirk like a sixteen-year-old. He cleared his throat and shifted his attention to her face.

"For God's sake, Morgan," Katie hissed. "What are you doing here?"

"Trying to help," he told Allison. "I was aiming at the chopper, damn it." He stared at her in disbelief. "You have to know that. I wouldn't shoot at my own sister."

Katie narrowed her eyes at him but remained silent.

"But how you got from Point A to Point B," Allison said, "is the part I'm currently interested in."

"Gordita," he said. "I intercepted a call from Valenti and triangulated."

"No way," Katie began, but Allison raised her hand.

"We *know* that," Allison said. "Morgan, we let you hear it. Do you really think we're that stupid?"

She thoroughly enjoyed the look of discomfort on his rough-hewn features. He was here, finally, and whether friend or foe, he was no longer after her. One source of anxiety she could cross off her list.

"You lured me here, and then you attack me while I'm helping you?" he demanded hotly, the veins in his neck roped with anger.

"I lured you here so I would know where you were. Then I see you facing my safe house, shooting in the direction of my people with an RPG-7, so I don't stop and ask you if you had a pleasant trip from Virginia."

"What are you doing with a rocket launcher?" Katie demanded. "I mean, why do you even have one? Holy cow, Morgan, why do you know how to use one?"

"It was a Christmas bonus," he said. "At work."

Katie huffed. "You're so dead."

"You're black bag?" Allison asked. "Who do you work for?"

Morgan made no response.

"Okay, we'll torture you later for the intel," Katie said, maybe only half joking.

Allison glided barefoot—she had no idea where her slippers had gone—and gazed down at the artillery he'd brought. If she had ever needed confirmation that Morgan was something beyond a codebreaker, she had it now. There was a duffel bag beside the rocket launcher, zipped open to reveal the barrel of an Uzi. She glanced farther down the road to see what appeared to be a black panel van.

"Disarm yourself," she told him, "and give every single weapon you're carrying to your sister."

"I'm on your side," he gritted. "I heard Katie vouch

for me herself on the phone. I'm sure she'll vouch for me now."

"Don't be so sure," Katie shot back. "Morgan, what the hell are you up to?"

"I'm here to help."

"Prove it," Allison said. "Give Katie your weapons."

He looked supremely frustrated. "I won't be able to help you if I do that." He gazed down at her nightgown. "And if I may make a suggestion, a few layers of protection beats racing into battle half-naked."

"Don't screw with me, Morgan. This is not your op and I am not your subordinate," Allison snapped.

"Me, neither," Katie said coldly. "You are so damaged, Morgan. We're in the middle of a firefight and all you give a damn about is...*boobs*."

"Right. Knowing she would drive here in her nightgown, I risked my life for a free peek," he replied.

Allison left them to it, loping toward the fiery structure. Sharp rocks and, possibly, bits of shrapnel sliced into the soles of her feet. She didn't care. She would have walked across molten glass to get to her people.

Nikki came from around the building, saw Allison and headed for her. Her wavy black hair cupped her dirt-smudged face and her dark eyes flashed with fury.

"Thank God you're all right," Allison said. "What about the others?"

"We're banged up, but we're basically okay." Nikki scowled. "God, I'm sorry, Allison. They came right in and took him. Bombed the tunnel and broke it open like a *piñata*." She slung her Uzi around her neck and raked her hair away from her face. "Approximately a dozen helmeted soldiers in full body armor. Three were shorter, I'm thinking maybe young girls." She gazed meaningfully at Allison.

"Maybe egg babies," Allison said. "Maybe they brought along girls with enhanced abilities they could use. Someone who can see through barriers, someone who can create explosives?"

"Sounds right," Nikki said, shaking her head. "Egg babies, being used against us. If Echo is collecting them and feeding them false information to pit them against us, we could be in big trouble. Thanks for the assist," she added.

"I didn't do anything except show up in my night-gown," Allison said unhappily.

Nikki jerked. "Oh, my God, is that Katie Rush's brother?"

Allison nodded. "Until I give the word, he's to be treated as a hostile."

"Roger that." It was clear that Nikki had questions, and equally clear that she wasn't going to ask them. "What's our next move?"

"Figuring out our next move," Allison riposted. "Someone should stay behind to lock this place down, then meet us back at Athena Academy. We'll need a driver for my truck and Katie can drive Morgan's van. I'll ride along and guard him." She was sorry to turn the school into their home base for now, but it made the most sense, and it would have to be done.

"Will do," Nikki said smartly. Then she turned and dashed back toward the burning building.

Now that the spigot on Allison's adrenaline had been turned off, the cuts in her feet competed with her bruised ribs for most painful injury. As she brushed her hair away from her face, she touched her nose, and a jolt of fresh pain rocketed through her. She could hardly breathe. She was a mess. She needed some downtime.

Katie had forced Morgan to put his hands on top of his head as Allison slowly and painfully approached them. Allison, the tall brunette ops commando, had an Uzi—probably his—slung over her neck and she was holding it at an awkward angle, as if she were trying to keep it from banging against her body. Her face was screwed tight as she picked her way across the landscape in her bare feet. When she ticked up her glance and saw Katie and him, her face relaxed into a dull, expressionless mask that reminded him of the Sphinx. Morgan understood; she was in some serious pain, and didn't want to betray weakness in the presence of a supposed enemy.

"I can't believe you," Katie growled at her brother. "What are you doing here? And don't tell me you came to help or I'll haul you off and shoot you."

He grunted. "Why don't I save it for one debriefing. I'm guessing you're Allison's subordinate, even if you aren't mine."

"That would be a good guess," she said frostily.

"So I may as well wait to tell you both everything at the same time. Meanwhile…what are you running? Is Athena Academy just a front?"

"Yup. I went there for four years and graduated with honors so they could pretend it was a real high school," Katie said, rolling her eyes. "Jeez, Morgan, did you take an extra dose of conspiracy theory with your vitamins this morning?"

"Don't be so touchy," he needled her.

"Don't be so patronizing."

Allison reached them. She was pressing her hand against her side, bunching the diaphanous fabric over her breasts, which were small and very firm, the nipples taut. The small triangle of darkness at her bikini line made him stir, despite his situation. Maybe Katie was right and his sexual drive was somehow unnatural.

Naw.

"Stop staring," Katie hissed at him.

"Can't," he said unapologetically.

Katie rolled her eyes. "You're disgusting."

"I'm a man, Katie."

"A very sick, wrong man." She raised her voice. "Hey, Allison, we have three vehicles plus your truck plus my brother's van. I can drive you back to…where your clothes are."

"My clothes are in a duffel in the truck," Allison replied. She turned her attention to Morgan. "We'll be riding in your van. But you won't be driving it."

He nodded. "Can I put my hands down?"

"Sure. After your sister cuffs you." Allison held out a pair of plastic cuffs that she'd no doubt also lifted from his duffel bag.

"Allison, this is…" He exhaled. He'd like to say it was crazy, but he completely understood her caution. "Okay," he said. "Want my hands behind or in front?"

"In front, where I can see them," Allison said.

"Put 'em down," Katie ordered him. As Morgan complied, Allison raised the Uzi and pointed it at him. He wondered if she would really use it on him. As Katie circled around and put the cuffs on, he gazed steadily at Allison. Despite the circumstances, he was very glad to see her.

"Heard anything from the office?" he asked her.

She moved to the left, keeping Katie out of her immediate kill range, and him in. "Have you?"

"Just from Valenti. I figure you've heard the same."

That it's bad. That we don't know where they're going to strike or when. That we don't know who, why.

Katie threaded the strips of plastic around his wrists and pulled tight. The plastic cut into his skin but he didn't complain. Big brother, little sister; complaining was probably what she wanted him to do, so he wouldn't.

"He's good and hog-tied," Katie said, then glared up through her lashes at Morgan as if to warn him against saying a word.

Allison stood down, easing the Uzi back around her neck. Without a word, she walked past him with a soldier's strut, acting as if it didn't bother her in the least that he could practically see her naked. Maybe it didn't. He liked that. It was sexy.

About ten minutes later, Allison returned to the van dressed in a black mesh long-sleeved top with multiple pockets, olive-green cammy pants and flipflops. She was braless because it hurt too much to put a bra on. The desert air was cold, not chilly, and she knew the outline of her nipples was visible. She didn't have time to care. She had given in to vanity and pulled her hair up and away with a ponytail holder, but that was it.

Allison had just hung up from talking to her brother, David, who had many choice words for her regarding her safety, and was willing to hear very few about why she had taken off with no warning in the middle of the night.

She put the phone in the pocket of her pants, so it would be accessible, and nodded at Katie, whom she had chosen to drive the van. If it was booby-trapped, she figured Morgan might be slightly less likely to allow his own sister to be blown up.

"Okay, let's go," she said, climbing into the back. Morgan was propped up against the panel behind the driver's seat, and Allison waited for Chesca to pull the door shut, then sat with her back to it. She kept the Uzi around her neck and showed Morgan her big, fat revolver.

"A .357 Mangle'em," he said. "Deep penetration."

"I'm beginning to think your sister's right about you."

"I chatter when I get nervous."

"The key-lock safety is on," she promised. "I figured if I accidentally shot you, I would never find out why you're dogging me."

Katie started the van and rolled away. Morgan closed his eyes wearily. Allison—an Allison he never knew before, kung-fu-fightin' hand-grenade-launchin' Allison— was safe. Katie was safe. If Allison did shoot him, he could die satisfied, if not exactly happy.

God, he was tired, down past his flesh and into his soul. And yet, if he let his mind wander back to the images of Allison silhouetted against the firefight, he woke right up.

Allison's cell phone trilled. Morgan opened his eyes to see her large, dark brown eyes widen as she took the call. She listened in silence, and then she went white, disconnected and put the phone away. She didn't say a word, but he knew she had just received some devastating news. He wondered if it had anything to do with the mission.

Which mission? he wondered. *What's she doing?*

"You got some e-mail while I was in your town house," he said, hoping to rattle her a little and shake loose what the call had been about. "I downloaded it."

For a moment he thought she hadn't heard him. Then she bobbed her head once. She looked tired, and hurt, and scared. And he had no doubt that if he tried to reach out and comfort her, she'd clock him over the head with her weapon.

So he sat facing her and didn't say another word.

"Hurry," she said loudly to Katie.

Chapter 12

Echo's island in Micronesia

"Target acquired," Schroeder informed Echo, his voice a soft purr in her beautiful diamond earring.

"Show me," Echo said, moving to the view screen in her bathroom. This time there was no one in her bed except her adored Persian cat, Ming, speaking of merciless. Echo stood naked, her toes digging into the soft circular rug on the marble floor and cocked her head expectantly, anticipating a much more luxurious visual than men with Uzis crammed into a van. What she expected was more along the lines of a glossy ad for a travel magazine: Champagne, caviar and a sexy flight attendant bending over from the waist.

Yes, there it all was, in the interior of one of her private jets. And there *he* was. Eric Pace's smiling, jowled face appeared on screen as Schroeder looped an earpiece behind Pace's left ear. The disgraced military man looked older than the photos in her dossier, which included his mug shots upon his arrest. He had certainly gotten fatter since his incarceration. She understood that American prison food was high in carbs and low in nutrition. *You are hereby sentenced to twenty years of macaroni and cheese.*

"Greetings, General Pace," Echo said.

"Madame Echo, I presume?" he said, touching the earpiece and smiling into the camera Schroeder or one of his lackeys was holding. Pace couldn't see her. The visual was not two-way.

She liked her privacy.

"Yes, General Pace. I understand your rescue went remarkably well."

He took a sip of champagne. "Well, there were a couple of hitches in the operation, but your people are good at what they do."

Hitches? Schroeder had mentioned nothing like that.

"As are yours." She understood that many tens of thousands of dollars had traded hands within the last week—guards paid to look the other way. Still, it always surprised her that people could throw away their lives so cheaply.

"How many girls have you been able to acquire?" he asked her.

"Thirteen." She couldn't keep the pride out of her voice. "The firestarter is my absolute favorite. I'm going to legally adopt her." Of course she would do no such thing, but it sounded good.

He chuckled. "I'm looking forward to meeting them all. How's the lab?"

"If you thought Lab 33 was a cutting-edge bastion of high technology and superhard science, you'll find *my* lab shatteringly brilliant," she crowed. "Everything is so shiny and new. I can't wait to see Jeremy Loschetter's reaction."

The general raised a saggy eyebrow. He was disgustingly flabby. She'd like to carve the rolls of fat right off him. "Oh? So you've already broken him out?"

"An hour ago. I'm just full of happy surprises today. He's on his way, just like you."

"That is outstanding," he said, beaming at her. "We can get right to work."

"Yes. But for now, relax and make yourself comfortable. You've had quite an ordeal. We'll see each other soon."

The camera went off. After a full minute, Schroeder's voice returned to her earring. "I'm piloting," he said. "We had heavy casualties. Apparently not all the guards Pace thought he had bought came through."

"I hope some of *them* died, then," she said, feigning a moment of respectful silence for her cannon fodder. It would be bad for morale if her men knew that all she cared about was the cost of replacing them. When one was involved with world domination—correction, world *control*—one figured in the replacement cost of operatives. She would have to have her accountants run some numbers and see if she was on track this year.

"Yes, indeed," Schroeder said offhandedly. "We gave ugly deaths where and when we could. ETA in twenty hours tops."

"Good." She smiled. Schroeder would pay for not filling her in immediately about the "hitches." She wasn't sure she should kill him but maybe she could give him a good healthy dose of food poisoning.

Since she was already up, she walked back into her room, buzzed a houseboy to start her bath and began the process of selecting an outfit for her morning meeting with Natalia LeClaire. Eventually she decided on a soft white silk blouse, a pair of raw silk capris and sandals—elegant but casual, decidedly not dragon lady. She would leave that to her dead half sister, Kwan-Sook.

She went into the Spider Room to show her mother.

In the forty-eight hours since her arrival, Natalia hadn't eaten a thing, which meant that she hadn't ingested the dosage of anxiety-reducing Xanax Echo's physician had prescribed for her. Since it wasn't water soluble, Echo couldn't fool her into taking it with her bottled water, which was the only food or drink she'd had since she'd arrived.

So maybe it was time for some talk therapy.

She nodded to the guards in the hall, both of whom looked amazed that she was walking into Natalia's cell supposedly unarmed. She didn't advertise her special gifts to her employees. With a swipe of her palm and a retinal scan, the lock clicked on the meter-thick door and she pushed the door open.

"Hello, Nat," she said, having read from the FBI FD-302 that her parents always referred to her as Natalia. They had been described as cold and detached, distinctly lacking in interest regarding their daughter's abduction. They should have had the good sense to at least fake some interest….

Natalia had pushed herself up against the back corner of the cell, rather like an octopus denied a place to withdraw in an aquarium. Her head was on her knees and she was wearing the dark blue pajama bottoms, tank top and sandals Echo had set inside her door on her last visit. The dear thing kept burning up her clothes.

"Do you feel better today?" she asked Natalia, which was a question designed to throw her off. Echo had visited her only three hours ago.

"How—how long have I been here?" Natalia asked. Echo felt a bit of triumph.

"It's been a while," Echo said, crossing her ankles and lowering herself gracefully to the floor.

"Are my parents—do they know…" Natalia trailed off, almost as if she didn't want to know.

"Nat." Echo pushed out her creamy, sun bronzed lower lip. "Hasn't anyone told you? I asked someone to break it to you gently." She took a deep breath. "We're an organization dedicated to the location and rescue of young people such as yourself. We've been looking for you for a long time."

Echo wrinkled her forehead and caught her bottom lip between perfect white teeth. "We wouldn't have intruded on your life in a thousand years if you'd been happy. Safe." She let the words sink in.

Natalia laughed bitterly. "Right. And I'm so much happier in *this* cell. At least at home, I had my stuff."

"You wouldn't have for long, my dear pet," Echo said. "We were monitoring your parents' e-mails. I don't know how to tell you this, but…your parents…" She looked down at her hands. "Well…"

"What? What happened to my parents?" Natalia demanded, her delicately shaped eyebrows shooting toward the ceiling. Echo could actually feel Natalia's increased body heat wafting toward her.

My, Red Riding Hood, what warm vibrations you give off.

"Nothing happened to them, darling. They're fine. Just fine."

"Then what are you talking about?"

Echo feigned great sorrow. "Well, as I say, we were monitoring their e-mails, and they'd been in contact with a number of…scientific organizations, shall we say. They had come to the conclusion that they could no longer care for you properly, and they were trying to figure out the most suitable…arrangements for you. They were very careful to limit the nature of the experiments that would be conducted on you—they didn't want you harmed—"

"What?" Natalia cried.

Echo went on. "You see, dear, quite frankly, your parents had a number of crushing debts after your father's 'accident' when the house caught on fire eleven years ago. I imagine that was before they put you in the cell."

Natalia's face glowed crimson. Her eyes darted left, right. She began to breathe hard. "You mean my parents were going to *sell* me?"

"No, no, darling," Echo said with a sincerity calculated to sound very false. "They knew they couldn't provide a decent environment for you. Constantly drugged, buried in a basement cell while other girls your age went to school, had dates…" She shook her head. "They were growing desperate."

"And so *you* bought me from them?" Smoke rose like a tendril of hair from the top of her head. Echo was dying to know why her hair didn't burn away when she turned into a human torch. She supposed it was the same reason Lilith didn't poison herself when she sucked on her thumb as a baby.

"No, as I said, we rescued you. We've rescued over a dozen special girls. We want to keep you free from government studies. If we can find a cure, that would be nice, but that's not our aim here. We simply want you to be able to be yourself for the first time in your life. No one has ever made *you* safe, have they?"

Natalia turned her face to the wall. She had such a beautiful profile. A tear slid down her cheek and Echo fought off a smile. Tears were usually a way in.

The tear sizzled and became a wisp of steam.

"I killed a man when you came for me," Natalia said. "I—I got scared."

"His death was a tragedy, but no one blames you, dear. As members of 'Arachne,' we're prepared to make sacrifices," Echo assured. "We're on a mission to keep all of you safe."

More smoke rose off the girl's skin as she gazed back at Echo. "My parents were going to sell me for medical experiments, and you…you…" She burst into tears. They evaporated on her cheeks.

"They were frightened, desperate. Did you know your mother was pregnant?"

Natalia made choked, terrified noises in the back of her throat as she scrabbled backward, as if Echo were some kind of actual monster that was physically threatening her. Teenage girls were so emotional. "Get away from me!" She threw back her head and screamed. "Oh, no. No! Get out of here! It's going to happen!"

"Go ahead, Natalia. Burn," Echo urged her, holding

her hands below her chin and unfurling her fingers. "You won't be able to hurt me."

"No! I kill people!" Natalia leaped away from her, slamming into the cell wall. "I—I killed that man." She sobbed hysterically. "I saw his face. He was…it *melted* and his skin peeled back. He was screaming. And his *eyes*…oh God, God! Get out of here!"

And then Natalia exploded into flame. Fire spouted from her like pinwheels and comets; it was spectacular. Any other person would have been incinerated in a matter of seconds—like Jones or Jackson, whatever his name was.

But not Echo. For at the precise instant that Natalia's biologically heightened survival sense triggered her gift, Echo's was activated as well. In her case, a pulse of energy created a protective field around her, effectively deflecting anything thrown at her, from bullets to firebombs to flames. It was a sci-fi geek's dream come true—danger told her body, "Shields up!" and she was, to all extents and purposes, invincible. The tongues of fire lapped at her, then bent back at sharp angles toward Natalia herself.

Natalia, however, wasn't seeing that. She was flailing in the center of a firestorm, shrieking unintelligibly, in an agony that she was immolating another human being. Echo let her carry on for at least a minute; then she cupped her hands around her mouth.

"Nat!" she bellowed. "Nat, dear, I'm fine!"

Natalia blazed away, wild and out of control. Then abruptly, as if someone had thrown a switch, she fell to her knees, gasping and naked, and the fire immediately vanished. She didn't have a mark on her. And neither did Echo.

"Nat," Echo said. "Look at me."

Natalia's head jerked up. Her mouth dropped open and she stayed that way for at least ten seconds, frozen in disbelief.

Echo opened her arms. "You see, darling? You can't hurt me."

Natalia stared at her. Slowly she got to her feet, swaying, her mouth working but no sound coming out. Echo twirled in a circle, much as she had done when she'd shown off her party dress to the twins.

"I'm completely fine," she said. She took a step toward Natalia. "I'm the one person in the world you can never hurt."

"Oh." Natalia's reaction was almost comical. Echo had never seen anyone quite so unnerved—except her sister Lilith, perhaps, when she, Echo, had shown up in India to take her spider necklace.

The necklace that her sister and Allison Gracelyn's stupid little spygirl had stolen from her at the airport.

I should like to see Natalia reduce both of them to cinders one day. Soon.

"Oh!" Natalia cried again, staggering toward Echo. "You're all right. You're…you're…can I…?"

With a sob, she sank into Echo's embrace. Echo didn't flinch, but the truth was, she hated being touched, unless it was during sex. Her skin was crawling even now, as she wrapped her arms around the overwhelmed girl and rocked her gently.

"We can be friends, real friends," she told Natalia, feeding the girl, who was clearly starved for affection. "You'll never have to worry about losing your temper, or being upset, because you can't hurt me. For the first

time in your life, you can think about yourself."
Actually she doubted Natalia had ever stopped thinking
about herself—monitoring herself and suppressing her
emotions so that she wouldn't start a fire.

The girl sobbed quietly against Echo's chest and
Echo held her, even though, frankly, she would rather
have held a boa constrictor.

"There, there, dear Nat," she said. "It's going to be
all right now, don't you see?"

Natalia whispered something. Echo bent her head
close to her ear.

"Thank you," the girl said brokenly. "Oh, thank you."

"You are very welcome. We at Arachne will do all
we can to make your life splendid from now on." She
hesitated, then stroked Natalia's hair. "But I must warn
you, darling, that because we deprive the scientists of
fine specimens like you, we are deeply hated. And they
might try to come after you. We might be attacked."

She sighed. "We recently freed a little girl named
Cailey. She's only five, and she doesn't understand that
we have saved her from a life of misery. She misses her
parents…the ones who never kept her safe…"

"I'll help you protect her," Natalia promised fiercely.
She pulled back and gazed into Echo's eyes. "I'll—I'll
hurt anyone who tries to hurt you, or anyone in Arachne."

"Well, we certainly hope it doesn't come to that," Echo
soothed. "We have some men coming to help us. A scientist of our own, and an Army general who could no longer
stand by and watch girls like you kidnapped and studied
like lab rats." Her nose wrinkled. "Someday we'll be free."

"We…?" Natalia repeated slowly. Then her dark
eyes got big as saucers. "Oh, my God, you're one of us."

"Indeed, love, I am," Echo said nobly. "And there are people who have been after me for years. They hounded my mother, tormented her…" She swallowed her crocodile tears. "And now she is dead."

Natalia inhaled sharply and covered her mouth with her right hand. Echo smiled in sad resignation. "So you can see why I have made it my life's mission to find those like me and offer them sanctuary."

"From now on, it's mine, too," Natalia swore.

"Oh, you're so wonderful," Echo stroked her. "But, Nat, you're too young. You need to enjoy life. Leave these terrible matters to me."

Natalia shook her head. "I'll be part of Arachne until the day I die. I swear it."

Echo chewed her lip, appraising Natalia, narrowing her eyes as if she needed to come to some sort of decision. "I've never told any of the others this," she said. Then she shook her head. "Never mind."

"What?" Natalia pressed. "You can tell me."

Echo made a face. "You probably wouldn't understand. All this is so new to you…."

Natalia lifted her chin and waited.

"Well, sometimes, if we get word where *they* are, we…we attack them first, before they can attack us," Echo confessed. "Sometimes, we…we kill them." Her voice dropped to a low, tense whisper. "Before they can kill any more of us." She looked off into the distance, as if seeing images from the past too terrible to imagine.

"The ones we failed to protect…I'm haunted by them, Nat. Tied down in labs, screaming…one little girl, cut open from sternum to pelvis…"

Natalia looked positively green. Then she licked her

lips and straightened her shoulders. "I'd be proud to fight against them."

"Maybe someday, darling. But for now…have you ever had mango ice cream? It's so delicious. I fancy a dish. How about you?"

"I haven't eaten since I got here," Natalia said. "I guess you know that."

"I do, and I was getting a little worried, but I certainly didn't want to add to your distress. I'll go and dish some up myself."

She turned to go. Natalia took a step toward her. Though she was facing away from the girl, Echo could sense the vibrations of her approach.

"My parents," she said again.

Oh, for the love of God, drop it! Echo wanted to scream at her. Instead she turned around slowly.

"How could this happen to me, if my parents are so normal?" She looked confused, and agonized, and far less certain about what was going on than she had been even ten seconds before. Echo understood that; it had to do with redefining one's entire reality.

"Well, here it is," Echo said diffidently, as if the last thing on her mind was hurting this poor, sweet, innocent girl any further. "I assume you know about the facts of life."

Natalia nodded impatiently.

"That will make this simpler, then," Echo said. "A long time ago, some very wicked people surgically harvested eggs from women—some who knew that it was being done, and others, who had no idea—mixed them with sperm in the lab—that's called *in vitro fertilization*—and created embryos."

"Did they do that to my mother?" Natalia interrupted.

"Next, they…did things…to these embryos, and either transferred them into the uteruses of the women whose eggs they took, or into different women altogether. Sometimes without the birth mother's knowledge, although in some cases, the women were paid to carry the baby to term. Such women are called 'gestational surrogates.'"

Natalia's mouth worked. Echo could have kicked herself. She was telling her way too much way too soon.

"My mother…?" she asked, agonized. "Whose sperm? Was it my father?"

"We could perform tests to determine that," Echo said smoothly, "if we had DNA samples from all three of you. However—"

"Oh, my God! They're not even my real parents?" Natalia wailed, horror-stricken. "They caged me like a freak! They told me if I didn't behave they'd get rid of me!" She covered her mouth with both her hands. "That man I burned…"

"He wasn't the first, was he," Echo guessed. "There were a few…accidents, weren't there? And they told you how dangerous you were. That they had to make your life a nightmare for your own good."

"Yes, yes, yes!" Natalia shrieked, bursting into flames again. And right on time, Echo's defense system protected her, forming a shield that deflected Natalia's fiery outburst back at her.

This could get tedious, she thought.

By the time Katie drove Morgan's van over to Athena Academy, Christine had been alerted to incoming, wounded and otherwise, and alerted the infirmary. Allison was seriously considering diverting the entire company to her family hideaway, except that her group needed a chance to regain composure after the battle... and she needed to check in with Oracle West as soon as possible. Lynnette had called with very bad news while Allison was sitting across from Morgan in the van.

At the exact same time that Jeremy Loschetter had been grabbed, a second flank broke Eric Pace out of a private military prison near Bethesda. The attackers had superior firepower, and a significant number of the guard had laid down their weapons and joined the opposing side—obviously they'd been bought, and the operation had been planned for a long time. The general in charge of the brig had been put on administrative leave, his career essentially over.

It had to be Echo, she thought. *I should have seen that one coming, made the obvious connection....*

"We'll get out of here as soon as possible," Allison assured Christine, as she oversaw a few stitches in Chesca Thorne's arm. The infirmary smelled of alcohol swabs, sweat and blood. It was a miracle that they had sustained no serious injuries, much less fatalities.

Lucy joined them. She had stayed behind to watch over the students, assisted by Kayla and additional police officers.

The three women observed Dr. Singh in action. "Does this have to do with the egg baby abductions?" Christine asked.

Allison nodded. "Very much so. A group of us had possession of Jeremy Loschetter, Christine." Christine paled. "We lost him. I think the person who took him is the same person stealing egg babies."

"'Possession of Loschetter,'" Christine echoed. "It was off the books?"

"Way off," Allison concurred. "I'm sorry. I didn't want any of this to happen anywhere near Athena Academy."

"I don't see how it can be helped." Christine looked at Allison full-on, her blind left eye not tracking, her right one red with tiredness. "I'm trying to decide if having you stay here would serve as a deterrent against potential kidnappers, or an attractive nuisance."

"I have the same dilemma," Allison said.

"As I do," Lucy added. She raised her chin a notch. "My detail is Athena Academy. I'm not thinking past that."

"Understood," Allison said.

Kayla Ryan approached with Jazz in tow. Allison was startled to see what a mature young woman Jazz had become.

"I could talk to the tribal elders about having you stay on the res," Kayla ventured.

"No, Kayla, but thanks," Allison said. Kayla didn't know the full extent of what was going on, and Allison wanted to keep her out of it. She wasn't Oracle and she had enough to deal with as it was, maintaining the security of Athena Academy and the outlying town as well.

Katie and her brother appeared at the opposite end of the hall. A blanket had been slung over Morgan's shoulders, concealing his handcuffs.

"Morgan?" Christine asked, startled. She looked from the Rush siblings to Allison and back again.

"Christine, I need a couple days to pull some things together, and then I'm getting my people out of here," Allison finally decided. If Morgan pulled any crap—called in friends, say—she definitely didn't want it happening here. "Three or four of us will stay behind to guard the school," she added. "I'll make myself useful and then I'll probably move off, too. Lucy will stay as head of security. If that meets with your approval." She took a breath. "Nothing in me wants to bring the battle to you, but I want to ensure the safety of Athena Academy as well."

"Thank you, Allison," Christine said. "I trust your judgment."

"Same here," Kayla added.

"We'll wipe the floor with anybody who messes with us, right, Jazz?" Lucy asked. She smiled at Jazz. Jazz smiled back, a little tentatively, but it was there.

It was settled, then.

"Let's debrief your brother," Allison said to Katie. To Lucy, "I'll give you any pertinent data later."

"Got your back, always," Lucy replied.

Together, Allison and Katie escorted Morgan to her bungalow, rapping once to give Lynnette warning, if she was still deep into the works of Oracle West.

"A moment, please," Lynnette called out. "Okay."

Allison opened the door and led the way in. Upon seeing Morgan in custody, Lynnette's green-gold eyes flickered with interest. Lynnette was NSA like Morgan and Allison, but she wasn't on Ozone. She had probably seen Morgan around, without parsing that she would ever see him out of the office.

"Do we need to speak in private first?" Allison asked her.

"No." Lynnette scooted back from the desk. "I'll check in with you later."

"Thanks," Allison said.

Lynnette walked past Morgan, eyeing him with frank curiosity, and left the room.

He sat down with the fluid grace of a martial artist, gazing around the room until his eyes rested on her once again.

"No pictures in here of Gordita," he ventured.

"Stop trying to bait her," Katie said angrily. "You have no idea who you're messing with."

"Oh, I do. I know exactly who I'm messing with." He looked hard at Allison. "The right hand of Delphi."

The room went dead silent.

"Katie, can you go get us something to eat?" Allison asked steadily.

Katie looked from her brother to Allison and back again. Then she strode out of the room and shut the door hard.

"What do you know about Delphi?" Allison asked him.

"Nothing, really. By the way, my cell phone went off about ten seconds ago," he added. "It might be important."

"I'm not uncuffing you yet." She perched painfully on the edge of her desk, invading his personal space. It was an old interrogator's trick, one he surely knew.

"You have a lot of knives in your duffel bag," she said. "Very exotic, strangely shaped—"

"Pentjak Silat," he said. "We use blades. I just got a second call."

"Stand up," she told him.

He did so, understanding dawning across his features. "Front right pocket," he informed her.

"Don't try anything. You know I'm injured but you should also know that sending Katie for food was our code to surround this bungalow. Lucy's probably got a laser trained between your eyes by now."

Then she slipped her hand into his pocket. The turgid heat of his sex gave her pause. He was turned on. She wondered if he knew that she was, too. Despite her anxiety—or maybe because of it. Maybe this was some kind of instinctual survival mechanism—*mate and reproduce before you die.*

She studied the veins in his powerful hands bound in front of his bulging jeans and imagined what it must be like to go to bed with a fellow warrior. She hadn't had sex in…was it years?

"Could it be McDonough? Are you still working for him?" she asked him, as her fingers found the warm metal of his cell. It was still vibrating.

"Not since your house blew up." He pulled a sad face. "A real shame, Allison. You had some nice things. Big vase."

"One of my parents' wedding presents." She snaked the phone out of his pocket.

"Damn," he said softly. "Well, it saved my life."

Then it served its purpose, she thought and she was surprised at her rush of passion. In her mind's eye, she saw the body bag wheeled out of her house again.

"Please, uncuff me," he said. "Allison, I won't jump you."

Setting down his phone, she crossed back to his duffel bag and showed him one of his exotic razor-sharp knives. He nodded. She returned to face him, placing her hand over his to steady herself. She smelled sweat and coffee; she felt his heat. She was trembling from head to toe.

He stared into her eyes. He didn't say a word.

She cut him free. He didn't move. Neither did she. The hairs on his arms brushed her knuckles as he rubbed his wrists to work up his circulation.

She handed him the phone. He keyed into his voice mail and listened. She didn't move away. She didn't respect his privacy.

He looked ashen as he closed the phone and put it away.

"That was Davidson." He was Morgan's junior staffer on the Ozone team. "Circle of Justice just got orders to proceed to Step Two," he said. A beat. "We have no idea what Step Two is."

He looked so worried and thwarted that there and then she made her decision to bring him on board. Maybe she should have checked in with someone…but there really was no one to check in with. There was no board of directors or advisors. Allison was the beginning and the end of the discussion.

"Oracle," she began. She moved away from him. She didn't want her sexual interest in him to affect how she was going to do this. "It's better than Echelon. It gathers intel from any agency you can name and it gives it to us."

He raised a brow and whistled. "Who created it?"

"Delphi." She kept the pride out of her voice.

"And you work for Delphi."

"Yes," she said without hesitating.

"Do you trust him? Delphi?"

"Yes." She turned around and looked hard at him. "With my life. With the lives of Oracle's operatives."

"Are they all Athena alums?"

"I don't think you need to know that, but if you're asking about Katie, the answer is yes, she's one of us."

"I knew it. That little brat." He smiled ruefully and shook his head. There were crease lines around his deep blue eyes, which were heavily lidded, very bedroom, very...distracting.

"What about your life?" she asked him.

His smile faded and he looked very serious. Dangerous.

Feral.

"I'm in real deep, and it's a lot of stuff no one wants to hear about, not even the people who send me out. It's DOD—Department of Defense—and a lot of it is wet, and dirty."

"I never guessed," she admitted.

"You've had a lot going on. Does Delphi know you're working on Ozone?"

"Yes," she said. "I didn't breach confidentiality, if that's what you're asking. I didn't have to."

His full, sensuous lips parted. "Holy shit, are you telling me Valenti is Delphi?"

"No, I'm not." They were still playing cat and mouse. Maybe it was reflexive. Maybe they'd never be able to stop.

He cocked his head. "Did you know she told me you were pregnant?"

Flushing a little, Allison closed her eyes and shook her head. "We worked it out together. We figured with all that testosterone floating around, you guys wouldn't be sure. She said you didn't take it well."

"I asked a friend to run a pregnancy test on the

A-neg I swiped up in that alley." He licked his lips. "Do you have any water?"

"Would you prefer a beer?" She crossed to the postage-stamp-size kitchen and opened the fridge. She grabbed two bottles of Dos Equis, two shot glasses and a nearly full bottle of tequila. She opened both of them while Morgan poured two shots of tequila and slid one over toward her.

She picked up her shot and her beer and held it up in a salute. They both threw back their shots and chased them with the Mexican beer. She let the liquor blaze down her throat and settle out her jangled nervous system.

"The call I got in your van was about Eric Pace. He just got busted out of prison," she said. "He's—"

"I know who he is," he said, looking shaken. "Who did it? And why?"

"We think it's the same person who snatched Loschetter."

"Spider files," he ventured.

"Spider files. Egg babies."

Then she remembered the downloads he had mentioned.

"Do you have that e-mail off my home system?"

With her nonverbal permission, he walked over to his duffel bag and fished out the drive. He handed it to her; she sat down at her desktop and plugged it in.

"It's spoofed six ways to Sunday. I assume it came from Delphi?" Morgan asked.

"Don't know yet," she said, although the answer was no.

She clicked it open.

"I'm running virus checks on it," she informed Morgan, taking a sip of beer.

As the programs ran, Morgan rose and walked around the small room, light on the balls of his feet. His body was hard, his shoulders and pecs well-defined beneath the filthy dark gray sweater he wore, angling to a pair of narrow hips. His jeans hung on the sharp indentations of his pelvis, revealing a swirl of hair around his navel; Morgan was so meticulous about his appearance at work that she figured he must be wearing someone's castoffs after having escaped the explosion.

"Whose van is that?" she asked suddenly.

"Team member," he said. "He's been flipped." If Zorba had still been on Morgan's side, he would have called him by now. He was glad Zorba wasn't going to try to bullshit him, pretend to be concerned about where Morgan was and why he had taken the van. He knew Morgan had his number. They were enemies now.

"That's hard to take," Allison said.

He looked over at her, the stubble on his cheeks accentuating the hollows there. He cleaned up nice but she preferred him this way, more feral, ready to bring the jungle to the battle. He was prowling; he couldn't seem to stay still. Edgy, like she was, and probably just as worn-out.

And yet, aroused.

She glanced over at the graph on the screen, indicating that the virus check was thirty-five percent complete. It moved to fifty percent. She became aware that Morgan had stopped moving. She turned her head to see him with his beer to his mouth, studying her over the lip of the bottle.

He caught her gaze and didn't look away. His long eyelashes fringed his deep blue eyes. Not for the first time in her life, Allison wished she was just a regular woman. She didn't even know what that meant. She didn't know very many regular women—the secretaries at work, maybe, who hated her for the most part, because she wasn't like them. Not that she pitied herself. It was what it was. But it would be nice to not have such broad shoulders, relatively speaking.

"So this guy who flipped," she said. "Do you know why?"

"Unsure. You know how it goes, in our line of work. We put a lot of drug lords out of business. There's this Russian guy, Monya Kishinev. We totally fucked up his operation last year."

She felt a chill. "We captured phony traffic from someone posing as me in a scheme to squeeze Monya Kishinev."

"Small world." He smiled thinly.

She turned back around to the screen. Eighty-seven percent completed. She was anxious about having him in the room; he was so smart, and his job was putting two and two together. He would probably figure out that she was Delphi. She wasn't sure why she was letting him stay.

The virus check was done. She doubled-clicked on the memory stick icon. It opened.

An e-mail icon appeared. She felt Morgan's body heat along her back, his warm breath against her neck as he gestured to the screen.

"Does Christine Evans know you've got a system like this at her school?"

She put her hands on the keyboard and pointedly waited, until he sighed against her earlobe and moved away.

She opened it.

It was a photograph. Backlit against a shimmering web, two spider necklaces, each slightly different, gleamed and sparkled. Allison touched the chain around her neck. The pendant that hung between her breasts was clearly the third of a trio. She had put it back on in the field, when she'd gotten dressed. It was concealed by her black mesh top. Her skin itched as if the necklace had been dipped in acid.

"Spider necklaces?" he asked.

She answered his question with another question. "Who are you really working for?" She looked away from the screen to him.

Morgan ran his cold beer bottle across his forehead and down the side of his face. It was chilly in the room; maybe he was fighting his fatigue.

"Who, Morgan?" she demanded.

"Delphi," he replied. "I'm working for Delphi."

She took a steadying breath. "Does Delphi know it?"

His gaze bored into her, deep and penetrating, willing her to believe him, know him, accept his help. Her body quivered.

He didn't blink or look away, didn't release her from his gaze.

"She does now," he said in a sandpapery whisper.

Chapter 13

He knows. Morgan Rush knows I'm Delphi.

"I'm right, aren't I?" he asked her.

"I need to take a shower." Allison turned away from him and concentrated on shutting down the desktop. Her stomach knotted; sweat beaded on her forehead. She tried to keep her hands from shaking, but she could barely type in the commands to quit.

"Who else knows? My sister?"

She rose, saying nothing, still not looking at him. He would read it on her face. All these years, no one had pried that secret from her. He was an outsider. He was not Oracle.

But he's Morgan.

"Don't push me," she said.

He raised his hands over his head in an I'm-your-prisoner stance. "Does this have something to do with the research you're doing on force fields?"

She blinked and her lips parted in complete and total shock. Then she remembered the printout in her dresser in her destroyed town house—the town house he had been searching when it had blown up.

Facing him, she stayed outwardly calm, but her mind was racing. This was why she hadn't had a lover or anyone else close to her. He had waltzed through layers of security as if they weren't even there.

"I can help you. I will help you," he promised.

"This isn't your fight." She licked her lips and turned to go.

"Oh, but it is," he insisted. He took a step toward her. "Let me in."

She left the room, practically running into the bathroom and stripping down before realizing that she hadn't brought a change of clothes or even her robe; she was used to being alone, and she was distracted.

A mild term for it, she thought. *Oh God, I can't let him know. Know that I'm Delphi and that I'm...*

She felt her barriers rise up around herself.

That I'm what? Attracted to him?

She knew it was more than that. She knew it.

No way. Not love. Not Morgan. Ever.

She turned her back to the hot, steamy stream of water. Her ribs ached abominably and washing her hair was an ordeal. She did it compulsively, unsure even why she was doing it. She was shaking so hard she was afraid she might be ill. Was she having an anxiety attack?

She sank to the bottom of the tub, heaving, fighting for control.

I am the center of the storm.

He is the storm.

No. I am fine. I am calm. I can figure out what to do next.

She took deep, steadying breaths. She let the water

run over her head, imagining herself beneath a waterfall in a garden paradise. Saw herself relaxed and at ease.

Talked herself down.

Composed at last, she wrapped herself in a towel and walked back into the living room, wet hair dripping over her shoulders and down her arms.

"Okay, your turn," she said, as if their previous conversation had never happened. She looked at his filthy clothes while his stare raked her body. Ragged, dirty and bloody—he had been through the war. Now came the battle. "I'll have your things washed and try to find something for you to wear in the meantime."

"Thanks." Eyes on her, he unabashedly unpeeled his sweater, revealing his naked, muscular torso, etched with a few scars that created bare spots in the tufts of hair on his chest. He placed the sweater on the floor like a peace offering…or an invitation to seduction. Eyes on her, he was easy in his skin, undamaged despite their skirmish.

Apparently she was the one with the wounds.

He was reaching for the fly on his jeans when he disappeared into the bathroom. She heard the shower go back on.

She grabbed her robe and slipped it on, glancing around for telltale signs of electronic bugs. For all she knew, he had wired her room while she was showering. She opened the door and moved to the porch, watching sunlight tint the White Tank Mountains like pastel opals. In the distance, her Oracle agents patrolled. Safety without…none within.

She went over to her desktop, which she had shut and locked before leaving the room. At least she had had the presence of mind for that. Morgan was hacker enough that he might have been tempted to go back in, but he'd refrained. He was probably trying to prove himself. Delphi's loyal lieutenant.

Then she retrieved her laptop and connected to the Oracle mainframe, looking to see if the picture of the necklaces had kicked out. It hadn't.

She called Kim to verify the announcement of Step Two.

"We think it might have something to do with General Pace's jailbreak," Kim told her on the phone.

"Oracle West spit out an interesting visual attached to an e-mail sent to my home," Allison said. "I didn't see it when I connected to the mainframe. Which is troubling." She described the jpeg to Kim.

"I'll go over to HQ and take a look," Kim said.

"How's McDonough?"

"He left work early today."

"I'm wondering when and where he'll surface," Allison grunted.

There was a light rap on the bathroom door— Morgan, letting her know he was coming out.

I forgot to get him something to wear.

"I need to go," she said to Kim.

"Copy that, what's the status on Morgan?"

"I've read him in a little," she said, wondering afresh if that had been the right thing to do. "You have anything on him?"

She smelled steam and soap, and heard him padding barefoot across the Mexican pavers, then onto the mohair rug. She deliberately kept her back to him, not wishing to give him the slightest impression that she was ogling him.

"Nothing has kicked out," Kim said. "When he works, he's in deep."

Warmth crawled up Allison's neck and fanned over her cheeks and collarbone.

"So I've heard," she said.

Kim chuckled appreciatively. "If you read him in, you have your reasons. I'm guessing you're not alone."

"You're correct. I'll check back in," Allison promised her.

She hung up and turned to Morgan. She blinked. He was wearing a towel wrapped around his middle, revealing not only his torso but his well-defined calves and bare feet. There were tufts of hair on the knuckles of his toes. Droplets of water glistened in his hair and absurdly long eyelashes. He looked like a commercial for home exercise equipment.

She daemon-dialed Lynnette's cell phone number. "Does Pat have any extra clothes he can lend Morgan?" She looked over at him and nodded. "Yeah, I'd say large across the chest, narrow hips."

He grinned at her. She didn't react.

"There'll be something here soon," she informed him.

"Thanks," he said. "Allison, let's stop it. Let's lay out our cards."

She shook her head. "I'm too tired." *And too scared. Too much is at stake.*

They regarded one another. Allison raised her chin. "It's not happening, Morgan."

"Guess I'll be doing research on force fields, too," he replied, not smiling. "Okay, you're on point." He let out a breath. "Now, I realize it's only ten in the morning, and we just lost an important prisoner, but I'm falling down exhausted. Is there by chance a bed in the brig?"

Of course there was no brig at Athena Academy. And she didn't want him out of her sight. So she gestured to her own bed, in a smaller room just off the living room.

"Thanks," he said.

He grabbed the bedspread off her bed and the extra pillow next to the one she always used and crossed to the couch. He spread half of the coverlet across the couch cushions and fluffed up the pillow, then lay down, pulling the top half of the coverlet over himself like a sleeping bag. He squirmed a few times, and then the towel he had been wearing appeared in his grasp. He folded it and set it on the floor.

He was naked.

She tried not to let that matter while she waited for his change of clothes to show up. By the time they did, Morgan was fast asleep.

He wasn't completely asleep, but he was so exhausted he couldn't do anything to prove otherwise. He could hear her moving quietly around the room; the soft rap on her door, which she opened.

"Thank you," she told someone in a low whisper. "These will probably fit him."

Then he smelled fresh laundry close to his nose, mingling with the scent of Allison's clean skin as she bent over him. And…did she reach out a hand and almost touch him? Did she hesitate, and then move tendrils of hair away from his forehead?

Couldn't be. Allison was not the tender type. And besides, he was too close to her secrets. He knew it.

He must be asleep after all.

And dreaming.

Morgan woke refreshed and ready to take on the world—or at least Delphi. Did everyone else pretend not to know Allison was Delphi, or did they honestly believe Delphi was some anonymous tactician calling the shots?

When Allison saw that he was conscious, she gestured to a tray on the coffee table. On it gleamed several covered dishes. He picked up the biggest one and gazed down hungrily at a thick New York cut steak, a baked potato and some thinly sliced French green beans.

"God bless you," he breathed. He moved the coverlet around his waist as he sat up, got his knife and fork and began to cut himself a bite of steak.

"Here's the deal," she said. "Josie and Diana are going to take some of the Oracle agents to Fort Huahuache. No one in the Army will know exactly who they are or why they're there, but the Lockworths get a lot of the things they want. The others will stay here and guard the school."

He parsed that as he spied a glass of red wine and took an appreciative sip. Then his attention shifted to the view of Allison's bed in the little room off the living room. It hadn't been slept in.

"What about us?" he asked her.

"We're going to my family's retreat."

He nodded. "Half of America's after you, and I'm probably being hunted, too. I'll finish breakfast and we'll go."

"It's dinner. You've been asleep for ten hours."

"You shouldn't have let me do that," he reproved her mildly.

"Is it possible there's a tracker on your van?"

"I swept it, but I wouldn't want to be overly complacent," he told her. "You know how it is. Spycraft changes by the hour. I have something strong and powerful, you have something stronger and more powerful."

"Like a nuclear weapon," she said.

"Yes, like that."

Morgan finished his delicious meal and had another half a glass of wine. After much discussion, they gave Morgan's van to Diana to drive to Fort Huahuache. She brought them back a khaki green Hummer.

Then Lynnette and Allison worked around the clock to stuff her laptop with as many Oracle applications as possible. Morgan was asked to leave, and Lucy Karmon accompanied him as he jogged around the grounds, trying to burn off some energy.

Then it was time to go. Allison had strong emotional ties with Christine Evans and her people. It was clear as she said goodbye to them.

They left by cover of darkness, Allison driving. Morgan was comfortable in a pair dark gray sweats, a navy-blue T-shirt and a gray sweatshirt. Allison had on another pair of cammies and a navy-blue sweater. She was wearing kicker boots; if someone had told Morgan Allison Gracelyn owned kicker boots, he would have laughed him out of the office.

Allison was constantly scanning; Morgan wordlessly

rode shotgun. He had his Medusa and his Uzi on the floor and she had a Glock placed in the drink console between them.

The stars were hard and brittle; they glowed a silvery-blue as the Hummer climbed the mountains. Morgan had seen this part of the country many times, but its stark beauty still mesmerized him. It was primal in the way that the lush forests of North Carolina were primeval; and he knew that beneath its seeming desolation, there were chilly caves and oases as if from the stories of the Arabian Nights.

The outline of a rustic stone house rose against the moon like a howling coyote. Allison rolled up to it and killed the engine.

She climbed from the truck and walked slowly to the back door. She held out her hand, telling him to stay, while she went inside. Chivalry was equal opportunity when it came to special ops, but it was difficult not to insist on taking the protector role.

"All clear," she announced, poking her head outside. "I've called in. Let's leave the lights off for now."

"Roger that," he said, following her in.

"We have staples," she announced, walking into the kitchen, which was dimly lit by moonlight flooding through a large rectangular window. "Cereal in the pantry, frozen food."

She got two bottles of water from the fridge and tossed one to him. Her face in the moonlight appeared luminous and otherworldly. God, Allison was beautiful.

She drank her water. He could see her mind working. She was stressed, and she was fatigued. At any other time, he would call her burned out. But he knew how it was when you were running an op. You didn't have the luxury of being burned out.

"I'll take first watch," he said. "I'm rested. You need to sleep."

He watched her bristle. She was so much like he was—had to be in control, didn't like being second-guessed. He'd take care not to cross her.

"Sure. Go ahead," she said. "Let me show you around first."

She showed him where his room was—nicely appointed, featuring a lot of Gracelyn family photos—and he set his small travel bag, purchased while he was on the road, coming after her, on the bathroom counter down the hall.

Then he went outside, guarding her as she rested. He had promised to wake her up in three hours to take a turn, but three became four became five became six.

She still hadn't let him in on what was really happening. He still had the version she had doled out to Christine and Kayla Ryan, which was galling. He thought back to his last mission with his team—how his people were content to wait for the information Morgan would provide in due course.

Maybe that was because all Morgan's ops were sharply defined by two requirements from which he never deviated: a definition of the purpose of the mission, and an exit strategy. At every point, if a wrench got thrown into their goal or their way out, Morgan called a halt. He either shut down the mission or called time out while he redesigned the series of steps most likely to get the job done and send his people home alive and intact.

He didn't know if that was how Allison worked. Her

mission was still a mystery to him, her end game unknown. And as for her people coming back alive, he had seen firsthand how intensely loyal they were to her. He could imagine someone taking a bullet for her, out of a deep and abiding sense that her survival was more important than their own.

So they have to know she's Delphi, even if they don't admit it.

Six hours became nine.

It wasn't unheard of for one of his people to disobey an order to wake him up when he or she thought Morgan needed more rest. But the bottom line was that when they risked his wrath for disobeying orders, it was not so much out of personal concern for him, but so that their CO wouldn't be fatigued and therefore, jeopardize the mission. But since he didn't know what the mission was, he had no way to support it beyond supporting Allison.

Or was it something else? Something deeper?

The colors of the awakening desert glowed down on Morgan's face like a soft blanket, and he yawned. He turned around to go back in through the kitchen when Allison appeared in the doorway. She was wearing her cammies and a maroon T-shirt with the NSA logo in a circle on a breast pocket. Her hair was wet.

"Good morning," she said. She didn't chastise him for letting her sleep, and she had taken a shower.

He unhung the Uzi from around his neck and handed it over. Their fingers brushed. His gaze dipped from her face to her chest. He couldn't help it; he was a man. She was an uncanny combination of athleticism and soft beauty, and he wanted to take all her clothes off then and there, ease her down on the soft wool carpet and lose himself inside her.

But he made no move to act on his urges. He brushed past her without saying a word.

He went into the bathroom, still steamy from her shower. He smelled spicy soap and shampoo. Stripping quickly, he turned on the water and stepped into the tub, sliding the glass door shut. The water was hot, and he adjusted the shower head, hard. A sigh of pleasure escaped him as his tired muscles uncoiled.

He soaped and washed his hair. Grabbing a fresh towel, he dried off and wrapped it around his waist. Then he padded down the hall to the room she had assigned him.

He cocked his head and slowly smiled as he observed the rumpled condition of his bed. Allison had slept in here, not in her own room. He doubted she had been waiting for him—she was a professional soldier, and she wouldn't have wanted him to compromise their safety—but maybe what she was saying was, "If I could, I would." He didn't know, but it was mind-bendingly sexy.

Even sexier was the scent of her on his sheets as he took the towel from around his waist and hung it on the doorknob. He laid his clothes on top of a bureau and slipped between the sheets, which still retained traces of her body heat.

He was hard by the time he had pulled the bedclothes back up underneath his armpits and turned on his side to face the door.

When this was over, he was finishing what she'd started….

But not now. Now, he had to force himself to stand

down; to relax and go to sleep. A tall order, but Morgan was exhausted; and after a while, after he was used to the smell of her and an almost atavistic reaction to the idea that he was lying exactly where she had lain, he closed his eyes and drifted.

An unnamed island in Micronesia

Since the acquisition of her most recent set of egg babies, Echo had discovered something very important: She wasn't cut out for motherhood. Children disgusted her. They were messy, noisy, demanding and unpredictable; and as for reasoning with them…better to collect their eggs and be done with it. Some of them might make useful additions to Team Echo, but she was highly doubtful. One thing she was sure of: She would render any girl she auctioned off infertile before she handed her over to the highest bidder.

"Try again, Cailey," Echo said between her teeth, as the little girl with caramel-colored hair and huge blue eyes burst into fresh tears. Echo had no idea why she hadn't simply shriveled up from dehydration. All the girl *did* was cry.

"I want my mommy!" Cailey shrieked, pulling at her restraints. She'd been strapped into a dentist chair only as a last resort. Her little fingernails and toenails were painted with sparkly pink polish. She was wearing a thin blue hospital gown and the halo of an EEG machine encircled her head. Eric Pace and Jeremy Loschetter huddled together on the other side of a thick panel of glass, poring over Cailey's readouts.

"I want to go home!" Cailey screamed. She threw back her head. "Mommymommymommymommy!"

God, this is tedious.

"You did *such* a good job helping us rescue Dr. Loschetter," Echo cooed. The girl had the most amazing eyesight. She had actually detected indentations in the ground, indicating the tunnel. The twins had confirmed it, of course, reading the minds of the little spygirls hidden inside.

"There was shooting! I hate you!"

Echo took a deep breath, sliding her glance toward Natalia, who had crossed her arms over her chest and stood hunched and frightened.

Echo turned around and raised a brow at Jeremy Loschetter. *"Well?"* she mouthed.

His goatee looked so idiotic. It was difficult to take him seriously, except for the fact that she knew he was one of the most brilliant scientists alive.

"Her corneas seem to be made of a different sort of material," he informed her through a microphone. "Organic, but the structures…I suggest we consider taking a sample."

"Of her eye?" Natalia asked in a high-pitched voice.

"Of course not, Nat. They need to collect some of her tears. She has rather a lot of them to spare," Echo said, as she forced herself to move forward and stroke Cailey's arm. The little girl thrashed and cried as if a snake had bitten her. Perhaps she had some kind of sensitivity to touch.

Or perhaps she simply didn't like Echo.

The feeling is mutual, you little bitch.

Natalia shifted uncomfortably beside Echo. Echo

turned to her, pulling a sad face. "Nat, this is upsetting you." She forced herself to trail her fingernails beneath Natalia's chin and smile kindly at her, even though she would really like to dig those nails straight through her jaw and yank out her tongue. "We're only doing this because something seems to be wrong with her. You saw that seizure."

A seizure Loschetter had accidentally caused by anesthetizing Cailey's eyes with something she was allergic to, idiot.

The firestarter sighed heavily and nodded. It was such bad timing that Natalia had been out on a walk with Echo, heard the little girl's cries and would not be placated until she was allowed to see what was going on.

The little girl—Cailey—jerked her gaze to Natalia and fought against the restraints around her delicate wrists.

"Help me!" Cailey shrieked. "These are bad people! Get my mommy! Get her *now!* I want Clown Bear! I want Mommy!"

"It's going to be okay," Natalia told her, taking Cailey's hand and stroking her forehead. "My name is Nat, and I live here. Echo is our friend. The bad people are out there. They want to study us…" She trailed off, staring at the halo around Cailey's head. Echo followed her train of thought to its logical conclusion: Cailey *was* being studied.

"Studied by people who want to harm you," Echo said quickly. "But we're Arachne. We're the good guys. Cailey, dear, we only want to know why you started shaking. We want to see if something is wrong with you."

"Call my mommy," Cailey begged. "Tell her where I am. She'll come and get me. Oh, please, lady, please, please, please! I helped you get the doctor! Please let me go home!"

Shut up, shut up, shut up! Echo screamed silently at her, smoothing her hair away from her forehead.

Natalia whimpered. Echo smelled smoke. Now *she* was getting more upset. As her face began to redden, she let go of Cailey's hand and turned to Echo.

"I need to get out of here," she said urgently.

"Of course, darling," Echo replied, lacing her fingers through Natalia's and turning her back to Cailey.

"Stop them!" Cailey screamed at Natalia. "They're hurting me! Get my mommy!"

"Oh God," Natalia whispered. "Oh, Echo…"

"She'll understand one day," Echo whispered, giving her hand a squeeze. With any luck, she might break Natalia's fingers. "And she'll thank us."

Natalia nodded and allowed herself to be led out of the room, slinking past Loschetter and Pace. Both of them looked at Natalia like vultures swooping down on a dead zebra, then surreptitiously at Echo. They hadn't missed a beat setting up shop and getting to work. Echo applauded their dedication, and she would do all she could to support it. In fact, she had some tranquilizers in the pocket of the wonderful taupe linen jacket she was wearing, which she planned to put into Natalia's lunch. She had gotten the girl to begin eating again. It turned out that she was fond of sweet and sour chicken.

Once Natalia was unconscious, they'd run a few preliminary tests in advance of beginning the drug therapy that would allow them to harvest her eggs. Echo already

had three advance orders for firestarters—one from
Vlados Zelasco; one from the Circle of Justice; and one
from a Chinese billionaire who preferred to be known
as "Goldeneye."

Echo felt chills at the thought of how much money
she would make—and how very deeply in her personal
debt the three would find themselves. And of course,
Natalia would have no idea any of it had been done.

As if in response, Natalia's flesh sizzled. A mousy
little lab tech—some local woman Loschetter had
hired—gave her wide berth as she dashed toward
Cailey's examining room.

"Hurry," Natalia whispered urgently to Echo, as
more smoke rose off her skin. "It's going to happen
soon."

Yes, Echo thought. *It is.*

Chapter 14

The Gracelyn hideaway, Arizona

A week became two.

Courtesy of the many Oracle agents in the field, Lynnette hauled powerful computer desktops and dupes of proprietary software and applications to Allison for configuring a desktop system to augment her Oracle laptop, so that she could work side by side on several tasks at once. Lynnette lent remote assistance at Oracle West, and Selena and Kim worked from Oracle HQ.

Faced with the need for more manpower, she brought Morgan in deeper. She explained Echo's shielding system to him, and he continued searching for an offensive weapon against it. They worked on strategy and tactics for any number of direct assaults on Echo, should they ever locate her. They had three objectives: to contain Echo herself; to rescue the egg babies; and to locate and take possession of "two" items of interest.

"Those two items have to be those necklaces," Morgan said. Allison did not reply, irritating him, she knew. She kept her own spider pendant around her neck, never showing it to him. What she could and couldn't tell him was becoming too complicated, and they both knew that.

She let him see some of the items Oracle brought to her attention. He was amazed by the sheer scope and power of the intelligence-gathering system, and incredulous that Oracle's creator had penetrated the firewalls of so many agencies.

"Delphi is a beautiful genius," he declared. She did not respond.

For Morgan's part, his analytical skills were uncanny, his ability to focus impressive. He gave a hundred and ten percent day after day, for a week, and then two.

"Valenti says Ozone's looking at New Year's Eve as the event horizon," he told her, absently stretching as he sat at the desk. "There's a tremendous amount of encrypted chatter coming out of Berzhaan. And by the way, we've been fired and the CIA's looking for us. Probably a hell of a lot of other people are looking for us, too."

Allison wondered if they could be considered to be living together. They ate most of their meals together. They jogged in the cold winter mornings and worked together. Clothes Lynnette ordered off the Internet for him hung in the closet. But in the final analysis, they were not together. They were separated by secrets and suspicions. She sent him out of the house when she needed to conduct top-secret business, or take calls with her voice modulator strapped to her phone. Maybe it was a waste of time. She didn't know. She just planted one foot in front of the other, and stayed on course as best she could.

The nights were hard. They were awkward. She could feel his lust, and her own, as they went to their separate rooms. Never again did she sleep in his bed, and she was sorry she'd done it. If she could have foreseen that they'd be working together this long, she wouldn't have.

On the first morning of the third week, Morgan came out onto the back porch of the house, as she went through her martial arts forms, staying in shape, preparing, honing. She was waiting for Lynnette to arrive with their mail.

"McDonough's body has been found floating in the Potomac," he announced, waving a printout. "They're blaming the explosion of your town house on him. They've found a diary that proves he was obsessed with you."

"Manufactured by his handlers, no doubt," she said, remembering that he had mentioned an ex-wife a few times, and his daughter, Alyssa, in college. "Did it implicate you?"

"It wasn't in the file," he said. "Also, Elle Petrenko checked in. She's dogging Monya Kishinev. I wonder if Wrobleski's floating facedown somewhere."

She wondered if Wrobleski had family, too. She smoothed back her hair from her sweaty forehead. There was so much to keep track of.

"I think I may have something that will work on Echo," he continued. A soft ping came from inside the house. Oracle. "Back to work."

"Thanks," she told his back as he went inside.

Lynnette arrived about forty-five minutes later in a nondescript blue sedan. She changed cars frequently in case she was being watched. Unfortunately there weren't many routes to the Gracelyn hideaway, but she dry cleaned as best she could.

"FBI came with a warrant to search the academy

again," she announced, as the two women greeted each other. "They didn't find a thing."

Allison sighed. "Thanks. Please tell Christine how sorry I am to put her in this position."

"I did, and she knows. And your movie rentals came." She handed Allison two familiar-looking small red envelopes. "And…this."

She held out a letter addressed to *Allison Gracelyn care of the Athena School for Girls.* That wasn't accurate; it was called Athena Academy.

"Thanks, Lynnette," Allison said. "Stay for dinner."

"I will."

They walked into the house, and Lynnette headed for the bathroom, giving Morgan a nod as she did so. He nodded back.

"Oh, good, our movies," he said, looking at Allison.

She snorted. "*Your* movies."

He touched his chest as if she had wounded him. "*Charlie's Angels* is a classic."

"Uh-huh." She walked over to him and laid the movie envelopes at his elbow. Then she sliced open the letter with her forefinger.

Dear Ms. Gracelyn:

It has come to my attention that you are seeking information regarding the murder of your mother. I have information regarding Jackie Cavanaugh. E-mail me at AGfriend@xmail.com and I will contact you.

A Friend

She sighed, feigning a nonchalance she did not feel,

and showed the letter to Morgan. "Xmail, blackmail. Someone's trying to flush me out."

He looked at her hard. Licked his lips. For a moment she thought he was going to hug her, or at least squeeze her hand. Tingles played at the small of her back and coiled in her lower abdomen, and she tried to swallow the flare of anticipation that jittered through her body.

"You could send that to Alex Forsythe," he suggested. Alex was a criminologist with the FBI.

"Good idea. I'll ask Lynnette to do that," Allison said, moving away from him.

Lynnette came out of the bathroom. She took one look at Allison.

"Go for a walk?" Lynnette asked casually.

I wanted him to comfort me, Allison thought. *He's taken up residence in my life, and he's beginning to mean something more than...whatever it is we are. When I'm upset, I turn to him. I've never turned to anyone before. It was me against the world.*

But he's in my world now.

She took a pair of binoculars off the table and joined Lynnette outside. They walked in silence to the rim of the vast canyon below, training binoculars on the washes and gullies for anything suspicious. Lynnette, perhaps sensing the direction of Allison's thoughts, turned to face her friend.

"Allison," she began, "I need to tell you two things. The first is that I get a good vibe off Morgan. The second is that if you tell me to take him out, I will, without a moment's hesitation."

Allison nodded. "So will I," she replied.

The two women regarded each other. Neither smiled.

The landscape was so beautiful, the sky so vast and clear. It was picture-perfect. A hawk wheeled against the sun, searching for prey.

Echo's lair, Micronesia

It was astonishing how much one could accomplish in three weeks. Even better, what one could do in a month.

It was the middle of the night, and Echo swept along the catwalk of her completed laboratory with a bottle of champagne in one hand and her shoes slung over her shoulder. There was still a little bit of blood under her toenails, but she'd have her pedicurist deal with it in the morning.

Glass-walled examination rooms shone beneath arc lights. Banks of computers chittered and, well, computed. It was fantastic.

She flicked on a few screens and studied her "nursery." Little Cailey was shrinking away into nothing. Well, she'd helped with the Loschetter rescue mission; maybe she was used up.

Echo clicked to another screen. Natalia LeClaire was asleep, too. Her drug therapy was progressing nicely. Once her eggs were harvested, they would be mixed with the sperm of several very wonderful donors.

She switched to two more bedrooms in the nursery. Ah, and there was Willa, the superhacker. Echo studied the sleeping mocha-skinned eighteen-year-old, given a lovely suite of rooms not far from Mary and Elizabeth, the psychic twins. Thus far, Willa had not been able to crack Oracle, which was Echo's supreme ambition for her. She allowed Willa to "hang" with Mary and Eliza-

beth in hopes that they might read something in her sub-
conscious mind that would help her consciously unlock
the complex system created by Delphi. To Echo's
private amusement, Willa had taken to calling them by
their Goth names, "Shadow" and "Silk." Children. Who
could explain them? Of course, even grown-ups gave
themselves silly names.

Delphi has to be Allison Gracelyn, Echo thought.
*Everything always comes back to her. Wherever the
hell she is...*

Echo had created so many phony blackmail and extortion schemes starring Allison that even she had
trouble keeping track of them. She was stunned that no
one had located that bitch and garroted her. Wrobleski
was the idiot who had tried to blow up her town house,
although he had successfully managed to pin it on his
lackey at NSA, McDonough. She knew Wrobleski was
hiding in Amsterdam; she'd let him dangle for a while.

*The only good thing about all this is that Allison has
no idea where I am, either,* Echo thought. *If she did, she'd
be here in a heartbeat, trying to break down the door like
some villager with a pitchfork in a horror movie.*

Something caught Echo's eye as she gazed at Willa's
room. She couldn't say exactly what. Then her innate
defense system alerted her that someone was coming up
behind her.

She glanced over her shoulder. It was Eric Pace. He was
wearing his ridiculous military uniform. For the love of
God, he'd been stripped of his rank when he'd been thrown
into prison. Some men grew more pathetic with age.

She smiled down at the blood beneath her toenails.
Some men never aged. Maybe they were the lucky ones.

"We got another burst," he informed her by way of greeting. "Someone sent out an electronic message two minutes ago."

Echo narrowed her eyes at him and tapped her fingernails against the champagne bottle. "That's your area of expertise. Why come to me?"

His cheeks reddened. He had such an issue with strong women. "I want your permission to interrogate Willa Goldsmith." His eyes moved from her to the screen filled with the image of the sleeping girl. "Until she talks."

"Pfft." Echo pointed at her. "Look at her. She's asleep."

"It could have been time-delayed, to be sent when she had an alibi," he pointed out. Echo bristled. As if she wouldn't know that.

"Fine," she spat. "Interrogate her."

His eyes flickered. "How far can I go?"

"Nothing permanent." She took a dainty swig of champagne from the bottle. "We'd best sell her off if you think there's a problem."

"Thank you," he said. He looked put out with her.

She knew she needed him on her side. "It's the least I can do for you, dear Eric," she cooed. "You've put everything on the line for me."

"Yes. I have," he replied. Then he turned on his heel and walked away, his well-polished shoes ringing on the catwalk.

Wait. Did she sense another presence in the area?

She cocked her head, feeling the vibrations in the air. It was part of her genetic gift, a survival skill that had paid off handsomely in the past. It was very, very hard to sneak up on Echo.

She whirled around, gliding along the catwalk,

squinting into the darkness. The vibration felt…small. Suspiciously, she checked all the nursery rooms on her screen, number one—Cailey—through number thirteen—a girl named Greta Von Edel, whose special gift was superhuman marksmanship. She was also the best pool player Echo had ever met, her gifted brain calculating angles and trajectories with the precision of a sophisticated supercomputer.

She flicked back through all the images, studying each girl in turn. Had one of them figured out a way to reach the outside world? Had that one just snuck into the lab to eavesdrop on her then scurried back to bed?

Impossible.

She was about to turn off the screens and go back to bed herself—surely her room had been cleaned of all the blood by now—when she caught sight of Eric Pace and two armed guards entering Willa Goldsmith's room.

Willa bolted upright and struggled, appeared to scream—Echo had the sound off—and the two guards aimed their Kalashnikovs at her. She didn't seem to see them; she kept flailing in Pace's grasp as he pushed a surgical mask against her face.

Her right arm rose straight up; her back arched; she went limp. She was very little for her age. Very fragile.

Pace glanced up in the camera as if at Echo. She chuckled and gave him a wave, even though he couldn't see her.

"Nothing permanent," she said.

The Gracelyn hideaway, Arizona

Day thirty since Loschetter and Pace had been snatched, and there had been no more abductions.

Allison switched out some of her operatives so they wouldn't wind up tired and hunted, as she and Morgan were. Others took extended leave, lied a lot, did whatever they could to make themselves available. Oracle captured at least six more blackmail schemes that Allison was purportedly running. Morgan was wanted by the CIA for questioning. No surprise there.

Now, on a night shortly before Christmas, Allison sat alone in the dark as the rain poured down outside the living room window. Morgan was asleep in his room. She had put her hair up in a messy bun; she wore an oversize T-shirt, no bra and a pair of sweats.

The face of Natalia LeClaire gazed back at her from the computer monitor. She was very pretty, with a classic oval face framed by dark, curly hair and a lush, bee-stung mouth. Her deep-set, velvet-brown eyes were wide and pleading; she looked at once both terrified and grief-stricken.

What would it be like, to grow up with people who kept you in a cage? To know that your own parents were afraid of you? Did they let her out for special occasions like Christmas? Had she ever had friends? Gone to a sleepover, or even a movie?

"I'll find you," Allison whispered, touching her hand to the screen. "And I'll give you some of those things."

The sad, silent face of Natalia LeClaire gazed back at her. Allison kept the window containing her image open and pulled up the list of abductees. Using a matching program she had created, Oracle had located another probable pair of egg babies—English twins born in a small village north of London. Their parents had reported them as runaways, but only after their school had investigated a lengthy absence.

Scotland Yard had become involved, and their thick dossier on the twins revealed that they were minor celebrities nicknamed Shadow and Silk, who had perfected a "mind reading scheme" whereby they bilked gullible locals at the village tavern out of money for beer and cigarettes. The detective who had investigated their case claimed that the twins were obviously faking the whole thing by means of tiny microphones and transceivers.

There was a photo of them standing together in front of a drab row house. They were very Goth, with white skin, black-ringed eyes and black lips. Their black hair was short. They were smirking at the camera. Allison wondered if they had been the two smaller figures holding hands above the tunnel when the safe house had been attacked.

The last picture she gazed at was that of little Cailey Anderson, just five. Her frantic parents had given the feebs dozens of pictures of her, as well as her handprints and footprints. And a copy of her birth certificate. Allison gazed at her sunny face and chubby cheeks, laughing and giggling. Her only unusual gift appeared to be that she had excellent eyesight.

The images on the monitor blurred. She was tired and she knew she should get some rest. But she couldn't stop looking at the girls, couldn't stop reading every scrap of information Oracle collected about them. She was standing vigil for them.

Morgan was tightly wound, too. He continued to work on his plan to take on Echo when and if they found her. He was steady and relentless, but she heard him at night, pacing.

"I will find you," she vowed to Natalia, in the dark, in the rain.

The back door opened. She grabbed her Glock and leaped into tripod stance, ready to fire off a shot; then Morgan appeared on the threshold. He was completely soaked from head to toe. His salt-and-pepper hair curled beneath his ears; his eyes caught moonlight, swirling silver in the blue. Rain clung to his sharp jaw and the hollows in his cheeks. Rain sluiced down his long neck and soaked into the black workout shirt stretched across his pecs and biceps. His black sweats molded his thighs and calves.

"Sorry, I thought you heard me say I was going for a jog," he said.

"If I had, I would have told you we were expecting a storm," she said, putting down her weapon. "I thought you were in bed."

"Can't sleep." He looked at her. Really looked. A muscle in his cheek jumped, as if he was seeing her for the first time after they had been separated for years, by war and other tragedies.

He stood in front of the storm and all she could see were his blue eyes. The movement of his chest.

The atmosphere in the room shifted. Altered.

Forever.

"I can't stand this," he said, his voice deep and gravelly.

"You've waited longer than this for the green light," she replied.

His eyes blazed. "That's not what I'm talking about."

"I know," she said.

He came into the room. She didn't move away.

She couldn't stand it, either.

Who walked forward first? Was it a walk, or a run?

She smelled spicy soap and fresh rain as he put his arms around her. His wet clothes soaked her T-shirt and made her nipples taut. He caught her at the small of her back and tilted his pelvis so that she could feel his erection. The fabric of her sweatpants molded against her sex as she rocked against him.

He put his lips over hers, soft; the stubble on his chin and above his mouth a reminder of his masculinity as his tongue stole into her mouth. Her knees buckled. She clung to him, gripped his shoulders, answered him.

"Oh God," he whispered. "God, Allison."

He bent down and slung his arms beneath her legs; she parted them and let him pick her up. She wrapped her legs around his waist and he began to walk across the floor, carrying her out of the room as he kissed her over and over again. She gathered up the curls of his hair in her hands and gasped as she kissed him back. Moaned in anticipation.

And then Oracle pinged. It had incoming.

"Oh, no," Allison whispered. "No. Not now."

Then amazingly, they both chuckled sadly. Morgan carried her not to her bed, but to her work desk, and set her down.

"Don't electrocute yourself," he said, taking a step away from her.

She opened the new offering from her data mining system. It was a MySpace page, for someone named Tasi Arejab. Tasi used an image of a genie as her icon, and her section was headed, "Shoutout to my friends!"

"Hello, BFF Willa Goldsmith!" she had written.

Allison's lips parted. "Best Friend Forever," she said.

"*Tasi* is a Chamoru name, meaning 'sea' or 'ocean,'" Morgan added. "Guamanian. *Arejab* is Marshallese for 'lagoon side of the atoll.'"

She and Morgan both leaned forward as Allison scrolled down the page.

"WG likes catS Or dogS."

SOS.

There had been no effort to hide the origin of the message:

Micronesia.

Morgan's hand came down on Allison's shoulder. She caught it. They held each other, staring at the screen, as if both were afraid to blink, equally afraid to believe that it had finally happened.

She dialed Selena back in Virginia.

"Get to the town house stat," she said.

"On my way," Selena replied.

Allison hung up and started making more calls—to Lynnette and Diana; to Elle and Sam out in the field. She put on her voice modulator and let Morgan see her do it. It was time.

After the last call, she set down the phone with shaking hands. Then she turned in her chair and gazed at Morgan.

"Last chance to bail," she told him. Tears spilled down her cheeks. She was overloaded. Jubilant and terrified, exultant and determined. This was it. She knew it.

"No chance, Delphi," he replied, bending over and kissing her.

Like a man who knew he was going to die.

Chapter 15

Echo's lair, Micronesia

"Wonderful news," Echo said to the little Goth twins, as she swept into their room. Their faces coated with their white clown makeup and black-ringed eyes and lips, they were lounged on Mary's bed, busy at a video game console. They smiled at her and set the game aside. They didn't hold hands, which was a tremendous relief. They wouldn't be able to read her mind, and she was under a bit of strain as it was.

"What is it?" Mary asked.

"We were able to reunite Willa with her parents," Echo lied, beaming at them. "She wanted me to tell you that she was sorry she didn't get a chance to say good-bye." She wrinkled her nose. "We had to keep it very hush-hush. I'm sure you understand."

"Oh," Elizabeth groaned. As she looked at Echo, her rapidly blinking eyes filled with tears. She turned her back and hung her head.

"She was so much fun," Mary said, moving away from her twin. "I thought she rather liked it here."

Elizabeth began to sob.

Oh my God, Echo thought. *Do they know I'm selling her? She's upstairs in my apartment right now, waiting for transport.* Then she reminded herself not to think around them. They might suddenly hold hands, and then where would she be?

"Well, you must remember that her only gift was being especially good at computers," Echo replied reasonably. "She could fit in quite easily with normal society."

"She didn't tell us," Mary muttered. She glanced over at her weeping twin. "We didn't read anything like that."

"She didn't know. I was afraid to give her hope, in case things didn't work out." Echo smiled sweetly, the picture of thoughtfulness.

"Oh," Mary whispered.

Echo held out her arms. "My poor sad darlings. I didn't realize you two had gotten so close with her."

"How could we?" Elizabeth wept. "We never get to go anywhere, do anything! We haven't any friends!"

"Oh, and perhaps you were hoping that she could become your friend?" Echo asked, feeling somewhat relieved that Elizabeth was carrying on because she was a petulant teenager, and not because she knew Willa Goldsmith was destined for Vlados's castle—to make up for the loss of his other psychic egg baby, Teal Arnett.

"We've wised up," Mary ventured. "We know we have to pass as normal, too." She picked at the cuticle on her left thumb. It was bloody and ragged. "So perhaps we could go back to England?"

"Don't *you* like it here?" Echo asked.

"I guess." Mary shrugged. Elizabeth's sobs grew heavier.

"Maybe we could have a little party with the other girls," Echo decided. "Cakes and punch, that sort of thing. Or is that too childish for you?"

"We'd love it," Mary said. She came up to Echo and kissed her cheek. "Thank you. We don't mean to be ungrateful. It's just, well, you know we had more freedom back home."

"Unless the school authorities had caught up with you. Then you'd be in prison, wouldn't you?" Echo asked, fighting not to wipe Mary's kiss off her cheek. "There'd be a lot less freedom then, wouldn't there be, Elizabeth?"

"I don't want you to call me that anymore," Elizabeth ground out. "I'm 'Shadow' and she's 'Silk.'"

Mary grimaced apologetically at Echo. "She's got her period," she whispered to Echo.

"Oh, I see." Echo was appalled that the girl would mention it. It was so…visceral. "We'll have some fun together. A lovely party."

It will be the last party I hold for you miserable…

Elizabeth rushed over to her sister and took her hand.

…beautiful, wonderful girls, Echo thought carefully, pushing warmth into every syllable.

They clung to each other and did not smile.

"I'll have party dresses made for all of you," Echo told them. "Here in…where we are, seamstresses are very skilled, and dirt cheap. Why, they're practically slave labor!"

"How…nice," Mary said.

Elizabeth burst into more tears.

The Gracelyn hideaway, Arizona

Allison and Morgan did not have sex the night of the SOS, and now that chance was gone. The hideaway had become Oracle HQ West as agents brought weapons and gear in preparation for shipping out to Micronesia. Using Diana's remotely controlled surveillance craft, Predator, they pored over navsat photos of every square inch of the hundreds of atolls and islands that made up that section of the world.

Allison activated a core group—her first wave—and prepared a second and a third in case Team One went FUBAR. She would be in the first wave. So would Morgan.

The rest of Team One was Jessica Whittaker and Diana Lockworth, who were already in Arizona; and Selena Shaw Jones, Sam St. John, Elle Petrenko, plus Dawn O'Shaughnessy, who would be accompanied by her husband, British Special Air Forces Captain Des "Ash" Asher, from outbound. Scattered arrivals would be harder to detect as they swarmed to their rendezvous point.

"As soon as we have a location, Morgan and I are flying out, ahead of you," she told Jessica and Diana, who stood in her living room. She had briefed each of the other agents by phone, and they were all a go.

"Copy that," Jessica said. "You say the word, Allison, and I'll swim to Micronesia if I have to."

That was a little bit of Whittaker humor. Jessica's gift was her ability to breathe underwater. Allison had chosen her for this mission specifically because of that. She had also asked Dawn's husband Des Asher to interface with the Special Boat Forces, the amphibious arm of the British Special Forces.

"I'll swim, too," Morgan said, coming up beside Allison.

She could feel his body heat, and her body responded. She felt both tantalized and crowded…and confused. This was not the time, or the place…or the man. There could be no man.

She was Delphi.

If we had taken that chance, gone to bed…how would I feel about bringing him on the mission?

There was no answer to that. It hadn't happened. And yet, as his arm brushed hers, she almost instinctually wrapped her hand around his—the way lovers did. But they were not lovers. They were teammates on an op.

That was all.

"Allison?" Lynnette said. "Did you hear me?"

Allison blinked. All eyes were on her. Faces were drawn, pale; the tension in the room was like the pressure before a thunderstorm.

"No, sorry. What?"

"Circle of Justice just checked in. They're moving into position."

"We'll stop them, too," she said reflexively.

Morgan nodded. "Damn straight."

And she fell in love with him just a little bit more.

Wrong. I am not in love with him at all.

Echo's lair, Micronesia

High above the festivities, strolling along on her catwalk, Echo listened to the chatter of her guests as hip-hop music blared over the loudspeakers of the lab. The twelve remaining egg daughters mingled, eating sandwiches shaped like hearts and sweet cakes laced with tranquilizers. The lab techs and Loschetter's staff of scientists were smiling, enjoying some time off. The guards watched everyone.

Perhaps she should have thrown a party before Willa Goldsmith had gone "home." The other girls seemed subdued, despite their pretty new dresses, manicures and pedicures. She loved her own black gown sewn with golden spiders. Not as much as her two spider necklaces, of course. They were upstairs in her vault. Willa was in a holding cell next to the vault, with a little piece of party cake and some fruit punch to keep her company. Also, six armed guards handpicked for their reputations as heartless bastards.

Echo's diamond earring picked up whispers. She touched it gently and listened carefully.

"I'll give you fifty Euros to take my place," a voice whispered in *bahasa gaul,* the Indonesian slang of the working classes.

"You mean taking the firegirl to Kestonia? Sori, bruer," a second voice whispered. *"I saw what that girl did to Johnson. No way am I going anywhere with her."*

Hmm, how did they know she was planning to ship Natalia out? That was very disconcerting.

Sensing vibrations behind her, she turned to find Pace and Loschetter approaching her on the catwalk, looking as somber as teenage boys who hated dances because they exposed them for the socially awkward nerds they were. If ever anyone was socially awkward, it was these two.

"Gentlemen," she said graciously, holding out hands to both of them. Only Pace realized that he was supposed to kiss the back of her hand. Loschetter shook her fingers and slid his hands into the pockets of his white lab coat.

"Echo," Pace said. As she straightened, he gestured to the crowd below. "Dr. Loschetter and I were wondering if this was wise. At least two of those girls are psychics, and we don't want any trouble—"

Echo glanced down quickly to reassure herself that the two little Goths still weren't holding hands. Good. They were standing far apart, not looking very jolly, unfortunately. As an added precaution, she gestured to the two men to move with her to another one of her dampening fields, this one located at the opposite end of the catwalk.

"Have you had any more transmissions?" she queried, knowing the answer.

He pursed his fat lips and shook his head. His jowls waggled. She could hardly stand to look at him.

"Then we know it was Willa who tried to communicate with the outside world, despite her insistence that she had nothing to do with it," Echo replied. "Besides, we're shipping out the most problematic girls within the next few days. So enjoy the party." *It will be your last, you blubbery cretin,* she thought angrily, furious with him for daring to question her.

It appeared to be Loschetter's turn to show his disrespect. He cleared his throat. "You yourself have pointed out that some of these girls may have more than one gift. Things we know nothing about…"

Blah blah blah. She almost told them then that she

was going away, too. By week's end, she would remove the entire operation to Kestonia.

Vlados Zelasco had made the offer to give her a new lab there. It seemed that he had located another scientist who knew as much about the creation of egg babies as Loschetter. This man, named Michael Vardeman, had masqueraded as a minor lab tech at the original lab in Zuni, Lab 33, but he was actually a brilliant geneticist who'd gone there specifically to plunder Lab 33's secrets. Dear Dr. Vardeman had remained underground until recently, and now offered his services to Vlados.

She had originally turned down Vlados's offer to work together on the superegg project. But Willa's electronic burst had bothered Echo more than she had let Pace and Loschetter think. Coupled with that, she loathed these two men passionately and she was sorry she'd bothered to free them. They thought too much, questioned too much.

She could do better, and she would. They had no idea that during the construction of the laboratory, she had prewired the entire complex to blow sky-high in the event of an emergency. All she had to do was depress a tiny button three times in fast succession, and strategically placed explosives would rip apart the lab, and fill the escape tunnels with debris. She would press that button soon…from a safe distance, of course.

She thought of the spider necklace that was her mother's gift to her. It and Kwan-Sook's hung in the Spider Room, tribute to the Black Widow, Arachne, dead queen of all she surveyed. Echo had attached the detonator to her necklace. All she had to do was press it three-two-one…

She smiled at Loschetter and Pace.

Ka-boom! You're dead.

Four days, tops. That should be enough time to get anything of value out of here.

She smiled at her little girls, with their sandwiches, cakes and sparkly dresses.

Oh, and while she was at it, she'd order the Circle of Justice to go ahead and blow up Fort Meade, Maryland—the home of the NSA. And to place the blame squarely on the shoulders of Allison Gracelyn and Morgan Rush.

Suddenly the cavernous lab erupted with screams. Echo placed her hands on the rail of the catwalk and looked down as Loschetter and Pace joined her. Everyone was panicking, shouting, pointing. Natalia LeClaire had burst into flames. Engulfed in tongues of crimson fire, she whirled in a circle. The tongues shot up straight to the ceiling.

"Hilfe!" Greta Von Edel, the little sharpshooter, shouted, circling Natalia. She started yelling in German for a fire extinguisher, for someone to help Natalia— as everyone else raced away from the human torch.

The same mousy lab tech who had scurried to Cailey's side in the examining room scooped the girl up in her arms and raced around a column, shielding her as Cailey screamed and carried on. The tech's messy bun unwound like a pinwheel as Cailey clawed at her, like a little monkey trying to climb up a coconut tree.

Cailey cried. "Save me! Save me!"

Then the overhead sprinklers came on, raining water over Echo, the two men, the partygoers…and her beautiful lab equipment. Cailey screamed louder.

Damn that girl, Echo thought. Meaning Natalia.

"You see? There's a problem," Pace yelled, as the three darted along the catwalk.

"Turn off the water!" Echo shouted to the lab tech clanging up the stairs toward her. "Turn it off!"

Echo balled her fists as her slow-witted staff moved to obey her. She threaded her way through the clumps of weeping girls to Natalia, who had stopped burning. Steam rose off her like mist. Greta Von Edel minced toward the girl, as if she wanted to comfort her, but was too afraid.

"Darling," Echo said, holding open her arms as she glided toward Natalia.

You ruined my party!

She gathered Natalia in her arms, but the girl held herself rigid. So upset, poor darling. Echo determinedly rocked her, forcing herself to appear concerned and motherly when, really, all she wanted to do was slap the stupid cow's face.

"I'm so sorry," Natalia sobbed against Echo's shoulder. "Oh, Echo, I'm sorry!"

"Shush, no harm done," Echo snapped, then took a breath and tried harder to find an empathetic tone of voice. "Look, darling, you see?" She pointed upward. "There's a sprinkler system throughout our entire complex. It activated just as it should, and everyone is just fine. Aren't they, Greta?"

Greta didn't answer.

Echo frowned and looked over at her. The German was staring upward as if studying the sprinkler system. Echo didn't like the look of that.

"Greta?" she demanded.

"Ja." Greta ticked her gaze over to Natalia and patted her back. "It's okay, Natalia."

"She likes to be called Nat," Echo informed her.

Across the room, Pace and Loschetter were speaking to a clump of technicians who were examining one of the mainframe computers that lined the room.

Oh God, I can't get out of here fast enough, Echo thought irritably.

The Gracelyn hideaway, Arizona

"Allison," Lynnette said. "My God, look at this. It just came in."

Allison crossed to Lynnette and studied the screen. It was a set of blueprints marked Echo Chamber.

To Tasi's MySpace page, also from Micronesia.

"Come here," Allison said, gesturing to Morgan, Jessica and Diana.

"Oracle keyed in on the word 'Echo,'" Lynnette said as she zoomed in on the images. "The sender had to know we'd catch it. It's for an indoor sprinkler system. In what appears to be a laboratory and a set of rooms. At least one of them is a fortified Kevlar-titanium cell."

"You could keep a firestarter in a cell like that," Morgan said. He found Allison's hand. They held on tightly.

The room was silent. No one breathed.

"We're in," Allison said. "Now where? Please, where?"

She sat down next to Morgan, who was already working on the message. She saw Lynnette log on. Back in Virginia, Selena joined the team. Four seasoned hackers. Computers with amazing capabilities. Something had to happen. Something had to break.

Echo's lair, Micronesia

Eric Pace barely waited for Echo's invitation to enter her exquisite private office before he pushed open the titanium-enforced door. The walls were gold and decorated with drawings and paintings of spiders. The wall sconces were black widows. The ebony furniture was accented with red, the colors of the Black Widow.

Echo looked up from her sleek black desktop computer, where she was reading a poem written by Vlados, who fancied himself "the Robert Frost of the Eastern Bloc." She found that far more amusing than his terrible doggerel.

"Yes, dear general," Echo said.

"I think the other girls are up to something," he informed her, looking over at Willa Goldsmith, who was handcuffed and unconscious, sprawled out on Echo's black silk sofa. Then he looked past Willa to the black door on the other side of Echo's office, the one guarded by a handprint scan alarm system that was shaped like a spider, installed to the left of the door. Of course she had never let him see past that door. She was the only one allowed in there. The men who had built it were dead.

She arched her perfectly shaped eyebrows. "Then you should take care of it. Willa's launch should be here in an hour, yes? Is there anyone else who should be on it?"

Like you, perhaps, destined for Vlados's deepest, darkest dungeon?

"They all should go. I don't like them. I don't trust them. They're hiding something."

"Then please, get to work." She returned to Vlados's poem:

"The trees are green, my spider queen..."

"I don't understand your lack of concern," Pace said, his jowls bobbing as he shook his head.

"It's because I delegate," she replied, placing her black stiletto heels on her desk and crossing her legs at the ankle as she leaned back in her chair. "Or is this something you simply don't know how to handle?"

He set his jaw and bobbed his head.

"Yes, ma'am," he gruffed, all military general and not an escaped felon.

He slammed out of her office.

She really didn't care. She'd be out of here in less than three days.

"You'll blow sky-high, and you will die," she said aloud, laughing. Leaning forward, she typed a response to Vlados.

"Your poetry is amazing. What a deep, old soul you are."

The Gracelyn hideaway, Arizona

A day and a night. There was practically nothing left to eat in the house. Another day. They catnapped at best, placed calls, made plans, tried to crack code. Morgan and Allison jogged instead of slept, went over lines of code together as they made fresh coffee, foraged for food and fielded calls from the Oracle agents in the field.

Kim Valenti said Ozone had cracked a message about a countdown: a hundred hours and counting. A hundred hours. Dear God.

Allison went for a run to keep down her panic level, her mind blurring a bizarre montage of images: Morgan's eyes, the world exploding…

Just once. I wish I'd had him just once, she thought.

She ran in the cold gray morning, sweating out her fear and desire.

As she approached the house, she heard a cheer rise up inside. She pushed the turbo and charged toward it, heaving, hoping…

Morgan threw open the back door and flew toward her. His eyes were ringed with fatigue and three-day-old stubble on his face. But he was glowing.

"We have it, Allison. We know the Micronesia coordinates."

He crushed her against his chest and kissed her hard, ground against her, wanted her in this moment of triumph…

Morgan, thank God, Morgan…

"We're a go," she said, pulling strength from deep inside her, from her roots—Athena roots. This was the moment she had prepared for; the moment when she knew why she was in the world. Why she was who she was. "Let's scramble."

"Roger that," Morgan said, grinning broadly at her, moving toward her.

She took a step away, centered herself. Got right with her soul. Then she smiled at him, simply smiled, and took point.

She ran past him into the house. At the sight of her, Lynnette and Diana broke into cheers.

"Let's hustle," she told her team.

Chapter 16

The world of Delphi

As planned, Morgan and Allison left first. They took a commercial jet to Hawaii and grabbed a prop from there. Both of them had private pilot's licenses, and Allison flew the first hop, to a small island in the middle of the ocean. They refueled and took off again, as the other members of the team began checking in.

"Nineteen degrees, eight minutes, latitude north… longitude one-six-six east," Morgan announced. "That's definitely our rendezvous point."

From the air, the atoll was horseshoe-shaped and very lush. Three small islands collectively comprising approximately seven kilometers of land clustered around a central lagoon of deep sea-green and dark blue. Coco palms and breadfruit trees lined their natural landing strip; a waterfall glittered in the distance, cascading from the collapsed cone of an ancient volcano.

"The recon photos were good," Allison mused, as Morgan found the ancient lava flow and headed in.

Morgan landed the craft with a smooth, dexterous touch and taxied down the length of the lava flow. Allison scanned the area with her binoculars. She knew a sniper could be hiding among the bowed trunks of the palms or the vines trailing down from the pandalus trees. Morgan turned off the engine and they scrambled out.

Allison carried her laptop in a fortified field case and set it behind some rocks. Together they unpacked the netting of camouflage. Morgan jogged to the nearest stand of trees; Allison hauled out a footlocker of SCUBA gear, radio phones, water and medical supplies.

Her ribs protested as she carried it into the shadows, then went back for another load as Morgan returned with an armload of palm fronds. He dropped them and assisted her with the second footlocker, which contained sea-worthy weapons made of plastic and/or stainless steel: .9mm Glocks and rubber-handled divers' knives with serrated back edges. Spear guns, .457 bang sticks, and underwater grenades.

"Hurting?" he asked her gently as they heaved the locker.

"A little," she confessed. She smiled crookedly. "You should have seen the other guy."

"I did. Handsome devil." He smiled back.

They unloaded a third footlocker and then three wooden crates. By then they were both very sweaty. Morgan unscrewed the caps off two water bottles and gave her one. She drank deeply.

"I haven't spotted any visitors," she said, gesturing to the binocs around her neck. "We're the first ones here."

"We're the only ones here," he countered, setting down his empty water bottle. "And we missed our chance before. I swore if I had another one, I would take it."

He pulled her into his arms. She flattened one palm against his chest, feeling the hard muscle and the thundering heartbeat. He was aroused. So was she. But she had to deny her impulses and take command. They were hurtling toward zero hour. Nothing was more important than the mission. Not Morgan, or her. No one.

"This is not a chance we should take," she said hoarsely.

"We'll come through it," he murmured into her hair. His hand moved down her back, settling on her hip.

"It's not that."

"It is. Or some version of it." He ran his thumb along her curve.

"The good guys don't always win, Morgan," she said, pulling away from him. "A lot of them lose."

"Then change the definition," he said, coming for her. "Maybe we don't have what a lot of other people work for all their lives. A nine-to-five job, kids, our favorite shows on TV and a lottery ticket every Friday. But we can have what they have when they turn the lights out at night." He nuzzled her forehead with his nose and stepped against her, letting her feel the hard bulge.

"We can have pleasure, and the comfort of being together before we go in," he said. "We're good together. Great, in fact." She heard the surprise in his voice. "Allison, I know this is your mission. I'm along for the ride. I won't get in your way."

But you are in my way, she thought. *You're tall and strong and I want you.*

But she knew that wasn't it. Not simple lust. He was right; they didn't have normal lives. They didn't really have lives. They had ops. Once they took out Echo—and they would, they had to—something else would come up. And something after that. She was Delphi. She knew things no one else knew, things no one else should ever know.

"Allison," he whispered, as he kept his hand on her hip and moved the other one up her side, his palm moving over the swell of her breast. "Sometimes the good guys *do* win. You have to allow for that possibility."

His lips moved over the crown of her hair. She closed her eyes, savoring his touch, smelling the coconut warmth of his sunscreen, the fragrance of his body. Her sex contracted; the moistness between her legs was undeniable as her body prepared for his, as her muscles tightened and her heart raced. She breathed him in, out.

I will die if you die, she thought.

Hearing herself, knowing that was her core truth, she pulled away from him firmly and turned her back to him.

"We should get camp ready," she said. "The others will be here soon. I have to go over our strategy."

He came up behind her, cupping her breasts with his hands and kissing her neck. His aggression caught her off guard and she arched against him, her bottom brushing his erection. Then, as he bent his knees, she came down with him, onto the sand, planting her hands in the silky, warm grains. She was on her hands and knees, and he knelt behind her, rocking against her body as he found the zipper on her parachute pants and pulled it down. He snaked the pants around the ankles of her boots and grunted low in his throat as her black lace thong was revealed.

"I see you dressed for battle," he murmured.

She wanted to say, *It's not funny,* and she wanted to tell him to leave her alone precisely because she was preparing for battle.

But what she said aloud was, "You might die."

"I will die," he said, easing her over onto her back. He reached down and pulled off his T-shirt, revealing a set of dog tags in the thatch of chest hair. "I don't know when or where, but I know I will. So your point is…?"

"I can't do this," she told him. "I can't. I—"

He unzipped his camouflage pants and slid them down. His large, hard penis bobbed, fully erect.

She was still wearing her thong, her olive-green T-shirt, her sports bra and her boots, and yet she felt more naked and vulnerable than she ever had in her entire life.

She put her hand over his. "It's like you said, Morgan. We're not like other people. I'm Delphi."

He shook his head. "You're more than Delphi. You're Allison." His eyes flared. "And you care about me, and that's what you don't want to admit. Because then I'll die."

"Oh God, Morgan, please, shut up," she said, as a tear spilled down her cheek. She looked away from him. "Just…shut up."

"Baby," he whispered, "I've sent guys out I knew weren't coming back. Men I've known for a long time. It's never been easy, but I've done it, and if I have to, I'll do it again. And you can send me. There's some things worth dying for, and I'm going to die anyway."

He laid his hand over hers. "But we're alive now. Don't deny us what other people have, just because we put it all on the line."

"When my mother died I..." She shut her eyes tightly against the onslaught of emotion. "I'll be watching you. If it comes down to it..." She gritted her teeth. "I can't be in this place now. I can't second-guess my motives. If I see you in trouble..."

"Don't deny me a good death," he said, "ever. Don't take my self-respect away from me, Allison. I'd rather die doing the right thing than live for a hundred years because I didn't give it a hundred percent. If you really..." He caught his breath, thunderstruck by the world that sprang into his mind.

"Allison, if you love me, you know I'd rather die than simply exist."

Her eyes flew open. He stared at her. He felt her shock and her uncertainty. But there was something there; it was electric, and it was real.

"I don't love you," she whispered. "I'm nowhere near that."

"I know." He pulled the thong off, exposing the shell-pink treasure it had barely concealed. "I know you don't."

But everything in him knew that she did.

He had never seen a woman as afraid to give her heart as she, and he loved her all the more for it. There, yes, he loved her, too.

He loved that she was so strong and brave. He loved that she had endured so much sorrow, yet could scarcely stop herself from loving all her women...and him. He loved the whipsaw strength of her heart and her soul. She was a warrior not just of the body, but of the heart.

"You can win this one," he said to her. "I promise you, Delphi, you really can win."

The tears slid down her temples. Her dark hair was a sharp contrast to the golden-yellow of the sand, just as her tears were a contrast to the joy he knew he would bring her, if she would just lay down arms for a heartbeat.

"If I love you, I lose," she whispered.

"You don't believe that for a second," he countered.

Then he put his hands on either side of her shoulders, making his intentions clear. He angled his lower body and poised himself just above her, the tip of his penis rubbing against the delicate, sensitive nub of her sex.

"Don't stop me," he told her, reassuring her that she had the final word. He had never forced a woman, and he never would. As much as his body cried out for release inside her, he would stop in a heartbeat if she told him to.

She widened her eyes, and the golden flecks were like glimmers of her soul. He felt a rush of tenderness for everything she had gone through, and everything she was. He understood at that moment how thoroughly she had put walls around her heart so no one could hurt her that much again, and he understood that he could hurt her that much. His own protective armor was just as thick, equally effective. She had been right all along. If they did this thing…

…they both could lose.

There's no way out, he thought. *And I don't want one.*

"You," he said, his voice hoarse with emotion. "I want you to be with me. I want you to know me in case I don't come back from this mission. No one has ever really known me. I haven't let them. So no one has ever slept with the real me before."

She caught her breath.

"This is me," he said. "I would rather die than not be me. I'm flawed, and I can be a bastard. I can be mean. I get scared. But I'm a man, and I'm alive, and I'm in love for the first time in my life."

Her lips parted, but she didn't speak. Silently she gazed into his eyes and tipped her pelvis up, inviting him to join his body with hers.

It was a sacred moment. In the ages-old sense of the word, she wanted to know him.

So he entered her world; his eyes wide-open, he slid into the wet heat of her, gasping aloud at the sheer pleasure. Allison, his Allison, his woman, his.

She whimpered once, deep in her throat, and her back arched off the sand. But she didn't close her eyes. She maintained her gaze as her body found his rhythm, as they moved together in the ancient dance of claiming.

I know you, and you are mine. I know you as no one else knows you; I am yours.

Every masculine impulse to protect rushed over him, and he gripped her arms as he thrust hard and slow. He brushed her hair away from her forehead and rested his chin against the damp, smooth skin. He thrust; she thrust back.

"It's all right," he said. He had been careful in the past with protection and she had nothing to worry about.

"It's all right," she replied huskily, adopting his code.

But he knew she was still holding back, afraid to take him; because if he was hers, then she might lose him.

Never, he told her, using his body and all its skill to push her past her fear. *Never.*

And all the words he had been afraid to speak to any woman poured out of him like breakers, like crashing surf, like a tidal wave. Tears and sweat spilled down his face as she took him; she possessed him; he didn't give, he didn't know how—

Damn straight I do. Damn straight, and I'm yours... Oh my God, I know it. I'm yours forever. Let me into your soul. Let me live there, and I will never die. And neither will you.

"Oh my God," he whispered, overcome, as she moved with him, rode him, her eyes flaring, her mouth in a passionate grimace. Then she raised her head to meet his and she kissed him, sliding her tongue into his mouth and wrapping her arms around him. She held him, cradled him. They moved together, and he could hear the roar of the surf on the beach and the tidal urges of his body, trying desperately to fill her with his immortality.

Send me into battle, he thought. *Use me. Don't waste a second of my life.*

"Morgan," she murmured, "I-I'm—"

"You're *not*," he insisted. "You're not afraid."

He thrust again, harder. She cried out, and began to move faster. All her muscles tightened. Sweat ran down her neck between her breasts, where the spider necklace glittered and gleamed. She clung to him, moving with him as he got closer, and closer, as their bodies fused.

"Allison," he pleaded.

Then he lost track of words, and he lost himself in her; it was the most terrifying moment of his entire life, and the bravest. No longer *I,* no longer *Morgan,* but *we*—this new thing, this paradise, this forever-moment—

We.

And he climaxed hard. Waves of pleasure obliterated him.

As Allison climaxed, she shattered. There was only being…with him. It was ecstasy, in every true sense of the word. She had no sense of where he ended and she began; she had never known such a thing could be. The pleasure he gave her transformed into the pleasure she gave him—looping, infinitely. It was something beyond them both; it was like feeling the universe inside her; it was…

…It was over.

With a groan, Morgan fell against her, still holding up his weight but spent and exhausted. His breath tickled her earlobe and she turned her head toward him. He kissed her, long and hard, like his lovemaking, and she felt a rush of panic, followed by a grief so intense she thought she might die. Now, more than ever, she couldn't stand the thought of losing him.

I shouldn't have done this, she thought. *I lost control. I can't do that. I can't do this, ever again.*

"Whoa."

Morgan raised himself up on his elbows and smiled down at her. His face was radiant, his lips soft with a delighted smile that cut her to the quick. Whatever they had created, he still held it. But she'd lost her grip, and she felt somehow like she'd failed him. Failed them.

His smile faded.

"You're sorry," he said.

She didn't want to say it. She didn't know how. In the throes of her passion, she had felt…completed. But now that it was over, she felt like he had taken some of her away with him…a heart she had barely dared to admit she possessed.

If she gave herself to him again, would she lose even more?

"This wasn't the right time," she said, shifting beneath him.

He clearly took that as his cue to move away. A soft tropical breeze took the place of flesh on flesh as he rolled onto his side and sat up.

"This was the perfect time," he countered. Then, gruffly, "For me."

"It's not you," she said. "It's me."

"No. It's us," he replied. He slid his fingers through hers and brought her hand to his lips. "It's the way we are."

She swallowed hard as he let go of her hand. There was a finality to it that pierced her to her core. His walls were back up…as they should be. He was right to guard himself against her.

"This…it wouldn't end well," she murmured, and she was grateful that he didn't hear her as he tore off the rest of his clothes and his boots, got to his feet and walked naked to the water's edge. He was magnificent, hard sinews and scars and all. As he strode into the water, she wished she could just hand everything off to someone else and be his, be with him and let it all go….

She wasn't there, emotionally, and she knew Morgan was aware of that, as she took off her boots and followed his footprints into the water. The sea smelled like Morgan's seed, trickling between her legs. Ironically she was on her last month of birth control pills, and she hadn't renewed her prescription. She hadn't had sex in so long that contraception didn't seem worthwhile.

He saw her, but he made no move to come near her. She bobbed under the surface, letting the surf rush over her. Then she left the water, drying off in the hot sun, and dressed, feeling invaded, aware that he was watching her. She picked up her bulky black radio phone and walked over to their cache of equipment. She turned her back to Morgan, grabbed an unloaded Uzi and cracked open a box of black-tipped ammo rounds. Time to prepare. She loaded the submachine gun and started on the next one. Finished that, got another bottle of water and picked up a third Uzi.

Then she cocked her head, suddenly aware that she was hearing something that didn't belong. She tried to ferret it out. Radio chatter? She skimmed her gaze over their setup and checked her radio phone.

"Armygirl to Gordita, over."

Then she looked past the phone to the ocean.

"Morgan," she whispered.

He was kneeling naked on the beach with his hands on top of his head. A man in a wet suit held a Browning to the back of his head while a second man fanned the area with the barrel of a Kalashnikov.

Chapter 17

The world of Athena Force

"Get here, danger, stat," Allison whispered into the phone as she pressed herself flat into the shadows, eyes on Morgan and the gunmen. "Armed men. At least two."

She set the phone down and grabbed up the Uzi she had just loaded. Her mind raced as she put the trio of men in her sights. If she took out the shooter, what would the guy with the Kalashnikov do? She doubted he would take out Morgan first. Self-defense would be his highest priority.

She formed a tripod—legs spread apart, elbows cocked—and forced all the air from her lungs. Then she drew in half a breath and held it. Her heart roared. She kept steady.

She aimed for the temple of the man with the Glock. When she hit him, would his finger reflexively squeeze the trigger, sending a death-dealing barrage of rounds into the back of Morgan's brain?

No way to tell. No time to find out. If she delayed, Morgan would probably die anyway.

She pulled the trigger. The report was more of a snap than the dramatic roar of movies and TV. So was the second round, when she saw that the shooter was still standing. She stood rooted to the spot, battling her impulse to run to Morgan and prepared to fire again.

Then, to her surprise, both assailants collapsed into the foam. The spear from a spear gun was centered in the back of Kalashnikov's neck; blood gushed from the wound. Morgan was on the shooter in a flash, pushing his head under the surf and keeping it there. The breakers fizzed to pink foam. She kept the Glock in her right hand and grabbed a spear gun in her left.

She didn't call to him; no need to advertise her approach to any additional hostiles she hadn't seen yet. Morgan would know she was on her way if he had any faith in her at all.

As she flew toward him, she saw someone in SCUBA gear rise from the water with his—her—hands in the air. She was holding a spear gun, and her hair was white-blond.

The diver yanked off her mask and looked straight at Allison. It was either Elle Petrenko or her twin, Sam St. John.

Or both…Allison saw a second diver breaking the surface, on the other side of Morgan, with a wickedly sharp knife in her fist.

"Morgan, friends!" she shouted, dashing toward them. She waved her own spear gun and the bang stick over her head.

"Allison!" Elle's thick Russian accent cut through the roar of the breakers. Then she and Sam grabbed one of the facedown floaters as Morgan dragged the other one—Kalashnikov—onto the beach. By the time Allison reached them, they had turned the two men onto their backs. Morgan, unconcerned about his nakedness, took the knife from Elle with a nod and started slicing the wet suit off the corpse.

"Slice deep, Comrade," Elle said, as Allison reached them and threw her arms around Morgan, dropping her weapons on the sand.

"This is Morgan Rush," she said, burying her face against his chest.

"Nice to meet you," Elle said politely, her mouth twitching as she shook his hand.

"The pleasure's mine," he replied, keeping his arm around Allison. "Thanks for saving my life."

"My sister, Samantha," Elle said. She gestured to the dead men. "These were the men I've been chasing. Monya Kishinev's thugs."

"Let's get them out of the water," Sam said.

Allison jogged back to the radio phone.

"Armygirl come in," she said.

"Armygirl on my way. Status?"

"Appears nominal, come in asap," Allison replied.

"Roger, over."

Allison put down the phone and returned to the group on the beach. Morgan had taken Kalashnikov's arms and was dragging him onto the beach, his wet heels carving deep ruts in the sand. Sam and Elle gathered up the shooter. Allison collected her weapons and walked beside Morgan.

"Diana's on her way," she reported.

"You said Echo implicated you in a scheme with Kishinev," Sam said to Allison.

"She knows you're here, then. We'll have to abort," Morgan put in.

"No, they were here because of me," Elle said. "So sorry I flushed them your way."

"Onto a deserted atoll in the middle of the ocean." Morgan slid a glance at Allison.

"They must have heard I was in the area," Elle argued.

"You have a leak?" Morgan asked.

"This is spycraft," Elle retorted. "There's always that possibility."

Morgan gave Allison a hard look, and she remembered that someone had known how to break into the Loschetter safe house and snatch Loschetter. Again she rejected the possibility that one of her agents was betraying her. It made no sense.

The four dragged the two bodies behind a stand of palm trees. Scatters of brightly colored birds erupted from the crowns of fronds.

"Allison, it is a little…" Sam waggled her hand in the air. "Coincidental."

"You might be right," Allison conceded reluctantly. But she had more forces on the way. All kinds of help. And Des Asher was bringing them a new superweapon that just might take Echo out. This was it. She could feel it. They couldn't turn back now.

"You have to be dispassionate about this," Morgan insisted. "Something's hinky."

"Morgan, we have less than sixty hours to stop her or that bomb goes off," Allison said.

"We don't know that she's behind the Circle of Justice. All we know is that we have two dead guys who shouldn't be here."

"I'm not calling it off," she said. "Echo would have sent in more firepower than two Russian goons with a couple of cap guns."

"Which were aimed at my head," Morgan reminded her. "Less than an hour after we landed."

Elle and Sam glanced at each other, then gave Morgan's nude body an appreciative once-over.

"Did they ask you where I was?" Allison asked him. "Did they ask about a necklace, or Delphi?"

He glared at her. Finally he shook his head.

"They spoke to me in Russian, but they didn't ask me any questions." He held up a hand to stave off her I-told-you-so. "Because they didn't have time."

"I beg your pardon for saving your life too early," Elle bit off. She looked straight past him to Allison. "Our Zodiac's moored a few feet out, beside a local vessel they rented off an island about thirty kilometers from here. There was no one else on the boat. I don't know who's waiting to hear from them."

"We should investigate." Allison turned and headed back to camp. "If they were working alone, we can sink the boat and move forward."

"Are you out of your mind?" Morgan said. "We need to abort. You cannot guarantee that they were alone."

"We can be reasonably sure," she replied. "Give me some time and—"

"We need to get in this plane and leave *now,*" he replied, standing with his feet wide apart, as if ready to take her on.

"This is my show, Morgan, not yours. I'm sending Diana to look around. And put some clothes on, for God's sake," she snapped at him.

"Why?"

"Because if you don't, I'm going to kick you in the balls."

"You can't touch me. What am I even talking about? This is insane."

"Morgan, Circle of Justice," she said.

"Goddamn it," he said, balling his fists and pressing them against his forehead. "Listen to me."

"It's happening," she yelled. Then she lowered her voice. "You can't deny me *my* meaningful death, either. Deal?"

Morgan clamped his jaw shut. Turned.

Nodded.

Diana Lockworth did a few flyovers, investigating the vessel—easily traced back to a small island, where no one was exactly checking IDs for rentals—then landed her Black Hawk on Allison's atoll. The copter bore Royal Australian Air Force insignia; Diana might be off all books, but she had friends in high places. Jessica Whittaker was with her, and she swam back to Elle and Sam's Zodiac with the twins. No radios, no cell phones.

"Those guys were off the books, too," Sam insisted.

"Okay, final analysis," Allison said. "Do we need to abort?"

"No way," Jessica argued. "We're too close."

"Those two Russians showing up, that's weird," Diana argued. She exhaled and ran a hand through her strawberry-blond hair. "On the flyover, I got a message from Kim. The Circle of Justice has gotten orders to move to Step Three. We don't know what that means, but the Ozone team has the impression that they're pushing up their timetable."

Allison looked at Morgan. He balled his fists and shook his head.

"Let's look at those blueprints again," Allison said, walking over to her laptop case. She picked it up while Diana, Jessica, Elle and Morgan got busy draping the Black Hawk with camouflage.

Sam met her on her way back to the group.

"A minute?" she asked.

Allison nodded, stopped walking.

"Morgan," Sam said. "What's going on?"

"He wants us to abort," Allison replied.

"I know *that*." Sam cocked her head. The tropical breeze ruffled her white-blond hair. "I mean, between you two?"

Allison shook her head. "It's nothing." Then she lifted her chin and smiled ruefully. "It's nothing if you're not out in the middle of the ocean on a mission to save the world." She clutched the laptop case against her chest. "I tried to stop it. I can't let him worry about me. He's got to stay focused. If he's worrying about me…" She left the rest unsaid.

"It's good for us if he's worried about you, *Delphi*," Sam replied. "We all know it, Allison. And we know you've got to make it through this. The rest of us are…expendable."

"That's wrong," Allison blurted out, even though until very recently, she would have agreed. "No one person is more important than another."

"That's an incredible statement, coming from a woman in love," Sam replied. She didn't smile. "I can see it. You love him. So...how expendable is *he?* Would you risk the world to save him?"

"No," Allison said instantly, but her cheeks blazed. She reached for the necklace, tucked inside her shirt. "I wouldn't. He would hate me if I did that."

"Then I'll follow you into battle," Sam replied. "And so will everyone else. Including him. Even if he thinks you should abort."

They gazed at each other, then melted into an embrace. Allison closed her eyes. She was scared.

Allison and Samantha St. John walked back to the camp. Morgan's eyes followed Allison's every move as she opened her laptop and linked it to the satellite Diana had succeeded in tasking for this very purpose. The group gathered around to study the Echo Chamber blueprints.

"It appears that the lab is located underground," Allison said, tracing her finger along the lines on the monitor. "See these? We think they're run-off pipes for the sprinkler system that drain directly into an undersea cave. It appears that there are a set of emergency controls and a fireproof hatch on a dense structure above the surface. Could be volcanic rock."

Chatter squawked on the Black Hawk, which was completely draped. Diana lifted up a section of the covering and scooted inside. She spoke for a minute, then returned.

"The Special Boat Service troops are approaching," Diana announced as she climbed back down. "Des Asher commanding, Dawn and Selena Shaw Jones are with him. There are six Futura Commandos. They hold six each. Plus we've got Elle and Sam's."

Morgan looked at Allison. So far the op was running exactly as she had set it up.

"You know your boats," Allison said to the group. "Jessica goes with Des, Selena, Diana, Morgan and me. Dawn, you and five of Asher's troops are coming with us. Load up your gear."

Everyone went to the weapons caches, gathering spear guns, bang sticks, revolvers, Uzis, neck knives, boot knives, grenades.

Morgan was equipped by the time the Zodiacs had arrived. Dressed in a wet suit, Allison greeted Des Asher, the CO, with short-cropped, burnt-pewter hair, and her two agents. Morgan recognized both Selena Shaw Jones, the blue-green-eyed brunette who had saved the bacon of friendlies in Berzhaan not once, but twice, and the super-egg baby Dawn O'Shaughnessy, with her thick golden hair and the remarkable green-gold eyes of Thomas King, the Navy Seal who had unwittingly been her sperm donor father.

Asher had brought fifteen British Special Boat Forces with him, square-jawed men who jumped to comply with each of Allison's commands. Asher was their point man, but Allison was their leader. Athena Force Team One had eight members; and Des and his fifteen men made twenty-four. The extra seats in the Zodiacs were for rescuees and prisoners.

They took to the sea, Elle in her Zodiac and four of Asher's men peeling off to the west, where they would try to make the beach to investigate the shadow on the Predator photo. Sam and another four headed in a British Special Boat Service Zodiac for the eastern side of the volcano. Wearing face paint and lightweight but effective Kevlar body armor, they were well-stocked with weapons, climbing equipment and explosives. Their mics were working fine, and Morgan could hear Elle flirting in her lilting English with her British escort as they motored away.

The remaining three Zodiacs clustered at a rendez-vous point in the shelter of an outcropping of stone and coral. Morgan picked up his binocs and studied their target across the water, a dormant volcanic island much like the one on which they had landed. Palms bowed in criss-crosses along the beachheads, sur-rounding a craggy volcanic mass that had long ago collapsed into its center. He picked out the shadows on the east and west flanks that Elle and Sam were headed for.

Echo had quite a flair for the dramatic—also unpar-alleled expertise and access to resources. A formidable foe, to pull off building a state-of-the-art high-tech lab in there; abduct over a dozen young women and break two enemies of the state out of prison.

And we are going to take her down.

Allison and Jessica went through a sound check on the underwater comm system. Asher had brought masks and packs for everyone aboard, along with his special present for Allison: two experimental Metal Storm pro-totype handguns, capable of electronically firing the equivalent of thirty thousand rounds a second. There was no way to know if they could take out Echo's force field until they were deployed in combat.

"Okay, Jessica, you're a go," Allison told the young woman.

Wearing a wet suit top, goggles and fins, and a

facemask for underwater communication with its accompanying backpack, which also contained alarm descramblers—but no SCUBA gear—Jessica Whittaker picked up her bang stick and spear gun for protection against shark attacks and gave Allison a thumbs-up.

"I'm away," Whittaker announced and flopped backward into the water. Half a minute later, from beneath the water, her voice came in clear on the hydrophone. "Swimming toward the target," she said.

"Roger. Be careful," Allison said into the mic.

All they could do now was wait. Morgan spent the time mentally running the op, examining the possibilities, predicting the things that would make everything go FUBAR. He was also wearing a wet suit, and he was sweating.

Time passed. They drank water, ate protein bars. He watched Asher and O'Shaughnessy, so clearly in love. He wished them well.

"Stolichnaya checking in," Elle Petrenko said in Morgan's earpiece. "We're here. Seeing a road about a hundred yards above us. Approaching."

"Understood," Allison said.

"Mermaid in a cave, breaking the surface, seeing a blinking red light," Jessica said.

"Roger," Allison replied.

Morgan felt her tense, and then saw the light on the screen. It sat squarely in the center of a control panel, to the left of a round hatch, increasing its frequency as Whittaker got closer to it. Jessica was about nine inches shorter than he was; he'd have to watch his head when he went in.

Then he saw Jessica's flashlight beam land on a set

of metal stairs. There was a Fiberglas motorboat tethered to the bottom rung.

"Use extreme caution," Allison said.

Morgan watched as Jessica broke open her wireless descrambler—a rectangular-shaped black plastic box—and beamed it at the panel. Rapid-fire readouts flickered in the display panel and he grunted in admiration.

"I want one of those for Christmas," he told Allison.

"Only if you're good," she replied. "Sam, where are you?" she murmured beneath her breath.

Then she ticked her glance back to Morgan and covered her mic. She looked at him hard.

"My spider necklace is in a capsule, buried where you and I…" She exhaled, as if she were relieved she'd decided to tell him. "Back on the island. Sam, Elle, Selena and Diana know, too. And I e-mailed Lynnette and Kim."

"I'm honored," he said, and he meant it.

"Don't screw up." The gold in her eyes glimmered. "If I go down, keep going."

"I will. You do the same."

She licked her lips. "I will."

And this may be the closest to a wedding ceremony people like us get, he thought wryly.

"Mermaid is in," Whittaker reported.

Echo's underground lair

Tap-tap-tap.

Willa had been picked up, and Echo had checked on all her girls, snug in their rooms. Everyone was very quiet. Maybe Pace was right; maybe they were up to something.

She felt tense. She needed to calm down…spend some time with her mother.

She pushed away from her desk and faced the black door behind her. Tears welled as she placed her hand over the print reader. It aligned with her hand and the door clocked open.

"Mummy," she whispered, pushing it open.

It was cool here, and dark. Dark as a womb, black as her soul. The octagonal room was fitted with ebony walls, a ceiling of obsidian and a floor of black marble. Hundreds of strands of spun gold hung from the corners, crisscrossing, swaying gently as Echo observed the torchlight flickering on them. No electric lights here, just smoke and flame.

It was also the safest, most heavily fortified place in her entire complex.

In the center of the web, standing on a black crystal globe ringed with black marble stairs, a life-size statue of Echo's mother gazed down on all she saw, like a madonna. She was formed of gold, and she looked so lifelike that sometimes Echo thought she could see her breathing. Did the two spider necklaces around her neck rise and fall against her chest?

Echo ducked beneath the elaborate golden web, easing away some of the silken threads. She mounted the stairs, stood on tiptoe and kissed her mother's golden lips. Tears formed in Echo's eyes.

"Aren't you proud of me?" she asked. "I'm so close, Arachne. Soon I'll be a daughter worthy of your legacy."

Echo reached around her mother's neck and lifted up the two spider pendants, showing them to the unseeing gaze of the figure.

"See? Soon there will be three, and I'll reweave your web, and carry on your work. The world will tremble, Mummy. It won't be long now." Tears washed down her face, marring her makeup, but she let them remain as a testament to her depth of feeling for the brilliant woman who had conceived her. "I wish you were here. I wish you hadn't had to die."

She kissed Arachne's lips again, then, and eased her way out of the room. She shut the door.

She sat down and began a note to Vlados, to give him a little advance warning, both of the nuclear explosion and of her imminent arrival in his lovely oppressed nation.

Tap-tap-tap. My Dear Demented Dictator, By the time you read this…

She smirked and deleted the "Demented Dictator" and replaced it with "Vlados."

"We'll be arriving sooner than planned. If you have any assets in Maryland, I suggest you remove them immediately."

Her long fingernails clattered on the keyboard as she typed in another message to the Circle of Justice. They were getting into place, waiting for her word.

ARACHNE@spiderweb.org: My Brothers, I give you the code to begin your operation.

Echo smiled. *Tap-tap-tap,* inputting the first two syllables of the three-syllable Berzhaani word for "forbidden fruit." Then she noticed something very peculiar: her cursor was blinking in an odd, rhythmic pattern.

"What is this?" she asked aloud, leaning forward and watching it.

Dit-dit-dit-daw-daw-daw-dit-dit-dit.

"What?" she said again, as a slow, terrible realization dawned on her: It was an SOS.

From my cursor? Is someone using my machine, my heavily protected, impenetrable machine, to send out secret messages?

With a sudden, terrible feeling, she opened up her cached files and started scanning them. Transmissions she had not made lay inside layers of protection. Three of them…all to a MySpace page for someone named Tasi Arejab. What the *hell?* From her computer?

Impossible!

Tasi Arejab. Who the hell was that?

She typed in the name. A window marked Personnel File: Laboratory Technicians, opened up, revealing the image of the mousy lab tech.

Her cursor blinked.

Another window popped open, revealing a file marked Armory. The full list of weapons for her security team scrolled down.

"Oh my God!" she shrieked, leaping out of her chair and racing for her door.

Allison, Morgan, Diana, Des, Dawn and five SBS troops crouched beside Jessica at the hatch. They had transported their weapons and body armor in a series of inflatables riding along the surface like sharks. Everyone had on state-of-the-art vests, helmets and headsets; Allison and Diana had the Metal Storms. Selena and two backup men were back with the Oracle laptop in the Zodiacs, linked up with Kim at Oracle HQ and Lynnette at Oracle West.

Elle and her people were stationed around the entrance to a tunnel. Sam and her squad verified that they had located a metal hatch. They'd wired it to blow with the British plastic explosive, PE4.

"On your signal," Sam whispered to Allison. Everyone was wearing earpieces; everyone heard her.

"We're in position," Elle reconfirmed.

Morgan gazed at Allison. She looked back at him.

"It's showtime," she said. "On my mark. Three, two—"

"What are you doing?" Echo shrieked at Eric Pace as she clattered along her catwalk. The general was dragging Mary the Goth by the hair, a SIG Sauer P-226 at the little clown's temple. Backed up to a wall beside a computer station, the mousy lab tech—Tasi the Traitor herself—held Cailey in her arms.

Pace didn't look at Echo. He kept his attention fixed on Tasi.

"I caught her at it," he declared. "She's the one who has been sending out the transmissions."

"Put Cailey down, Tasi," Echo said calmly. "The general won't hesitate to shoot her to get to you."

"No, no!" Cailey screamed. "Help!"

"No one will help any of you," Echo shouted. "No one!"

Mary started screaming.

"One!" Allison shouted. "Go, go, go!"

Two of the SBS men pushed open the door and barreled down a dimly lit tunnel, Allison next, followed by Morgan and the rest. They were about twenty-five feet in when a tremendous explosion threw Allison against the side of the tunnel. Debris rained down. The lights went out. Alarms whooped and the sprinkler system blasted on.

Sam had blown the hatch.

"Report, report!" Allison yelled.

"We're in! We're in!" Sam reported. "Rappelling down now!"

"Grenades in!" Elle shouted.

In the distance, Allison heard more explosions, roars of gunfire, yelling; noise and shouting and alarms. She kept going.

Suddenly the tunnel blazed with light. Armed men in black appeared at the other end, weapons drawn. The two SBS men fired; the attackers returned it. Her two men went down, and Allison stood to be next.

"Get down, Allison," Morgan yelled at her.

"Stay on target!" she shouted back, as she opened fire with the Metal Storm. It sliced through the first wave of hostiles like butter; blood flew as they went down, and more went down again. She kept firing, registering the lack of recoil.

Then the hostiles started yelling and she realized someone had come up behind the hostiles. They collapsed like dominoes and Allison stopped using her Metal Storm, saving it, letting the others take out the baddies with more conventional weapons.

Racing over the dead and dying, her group made it in, less the two SBS men. They fanned into what had to be the lab, firing, taking it; Sam was there with her men—one was missing—as more hostiles poured in from other tunnels and doorways. The water was rushing down; looking up, Allison saw General Eric Pace on a catwalk with a woman crumpled at his feet, and two girls—one dressed like a Goth; the other one had to be Cailey Anderson—running in the opposite direction.

Pace saw her, too, and darted after the girls. He grabbed Cailey and threw her in front of himself like a shield, smacking her against the temple. She staggered and wobbled.

Then Allison ticked her gaze to the left, and saw *her*. Echo.

Nothing was touching her, not bullets or rain or smoke, which had begun to billow throughout the enormous room. Echo stood in the center of her force field, staring at Allison as if she could kill her with a look.

There you are. I'm in your lair, and I'm going to get you and you and your dead mother are going to be so very, very sorry you tangled with Athenians, Allison thought fiercely.

Morgan raced up beside Allison.

"I'll get Pace," he said. "I'll get his hostage. You go for Echo. Get some cover. Take her out."

"Roger that," she replied, and she wanted to say more. She wanted to say, *Morgan, don't die. I do love you. I do.*

That chance was gone.

"Diana," she yelled, "with me."

"On it!" Diana shouted. She shouted out names. "Jessica, with us! SBS Team One, with us!"

Allison didn't know how they found each other in the surging mass, but there was intention in the chaos. Enemy recognized enemy, death found victims. As her people streamed toward her, Allison watched Echo glide along the catwalk, unhurt, and traced her route with her gaze.

"Stairs! Find them!" Allison shouted.

To the sound of explosions, screaming and gunfire, Echo flew into her office and picked up her phone, pressing #23 for the hangar. "Get my plane ready!" she yelled—into dead air. She depressed the button, tried again. *Communications system cut off,* she thought, reaching for multiple lines, finally having the presence of mind to open a drawer in her black desk and grab her radio phone.

"Get my plane ready now!" she yelled.

"We're under attack!" her man yelled back at her.

"Fight back!" she screamed at him.

"We surrender! Stop, don't shoot!"

"Don't do that, you idiot! I need you!" She hurtled the phone across the room, smacking a framed oil painting of several spiders crawling over a guava, shattering the glass. She whirled in a circle and grabbed her hair, shrieking. "You stupid moron! I'll kill you!"

Calm down, she told herself, her chest heaving. *Calm down now. Emotions are a waste of time. Think, Echo!*

My necklaces. That's what she's after.

She pressed her hand into the handprint screen and raced into the Spider Room. The golden statue of her mother gleamed like a candle in the darkness.

"Mummy," Echo said, running up the stairs. "She's here. She's going to die before your eyes."

Echo grabbed the necklaces like scalps and yanked on the gold chains. Staring down at the tiny detonator on the necklace Arachne had given her, she smiled. Three taps, and it was all over.

She pressed her finger down. *One, two…*

"Stop," the statue of Arachne told her.

Echo's mouth dropped open.

"Did you…did…?" She was stunned.

"Yes, I'm here, darling," the statue whispered, although its lips didn't move, and its eyes didn't blink. "Think a moment. What if she has the third necklace, and you blow her to bits?"

"She wouldn't do that," Echo replied. "She wouldn't bring it with her onto my territory. She's far too cagey." She smiled. "I know you aren't really speaking to me. I know I'm feeling a bit of stress. Crazy people don't rule the world. *Control* it."

Still, she took her hand off the detonator and tried to think about what to do next. First order of business was to shut the door. Shut out the war. *Kaboom, kaboom, kaboom.* Such a racket!

She clattered down the stairs and pushed a switch on the base of the globe. The door began to swing shut.

"Oh, damn it!" she said, clapping her hand to her forehead. She'd forgotten to finish typing the code to the Circle of Justice!

She hit the off switch and pushed through wave after wave of golden spiderweb as she headed for her outer office.

"Diana!" Allison shouted, as Diana crumpled on the stairs and slid facedown. Blood mushroomed in a pool beneath her torso.

There was no one left in Allison's detail. Jessica had fallen back. The soldiers were engaged with pushing back the enemies.

I have to keep going. I can't stop for anyone, not even Diana.

Deeply regretful, Allison turned and raced on, scanning for signs of Echo. She had no idea how many flights of concrete steps she'd gone up. The lights were out. Everything around her was shaking like an earthquake.

A bullet whizzed past her right shoulder and she jumped to the left, tumbling into a hallway buzzing and flickering with artificial light. She was taken back in time to the alley behind Jade's Bar, when she had started her run. It had led her here.

She pushed herself to her feet and staggered, aware of a coldness spreading throughout her limbs.

I've been hit.

She looked down to see a hole in the material covering her thigh. Blood streamed from the wound to the floor. She slipped on it as she moved forward and the floor clunked her nose, hard. She felt blood. Cursing, she tore off her helmet and wiped her fist against her nose. Then she let loose with a burst of rapid-fire pulses, the equivalent of sixteen thousand rounds a second, taking out most of the wall in front of her.

Yikes. What the hell was that?

Listening to a hail of practically supersonic explosions, Echo leaped up from her chair and darted back into the Spider Room. She'd have to tell the Circle of Justice to blow up the NSA at a more convenient time. Just three letters away from Armageddon! It was so frustrating.

She stood behind her mother's statue and unaccountably began to laugh. It was all so…*much*.

"I can feel her coming for me," Echo told the statue. "It's her. I know it is." She gripped the necklaces and peeked around the golden figure. Her protective shield activated.

The supersonic explosions resumed—*blamblamblamblamblam*—and the outer door blasted away into metal toothpicks.

Allison Gracelyn stood in the doorway. The lower half of her face was covered with blood, and all of it was filthy. Best of all, she was alone.

What a lunatic.

Allison stared first at the intricate golden web, then at the statue.

"Come out, Echo," she said. "It's over."

Echo covered her mouth to stifle her laughter.

Then *blamblamblamblamblam* her mother's statue disintegrated, as if it had been made of sawdust. The shards ricocheted against Echo's force field, pushing her backward. That had never happened before, ever; Echo threw back her head and screamed.

"You bitch!" she cried. "What did you do?"

"That's going to be you next," Allison said, walking into the room, taking aim. "Give me the flash drives."

Echo hid her hand behind her back. "What makes you think I have them?"

Allison didn't reply, just kept walking forward steadily. Echo started laughing again. It was *so* inappropriate.

"I think you should know that I have a detonator in my hand," she informed Allison. "If you come any closer, I'll blow up this place."

"You wouldn't," Allison dared her. "Even your shield has its limits. I just saw…" She staggered sideways.

"Oh, good!" Echo cried, delighted. "You're wounded." She wrinkled her nose. "You're probably dying."

Allison Gracelyn, her nemesis, the one woman in the world who might have stopped her, drew herself up with all the nobility of the hopelessly heroic.

"We all die," Allison said, opening fire.

"You might have *warned* me!" Echo shouted, as her shield wrapped her in its protective cocoon.

The Metal Storm pulsed as the room dimmed; *blamblamblamblam* as Allison felt all her muscles trembling violently. *Blamblamblamblam* as she stopped feeling anything...

Except the plosive force of a huge explosion, throwing her at Echo. And Echo, screaming, as Allison pushed through her shield and landed on top of her in a bone-crushing heap.

Not really seeing, but sensing where her enemy lay beneath her, Allison grabbed Echo's wrist and yanked the necklaces out of her fist.

Echo laughed hysterically. "Ouch! Ow! It's too late! They're all dead!" she screamed.

Morgan, Allison thought.

And then she collapsed.

"Mayday, mayday," someone shouted from far away, as Morgan balled himself around the little girl, and the laboratory tumbled down.

I'll see you soon, baby, he thought, imagining that Allison was dead.

Epilogue

Delphi sat alone in the darkness with her phone. She had no voice distorter attached to it.

"Echo's remains are secure," Katie Rush reported.

"Very good," Delphi said. "Diana and Josie gave me the status of the egg babies. We've returned the ones we could. The others will stay with Christine at Athena Academy."

"Roger that," Katie said. She paused. "How's my brother?"

"Allison's gone to check on him," Delphi told her. "I'll let you know as soon as she calls me."

"Thank you," Katie replied.

"You're welcome," Delphi responded.

It was nearly Valentine's Day, and it was snowing heavily. Allison could feel the cold in her bones as she slowly climbed out of the cab. The cabbie fetched her crutches as she slung her laptop over her shoulder.

"You want me to get you some help?" he asked her, gesturing to the hospital entrance.

"No, thanks." She handed him double the fare. "Thank you."

Slowly she approached the hospital. Though feather-light, the laptop seemed to weigh a thousand pounds.

The three flash drives in her pocket jostled together like grenades.

Mayday, mayday, mayday.

Wounded women coming for her; lifting her out of the debris. Choppers, Jessica over her, yelling at her to stay with them. All her women, some on stretchers. Elle, swearing in Russian. Sam's arm in a sling, shouting at her to fight it, fight. Medics in the helicopter working on Diana. Dawn and Asher quarreling with the pilot: Guam is closer, get them to Guam for God's sake, or Allison's not going to make it... Rush's heart has stopped again, where's the defib? Is anyone religious? Does anyone need a priest?

Echo needed more than a priest. Who knew where a dark, crazy soul like hers would go? She was dead, bloodied and shredded; yet her eyes had been open and she had been smiling.

It was so hard to believe. Dead, just like anyone else on the planet.

But Arachne's web of evil had survived.

For now.

Allison made her way into Morgan's private room. He had remained unconscious, and they didn't know if he would wake up. They told her that if it was any consolation, he had saved the life of the little girl huddled beneath him.

It was.

She sat down beside his bed, listening to the beeping machines, tracing his profile with her gaze. He was as gray as the sky.

She flipped open the laptop and booted it up. She knew that back in HQ, Selena was seeing what she was seeing. Out in Arizona, so was Lynnette.

Delphi One, Delphi Two and Delphi Three.

She put the first drive in USB port A. It was Lilith's. Nothing happened. No icon appeared on the screen.

She added the second drive, Kwan-Sook's. Still nothing.

The third. Echo's.

A screen popped open. An enormous black spider filled her screen. Then it slowly melted into letters, numbers, letters, names, scrolling crazily. A rapid-fire list; she saw names—

Catching her breath, she yanked out the three drives and gripped them in her hand.

Her phone rang immediately.

"Delphi One?" Selena said. "What happened? Are you all right?"

"I aborted," Allison told her. "I know we discussed it, but I really don't know."

There was a long pause.

So much tragedy, and sacrifice. Needless.

Necessary.

"Let me call Delphi Three," Selena said finally.

"I—" Allison began, then gave her head a shake.

She had been the one to suggest a triumvirate, three Delphis, three votes.

"Roger that, Delphi Two. I'll wait for further instructions." She closed her phone.

She watched the shadows of falling snowflakes as they washed over Morgan's still features. The world outside was busy. The Circle of Justice had been quashed. The threat was over. The various intelligence agencies, at home and abroad, were rounding up the men and women "she" had blackmailed. Contracts to take her out were being canceled. She and Morgan had their jobs back.

A scenario got floated that she and Morgan had been tasked to another arm of Project Ozone, which they had successfully completed. They were given credit for terminating the threat posed by the Circle of Justice, and they came back to NSA as heroes.

Her broken body was mending.

But her heart? She stared at Morgan, almost hating him because she was so terrified that he was never going to wake up again.

"I can be with you now," she whispered. "I've got help." She heard the pleading in her voice, and she gave in to it.

"Please, Morgan, oh my God, please don't die," she whispered. She carefully slid her arms around him and rested her head on his chest. She heard his heart. "I've come such a long way to be with you."

As she closed her eyes and listened to his heartbeat, she thought of the tragedies and sacrifices so many women had made, to make a world where she could love Morgan Rush. Athenians, Oracle agents, shining light into the darkness, pushing against the shadows. Daring everything, putting it all on the line.

Miraculously none of them had died in the explosion at Echo's lab. Des's troops had sustained nine casualties.

And Natalia. I failed her.

Natalia had died. Knocked out by Eric Pace and left alone in her fortified cell, she had been found too late. Allison's chest squeezed painfully as she mourned her.

She rested against Morgan's chest as the snow drifted down. No one outside Oracle knew about the flash drives. Arachne's web was their web now. But it was a web of evil and terror. If they looked at it, what would that do to their souls?

If they didn't, what would it do to the world?

Her phone rang and she moved to get it. It was probably Delphi Two, wishing to discuss what to do with the three drives. She shifted her weight to reach her phone.

And Morgan grunted.

"Stay," he whispered.

"Morgan? Oh God, Morgan?" she said, lifting her head to stare up into his face. His eyes were still closed. The shadows of the snowflakes dusted his sunken cheeks, the cleft of his chin, his eyelids.

"Yeah," he managed. "Stay, 'lison."

The phone rang again.

"Love you," he slurred.

"I love you, too, Morgan," she said hoarsely.

She laid her head back against his chest and gave in to it, gave in to her love, her deep love. She was there now. She had gotten back what she had possessed so fleetingly on the beach. She had broken the code.

"I love you," she said again, weeping.

"Mmm," Morgan said, his hand searching for hers. She found it, grabbed it, held on with all her strength.

Delphi would answer her phone. She would do what should be done with the flash drives. She would keep the world safe from other monsters like Echo. For of course there were others. Of course.

She would do all that.

After the snowflakes stopped falling.

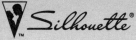

Romantic
SUSPENSE

**Sparked by Danger,
Fueled by Passion.**

Cindy Dees
Killer Affair

Seduction in the sand…and a killer on the beach.

Can-do girl Madeline Crummby is off to a remote
Fijian island to review an exclusive resort, and she hires
Tom Laruso, a burned-out bodyguard, to fly her there
in spite of an approaching hurricane. When their plane
crashes, they are trapped on an island with a serial killer
who stalks overaffectionate couples. When their false
attempts to lure out the killer turn all too real, Tom and
Madeline must risk their lives and their hearts….

**Look for the third installment
of this thrilling miniseries,
available August 2008
wherever books are sold.**

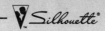

SPECIAL EDITION

A late-night walk on the beach resulted
in Trevor Marlowe's heroic rescue of a
drowning woman. He took the amnesia
victim in and dubbed her Venus, for the
goddess who'd emerged from the sea.
It looked as if she might be his goddess of
love, too…until her former fiancé showed
up on Trevor's doorstep.

Don't miss

THE BRIDE WITH NO NAME

by *USA TODAY* bestselling author
MARIE FERRARELLA

*Available August
wherever you buy books.*

REQUEST YOUR FREE BOOKS!

2 FREE NOVELS PLUS 2 FREE GIFTS!

◆ HARLEQUIN®

INTRIGUE®

Breathtaking Romantic Suspense

YES! Please send me 2 FREE Harlequin Intrigue® novels and my 2 FREE gifts (gifts are worth about $10). After receiving them, if I don't wish to receive any more books, I can return the shipping statement marked "cancel." If I don't cancel, I will receive 6 brand-new novels every month and be billed just $4.24 per book in the U.S. or $4.99 per book in Canada, plus 25¢ shipping and handling per book and applicable taxes, if any*. That's a savings of close to 15% off the cover price! I understand that accepting the 2 free books and gifts places me under no obligation to buy anything. I can always return a shipment and cancel at any time. Even if I never buy another book from Harlequin, the two free books and gifts are mine to keep forever.

182 HDN EEZ7   382 HDN EEZK

Name _____ (PLEASE PRINT)

Address _____ Apt. #

City _____ State/Prov. _____ Zip/Postal Code

Signature (if under 18, a parent or guardian must sign)

Mail to the **Harlequin Reader Service:**
IN U.S.A.: P.O. Box 1867, Buffalo, NY 14240-1867
IN CANADA: P.O. Box 609, Fort Erie, Ontario L2A 5X3

Not valid to current subscribers of Harlequin Intrigue books.

**Want to try two free books from another line?
Call 1-800-873-8635 or visit www.morefreebooks.com.**

HI08

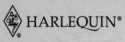

KATHERINE GARBERA

BABY BUSINESS

Cassidy Franzone wants Donovan Tolley,
one of South Carolina's most prestigious
and eligible bachelors. But when she
becomes pregnant with his heir, she is
furious that Donovan uses her and their
child to take over the family business.
Convincing his pregnant ex-fiancée to marry
him now will take all his negotiating
skills, but the greatest risk he faces is
falling for her for real.

**Available August
wherever books are sold.**

Always Powerful, Passionate and Provocative.